SING, I

Also by Ethel Rohan

In the Event of Contact

The Weight of Him

Goodnight Nobody

Cut Through the Bone

SING, I

A NOVEL

ETHEL ROHAN

TriQuarterly Books / Northwestern University Press

Evanston, Illinois

TriQuarterly Books
Northwestern University Press
www.nupress.northwestern.edu

Printed in the United States of America

10   9   8   7   6   5   4   3   2   1

ISBN 978-0-8101-4717-1 (paper)
ISBN 978-0-8101-4718-8 (ebook)

Cataloging-in-Publication data are available from the Library of Congress.

For Nicole McRory. Rest in Power.

That's the lesson stone teaches:
even after it falls, it endures.

—Emma Donoghue, *Haven*

CONTENTS

SING, I

The Holdup

Kevin entered the kitchen, his hand grabbing the hair at the top of his head and explicit lyrics thumping from his phone.

"Good Christ. Turn that off." Ester returned her attention to the bread she was briskly spreading mayo onto.

Kevin located his earbuds on the island and inserted them. "Happy?"

"It'll take more than that," Ester said.

He flashed his smile, the one that worked on her like those videos of rescued dogs finding their forever home. Seated at the island, he helped himself to cornflakes while reading his phone, his head bopping to the expletive-laced outrage that remained audible through his earbuds. Ester was tired of telling him he would damage his hearing. She sliced his and Jason's lunch sandwiches in two, exposing lines of orange cheddar and slick turkey.

Simon appeared, making straight for the coffeepot. Slurping his coffee, he poured boiling water over a bowl of instant oatmeal and stirred the mixture with unnecessary force. He situated himself at the island next to his firstborn and pulled out Kevin's nearest earbud. "The whole point is a concert for one."

"Hey." Kevin returned the earbud to the designated hole in his head, his cranky gaze never straying from his phone. He did at least turn the volume down.

Ester plucked the stems from the blueberries, their growing stack on the counter like kindling. She pictured a tiny bonfire, the stems twitching in the flames as though alive. Simon attacked his oatmeal anew, his spoon clacking and scraping. How many times had she asked him to not? It was like he was trying to break the bowl.

She moved to the doorway and shouted upstairs to Jason. "Don't make me go up there."

She returned to the counter and topped off her tepid coffee. Her teeth tugged her limp toast. Overhead, there remained no signs of life. "He's going to put me in an early grave."

She received no response, Simon also lost inside his phone. A technical writer, he created software programs and fixed bugs all day long, and still he succumbed to the grip of technology at home. She added potato chips and beheaded strawberries to the boys' lunch bags.

Jason plodded in, his eyes underscored with mauve and his hair standing up in back like a bloated middle finger.

"What have I told you about playing video games late at night?" she said.

Jason ignored her and continued to the island, gangly and morose. At thirteen, he was already taller than her and quickly catching up to his big brother and dad. He dropped onto his bar-stool and reached for the cereal box, his free thumb scrolling his phone. He poured milk, and orange juice, managing to splash both onto the white countertop. Ester ordered him to clean up his mess, trying to remember the last time a smile had cracked his narrow face.

Simon and the boys continued to eat and slurp on automatic, all three now disappeared into their phones. She pushed down the urge to wave her arms like those airport agents with green vests and orange batons, the ones on the tarmac who direct planes to a complete stop.

Ester parked in front of Rich Goods, surprised to see its noxious-looking lights already on. It had to be Rich inside, but there was no sign of his banged-up truck. The Ford Transit was likely in the garage. Again. That thing had more lives than Ester's rattly fridge. She exited the minivan and approached the convenience store, like wading through water. She reminded herself she could handle Rich, and the job was easy local employment until she found something better.

She entered the store, triggering the bell overhead and sending the Closed sign swinging. To her relief it was Crystal standing behind the counter. "Hey, you."

"Hey. What are you doing here?" Crystal said.

"I was about to ask you the same thing. I'm on today's schedule."

Crystal scanned the handwritten worksheet. "Shit. Rich put us both down for this morning."

"He probably did it on purpose," Ester said.

"It wouldn't surprise me."

Ester joined Crystal behind the counter and readied to flip a quarter. Crystal called heads. Ester rescued the tumbling coin midfall. Right as she slapped the quarter onto the back of her hand, the store bell disturbed the air. A man in a giraffe mask rushed forward, a handgun aimed. Ester glanced at the red alarm button beneath the counter.

"Don't move!" The intruder panned the gun to Crystal, who was standing nearest the cash register. He fired a cloth tote bag with a cartoon Superman on its front, hitting Crystal in the chest. "Money. Cigarettes. Now!"

Ester's eyes fluttered, wanting to dart to the overhead security camera. Rich routinely spied on her and Crystal through it. She trained her sights on the gunman. *Please let Rich be watching right now. Please let him be calling 911.*

"Her name's Crystal, I'm Ester." Her pitched voice seemed to belong to someone else.

"Shut up." He sounded like his teeth were cutting into something.

She pressed on, knowing victims fare better if perps see them as people, not liabilities. "Take whatever you want. We just want to get home to our kids—"

"I said to shut your mouth." He vaulted over the counter and touched the gun to Ester's temple. She clenched her insides, about to pee herself. Beneath the mask's supersized giraffe eyelashes, the gunman's actual lashes reached through the eyeholes. Ester resaw the bonfire she'd imagined earlier, and the blueberry stems writhing while burning. Every time the gunman blinked, the scratching sound grated the back of her throat. He whiffed of something pungent too, like the childhood smell of her grandma's sour air conditioning.

Crystal started wheezing. The gunman whirled around. Ester hoped this was a moment of brilliance and Crystal was faking the asthma attack.

"She needs her inhaler." Ester stepped toward the alarm.

He spun back to her. "I told you not to move."

She nodded to the shelves below the counter. "Her purse is right there, her inhaler's inside."

He grabbed the tote bag from Crystal and shoved it into Ester's middle, knocking the air out of her. She doubled over, letting the bag fall to the floor. Superman watched from the faded linoleum, his gaze tender.

The gunman lifted the bag, choking its neck. "Fill it."

Ester accepted the bag with a sharp tug, trying to see the color of the gunman's hair beneath the hood of his navy sweatshirt. Crystal's wheezing worsened. If she was faking, her performance was spectacular. "She really needs her—"

He brought the gun to Ester's face and traced her cheekbone with its bottom lip. "I could shoot both of you and help myself."

Ester opened the cash register, her stomach dropping. Crystal had already added the morning's starting balance. The gunman was going to get away with two hundred dollars in notes alone. She rushed the bills and coin rolls into the bag and toppled an armful of cigarette cartons from the shelf, stuffing Superman to bloating. She eyed the wall clock and risked another sideways look at the alarm. Five minutes to opening and who knew how long before their first customer. Her hopes remained pinned on the security cameras. *Come on, Rich.*

Crystal stumbled backward into the shelves of cigarettes, her breathing a terrifying rasp. Ester dropped the bag, seeing a flash of her college boyfriend Marcus, unable to get to his inhaler and dying alone at only twenty-three. Crystal emitted strangled sounds and grasped for the gunman like she was drowning.

"Get off me." He twisted free of Crystal's frantic reach and whacked her with the gun, cracking open her hairline. She slid downward, cigarette cartons dropping as she fell and surrounding her on the floor where she sat slumped. Blood spilled down the side of her face, a half mask.

"See what you made me do," he said with rage and relish.

Crystal's starved lungs issued a huge sucking sound.

"Please, she could die." Ester didn't know she was crying until she tasted salt.

He pushed the gun against Ester's mouth, mashing her lips to her teeth. Just as quickly, he lowered the gun and pressed his harsh mask to her face, the plastic hurting her lips less than the metal, and yet more. He pulled away, grabbed the fat tote bag from the floor, and dashed out from behind the counter. Almost at the exit, he cracked a jubilant laugh and jumped through the air like a buck that's just gained his first antlers.

"You won't get away with this." Ester's furious threat caught him as he burst through the double glass doors. She smacked the alarm, then rifled through Crystal's purse. She rushed the inhaler to Crystal's bloodied mouth, picturing Marcus as the last of his air left him.

While Crystal pumped her lungs back to working order, Ester phoned 911, her lips and cheeks stinging. The only other time she'd made an emergency call was as a teen, when her mom died. She dragged her hand down her face, wiping the gun and mask traces, and ignoring how her bruised lips protested. The quarter she'd been about to flip lay next to her foot. It had landed tails up, making her the winner. She shivered. What if the coin had turned up heads? Would she be the one lying injured and bleeding?

She knelt down next to Crystal and eased a wad of paper towels to her slack face, sopping up the blood while taking care to avoid the oozing gash. She wiped Crystal's left eye clean. It stared out, dazed, empty. She wondered if she should try to pinch the wound closed. Sirens winged toward them.

"You hear that? Help's almost here. Just keep breathing nice and steady. That's it. Well done. It's over, okay? It's all over."

She continued to coax and nurse Crystal as best she could until the police and paramedics arrived and ordered her to stand clear.

Imalive

The ambulance whisked Crystal away. Officer Garamenchi escorted Ester back inside the store.

Seconds into scribbling down her statement, the short, knobby policeman paused. "Ester Prynn. Why's that so familiar?"

"You're thinking of Hester Prynne, from *The Scarlet Letter.*"

"The what?"

"It doesn't matter. Can we get this over with, please?"

"Sure." He aimed his pen. "You said he's about six foot?"

"Yeah." She listed the gunman's build and clothing. "I'm pretty sure he's middle-aged, if not older."

"What makes you think that? His agility, and the Superman bag, suggest otherwise."

"He has a creaky voice." Heat climbed her face. "And he kissed me. There's not too many kids up for that."

His oversized head jerked backward. "He kissed you?"

"Did he ever. Here, see for yourself," Rich said, almost gleefully, from the customer side of the crime scene.

A burly officer crossed the store and confiscated the security tape.

"I want that back," Rich said.

Ester finished her statement. Garamenchi flipped the small spiral notebook closed. "Great, thank you."

Rich grumbled about his losses. On Ester's first day on the job, she'd told him to invest in a locked case for the wall of liquor and cigarettes. He was sorry now.

"That's what insurance is for," Garamenchi said.

"You want to fill out that paperwork for me? Track down the trail of receipts they're going to want?" Rich said.

Out front, the fire engine, squad cars, and convoy of news crews continued to draw onlookers. Rich piped up again. "Where's that crowd every other day, huh? I'm lucky if I see that many people around here in a month, never mind in one morning." The officers laughed. "You think this is funny? Think I'm a comedian?"

"Yeah, you're a comedian," the burly officer said.

"I'd probably make more money," Rich said. The officers laughed harder. "Can you at least let me open up, maybe snag some of these rubberneckers?"

"As soon as we're done," Garamenchi said.

"How long's that gonna be?"

"As long as it takes."

"Man, I can't ever catch a break."

"Your head's in one piece, isn't it?" Ester said, quaking. "No one cracked it open with a gun, did they?"

"Ma'am, you sure you don't want to go to the hospital? It's never a bad idea to get checked out after something like this," Garamenchi said.

"She's fine. Crystal will be too," Rich said.

Ester addressed Garamenchi. "Am I free to go?"

"Yeah, sure. We have your details if there's any follow-up."

She hooked her purse onto her shoulder.

"Where do you think you're going?" Rich said.

As she walked out, his voice climbed. "Hey, I'm talking to you."

She pushed the door wide open, so it closed behind her with a satisfying *thwack*. Reporters and camera crews surrounded her.

Ester awoke to a beating drum. *Mom. Mom. Mom.* She jerked upright on her bed, fully dressed.

"I've been calling you for ages," Jason said from the doorway.

"What's up?" She hurtled clumsily to her feet.

"I'm hungry and there's nothing to eat."

She lifted her phone from her nightstand, shocked to find she'd slept for most of the day. There was no word from Crystal. Rich had discharged a series of increasingly furious texts, ordering her back to the store.

"Mom."

She hadn't realized Jason was still standing in the doorway. "Give me a sec."

He took off down the hall to his bedroom, his heels striking the hardwood. It needled her that he couldn't tell something was wrong.

"I'll make pasta," she called after him. "It'll be ready in a few."

She phoned the hospital again, knowing this time to pretend she was family. A nurse informed her that Crystal was in stable condition. Ester pressed her for details. "You'll have to talk to her doctor, but he's not available right now."

Ester ended the call, catching her skittish reflection in the mirrored closet doors. She wondered who was taking care of Crystal's three young children. She would check on them if she had a home address, but her only contact information was Crystal's cell phone, which had traveled in the ambulance with her, along with her purse and the bloodied inhaler.

In the kitchen, Ester set about fixing chicken Caesar salad and penne pasta drizzled in butter and Parmesan. Kevin arrived home. She braced herself, sure word of the holdup would have spread by now. But Kevin, like his brother, remained oblivious. The two siblings plated up and carried their heaped meals and glasses of water out of the room, the ice cubes colliding.

Kevin continued on to the TV in the living room and Jason to his bedroom and video games. She eyed the remaining salad in the bowl and the filmy pasta in the pot. A craving came over her for plummy wine, a juicy steak, and a slice of chocolate cake. She returned to her bedroom to tie up her frizzy hair and change out of her crime-tainted clothes. In the bathroom mirror, she removed her mascara stains and rubbed her mouth hard with the clean side of the face wipe. She painted her swollen lips a potent red and smacked them together, the popping sound remarkably loud.

Ester waited at the living room window until Simon's car turned into the driveway. She rushed outside, meeting him while the wheels were still rolling, and pulled open the passenger door. "We're going out for dinner."

"No. Please. I'm too tired."

"If we hurry, we'll catch happy hour at Capitanis." She dropped onto the front seat, relieved that he also knew nothing about the holdup. Until she said something about it, it was in the past.

"Capitanis? Wait, it's not our anniversary, is it?"

"That was last week."

"Crap, I'm sorry."

"I'm kidding. It's two weeks away."

"I knew it wasn't this early in March. Is there another occasion I should know about?"

"I just have a hankering." She turned the radio dial, raising the volume on Bon Jovi's "Born to Be My Baby."

"Notice how I always entertain your cravings?" Simon said, putting the car in reverse.

Inside Capitanis, Ester and Simon ordered from the happy hour cocktail menu. She repeatedly checked her phone for an update from Crystal. Repeatedly tried to work up the words to tell Simon about the holdup, and her walking off the job, but she still didn't want to bring it into the here and now.

They were drinking a second margarita each when the ribeyes arrived, Gorgonzola sauce for Simon and pepper sauce for her. They were cutting into the meat, spilling blood, when Simon froze, staring at something beyond her shoulder. She started to follow his gaze but paused, clapping sight of herself inside the three mega-screen TVs behind the bar. Her scalp tightened. She was giant, and in triplicate, on the local six o'clock news. Simon continued to gape at the TV behind her, his freckles fading. Her adrenalized voice, amplified by the reporter's furry black microphone, carved through the restaurant's noises. "I thought he was going to kill us."

"Jesus, Ester. Why didn't you tell me?" Simon sounded as salty as the rim of their margarita glasses. She didn't know what she expected from him in that moment, but certainly not a scolding. She furtively scanned their fellow diners and the roving staff, worried they'd recognized her. It appeared not.

Her phone shuddered on the table, vibrating with a text. Her Meat Loaf ringtone also went off, a call from Rachel. She hit decline, putting a stop to the chorus of "Bat out of Hell." She scrolled the incoming deluge of texts from more friends, neighbors, and fellow school parents. Her ringtone sounded again. She silenced her phone and turned it facedown on the table.

Simon's phone rang. "Please don't answer it," she said. He declined the call.

The calls and texts kept coming to their silenced phones, but nothing yet from or about Crystal.

Simon squeezed her hand. "Are you sure you're okay?"

"It's Crystal we need to worry about. I got off lightly."

"She'll be okay."

"You don't know that."

Stuffed on buttered bread, steak with fixings, and slushy cocktails, Ester and Simon ordered the chocolate dessert to share.

"I don't know where we'll put it," Simon told their server.

Yet he and Ester devoured the wedge of warm, gooey cake with athletic aptitude. She drained her glass of red wine, which tasted more of oak than the longed-for fruit.

"Molten, that's such a great word," she said, gripping her knees below the table.

Simon rubbed his stubbled chin, making his lips squelch. "You're not okay, are you?"

Her elbows jumped to the table and her hands pressed her face, their tips hurting her forehead, her cheekbones. "What he did to Crystal, it was horrible."

Simon eased her hands into his. "Hey. Hey."

Outside, the sharp air lifted Ester's hair off her face and the nape of her neck. It felt cooling, clearing.

Simon carried the reek of blue cheese into the car. Thanks to that and the twists in the road, Ester's stomach reeled. It didn't help that she'd made a pig of herself. She clenched her teeth against the urge to retch and gripped her seatbelt at her chest with both hands. Simon kept asking her to talk to him.

She considered telling him the gunman had kissed her. "Please, you're not helping."

At home, Kevin and Jason also quizzed Ester, their phones similarly crawling with texts and social media posts and messages. She reassured them she was completely fine.

"In broad daylight too," Simon said.

"Was he supposed to wait until it got dark?" Jason said.

"You're such an ass," Kevin said.

"You're the ass."

They didn't seem to notice her leaving the room.

Upstairs, her phone pinged with a text from Crystal. She read, softening with relief. *back home   outta it   talk tomo   thanks 4 ur help*

Rich had fired off another ultimatum. *B here to open up tomorrow r else*

In bed, in the thick dark, she straddled Simon and rocked her hips in time to *Imalive, Imalive, Imalive.*

Blow Your House Down

Simon left for work, and the boys for school. Ester settled on the living room couch with a second bowl of cornflakes and powered on the TV with a flicker of guilt. She hadn't disabused her family of the idea that she was merely taking a day off work to rest and recover.

"Good for you," Simon had said. "And you know, if you're not up for it, you don't ever have to go back."

Well-intentioned, she knew, but he'd made her feel like she'd failed at something. She had felt the same way three months back, when her short-lived sales career at the solar panel company ended due to downsizing. The job had been her biggest and best role since returning to work full-time after Jason started middle school. Now it was more like a black mark on her résumé. When she'd told Simon she was let go, a dull knowingness had flickered across his face, like he'd expected as much.

She surfed the glut of TV channels, finding nothing. Rich texted seconds after 9:00 A.M. *UR FIRED BITCH!!!!!*

She blocked his number, picturing him muttering to himself inside the empty store. Thankfully, he'd already paid her through her last shift. Throughout the morning she watched back-to-back episodes of *Family Feud,* dispatching responses out loud and cussing when she got the answers wrong. The show was trite and sometimes sleazy, but often hilarious. Her phone pinged with calls and texts from various friends and school parents checking in. She couldn't muster the energy to reply.

At noon, she phoned Crystal for the second time. The call again went to voicemail. She left another message, trying not to sound overly concerned. Hopefully Crystal was still sleeping and there weren't any complications overnight. She wondered how Crystal would feel on finding out she'd quit the store. She hoped Crystal might do the same but knew the single mom of three, and a high school dropout, was short on options.

She considered heading to Daisy's Salon for a mani-pedi and paying the extra for a shoulder massage. After, she would go to Submarine 'n Some for an iced tea and their melt-in-your-mouth pastrami sandwich. Instead, her feet took her to the kitchen island, and her laptop. She searched the sizable online inventory of face masks until she found one closest to the gunman's. She ordered the replica in a single click, tempted to pay the additional six bucks for same-day delivery, but decided she didn't want the mask to arrive that evening, when Simon and the boys would be home.

She searched the faulty fridge for chocolate, finding none, and scrutinized the pantry shelves for an alternative sugar rush. Maybe she should have taken Rachel and Donna up on their offer to stop by, but she hadn't wanted them to ditch work on her account. She would see them soon enough. She closed the pantry door, empty-handed, peeved. Simon and the boys had eaten every treat in the house. They'd even scarfed the kettle corn.

Popping. That was the best way to describe the unnerving sensation in her head since she'd woken up. She could almost smell oil burning behind her face. Inside her brain, yellow kernels turned hot and rapid-firing, bursting into white, trembling masses.

Ester arrived at the strip mall, intent on the nail salon and later a deli sandwich, but her foot remained on the accelerator, taking her clear across the parking lot and toward the freeway. She'd lost count of the number of times she'd made this trip from Half Moon Bay to Daly City to see her demented dad, and could do it blindfolded. She closed her eyes. *One. Two.* Her eyes flew open, refusing to stay shuttered. She'd hoped to count to at least three while driving blind, thinking it might ease her angst to court danger on her own terms.

It was never solely a visit with Dad inside Golden Leaves' Alzheimer's wing, but a tour of the entire population. Ester walked through the cavernous dayroom, greeting the rows of residents parked in chairs and daybeds along both walls. Despite the high rate of turnover she knew every patient by name, even when most didn't know it themselves.

She entered the small back room, finding Dad stationed in his usual spot alongside Tom, Joan, and Roberto, a trio who tended to be almost as loud and disruptive as him.

"Dad," she said with resounding delight, as if it had been months and not days since she last saw him. For him, it had been three years since they last met. She kissed his florid, fallen-in cheek, also to zero response. It hit her that it was over a year since he'd last spoken. She dropped into the visitor's chair next to him and babbled about the weather, and Simon and the boys. His expression remained glazed.

"Right, let's go," she said, coming out of her chair and its cushions that seemed to want to suck her in.

She unlocked the brakes on Dad's wheelchair and rolled him into the main dayroom. She returned for Tom. Stella, a veteran caregiver, appeared with her broad smile and loose black hair that looked wind-tossed. She ferried Joan from the back room while Ester followed with Roberto, and lined him up alongside his three partners in crime.

Tom wailed for his dog. Stella lifted the plush pet from Tom's stick lap and placed it in his bony hands. Joan also fussed, similarly missing her most treasured belongings. Ester located Joan's striped shopping bag, forever stuffed with rolls of toilet paper. She placed the bag on Joan's much sturdier thighs, pushing away thoughts of the Superman tote bag. Joan removed a toilet roll and wound its length round and round her gnarled hands, their skin the color of pork.

"We saw you on the news last night," Stella said. "That had to be terrifying."

"Right now I'm more frightened of getting booed by this lot."

Stella laughed. "When have they ever? And even if they did, you'd survive. We staff get it all the time."

Ester moved to the front of the dayroom, in full view of the residents who were at various stages of erasure, and opened her phone's bookmarks to Shel Silverstein. It had taken some trial and error, but she'd discovered her audience, like toddlers, responded best to short poems with repetition and rhyme. When sparks landed, some in the group clapped and grunted and stomped their feet. Sometimes the more animated among them shuffled over the linoleum, twirled about, and waved their arms in a terrible-wonderful dance. On rare occasions, Ester swore she could feel some of their resurrected spirits ricocheting off the ceiling and walls.

This day, Silverstein's poems and Ester's stage-worthy antics received a lukewarm response. Almost as though the residents could tell her mind was elsewhere. She considered her arsenal of nursery rhymes and fairy tales, and launched into a robust telling of "The Three Little Pigs." The more the residents reacted, the more she delivered. Their animation climbed with the story's climax and several faces split open with gummy, drunken grins. By now the majority were flailing and rocking, parroting Ester's extravagant gestures. Others, including Dad, remained like mannequins.

When Ester delivered the wolf's final threat, many in the group bucked and raised guttural noises. It seemed, in some deep part of their remains, they knew the wolf had come for them too, and they wanted nothing more than to see him outsmarted, and destroyed.

On the drive home, Ester at last received a text from Crystal.

im alright in pain still shocked 10 stitches!!!!!!!!!!!! back to work tomorrow UGH how are you?

Ester was still mulling over Crystal's question when the minivan swept over the San Mateo County line. The name of her hometown hit her again. How Half Moon Bay suggested fracture, and the unfinished. More and more of late, she imagined packing up and starting over someplace new, where no one knew her. It would never happen. She had Simon and the boys, and her dad and dear friends. Her entire life was here. And yet.

Maybe she would move away when both boys were in college, if only for a while. Possibly travel for a year—spend a month in New Zealand, another in Australia, and ten months exploring the best of Europe. If she was going to do it, she would have to adventure alone. Simon would never agree to taking a year out of his life and work and wouldn't understand why she would want to. He never seemed to need more than what he had, except for money, and sex. Never seemed to worry that he was in the wrong life.

How Not to Love Them

Ester arrived at the store, relieved to not see Rich's truck. The jitters returned as soon as she exited the minivan, her nervous system still keyed up two days after the robbery. Two days. In her mind it seemed like the holdup had happened longer ago, and yet in her body it was still occurring.

She pushed the entry door open with her back, careful of the glass bowl she was holding, its resident a hyperactive goldfish. The store was empty of customers and Crystal was sitting on the barstool behind the counter. Borrowing from *Hairspray*, Ester belted, "Good morn-ing, Crys-tal-more."

Crystal's face lit up below her partially shaved head. Ester's throat constricted on seeing the raw wound up close, with its lace of black stitches and the surrounding skin a hot pink.

She lowered the fishbowl to the counter. "I thought you might like some company around here. Meet Jerry the Second, or whatever you want to call him. Jerry was the name of my goldfish when I was little, and he had this wild near-death experience—"

"Do I want to hear this?" Crystal said.

"Absolutely. I was draining the dirty water from Jerry's bowl when he slipped out and dropped into the garbage disposal, while it was running."

Crystal's hand pressed her mouth and she looked both amused and horrified. "No."

"I dived at the wall switch, turned off the blades, and scooped Jerry out, sure he was a goner. But somehow he was alive and in one piece." The memory of Jerry's wriggling, victorious body feathered Ester's palm.

"That is wild." Crystal watched the goldfish part the water. "Look at this one go. Reckon he's also a fighter."

"A torpedo."

"Torpedo, that's what I'll call him," Crystal said.

"Nice."

Crystal's smile dropped. "There's no way Rich will let me keep him here."

"Tell him the customers like him and that he's a draw for business. That'd make Rich display his own mother on a shelf."

Crystal chewed her lower lip, favoring its left side. "It's worth a shot. He's no substitute for you though."

Ester's right temple pulsed with guilt. "I'll keep sneaking in to see you."

"I'm not sure how long that'll last. There's not much gets past Rich."

Ester pictured him seething right then on the other side of the security cameras. Crystal dropped onto the barstool, more sinking than sitting.

"You shouldn't have come back to work so soon. You should be at home, taking it easy," Ester said.

"My bank balance disagrees."

"What did the doctors say? Did they clear you to come back already?"

"It's more what the debt collectors are saying." Crystal's expression brightened. "Well done you for quitting. What I'd give to have seen Rich's face."

"I didn't see it either. I walked out while he was shouting at my back. And yesterday morning, when it was clear I wasn't returning, he sent me a choice text." Fresh anxiety nipped. Rich could walk through the door at any moment.

"Oh. I thought you two had like a showdown. That doesn't make me feel so bad then."

"What do you have to feel bad about?" Ester said.

"I'd love to tell him where to shove it, but all I can do is shut up and put up. Makes me feel like shit on a shoe."

Ester remembered Crystal had a police record, which further limited her career choices. "Fierce, that's how you should feel. You're doing what you need to, so you and your kids can get by."

"Thanks for that spin." Pain cut Crystal's laugh short. Her fingers fluttered above the angry laceration.

Ester resaw the gunman pistol-whip Crystal. His plastic face was grinding Ester's mouth. His handgun drilled her temple.

"You all right?" Crystal said.

"Me? Are you all right?"

"I could do with some more painkillers, but I gotta wait a couple of hours."

Ester searched her purse, hiding her upset. There was no way Crystal should be back to work this soon. She handed over the plastic tub of fish food. "Don't overfeed him. People think it's how to love them, but that's how most fish die. If you want to spoil him, talk to him. It works for plants and most everything else."

"Got it, thanks."

"The first sign of green, you need to change the water. Dirty water, that's the second leading cause of death."

"You sure know your goldfish."

"Maybe better than I know children."

"Jason?"

"Who else?"

They traded fresh grievances about their kids, pausing the conversation whenever a customer arrived at the counter to check out.

They landed on lighter talk of their offspring's pickiness and phobias. Ester exaggerated her boys' neuroses for comedic effect, in particular Jason's terror of blue mold on food.

"My Jim won't keep his toothbrush in the bathroom," Crystal said. "Nothing I say can convince him a dump won't contaminate it."

Ester maintained her smile, but she was thinking about how the gunman had contaminated things.

Crystal also turned somber. "I can't help thinking this is my punishment for stealing stuff in the past."

"That's crazy, there's no comparison. You shoplifted what? Groceries? Clothes?"

"And then some."

"Hey, don't go there. I'm supposed to be cheering you up, remember?"

"You are, and Torpedo was a brilliant idea, thank you. Now get out of here before Rich shows up," Crystal said.

"Yeah, all right. Best if I live to return another day."

"You heard that Blazers is looking for a hostess, right?"

Ester had not.

"You should apply," Crystal said.

"I'll check it out, but I don't think I'm much of a candidate. Maybe twenty-five years ago, when my rack was still in the right place, and rather glorious."

Crystal laughed, her hand rushing back to her stitches.

"Right, I'll leave you in peace."

As Ester exited the store, Crystal waved from her post at the cash register, the goldfish parked on the shelf behind her. Ester waved back, her smile flimsy. Crystal could have died in that same spot—from battery, gunshots, or something as stupid as asthma.

Ester returned to the minivan and allowed the engine to idle, stuck on what Crystal had said about just deserts. Maybe the holdup, and her witnessing Crystal's breathless ordeal, was her cosmic punishment. For cheating on Marcus in college and causing him to move across the country to Chicago, where he died alone from asthma, criminally young and with a hurt heart. Or the holdup was random. Plain dumb luck. Whichever way, she needed to turn things around. She killed the engine and searched online on her phone. She dialed.

"Blazers." The voice was deep, gruff.

"Yes, hi, hello—"

"Blazers." He didn't repeat the word so much as hurl it.

"I'm calling about the hostess job—"

"Go to our website and complete the application online."

"So I don't need to apply in person?"

"No."

"I presume there'll be information on the website regarding—"

"Everything you need to know is on there." He hung up.

Ester gripped her phone like it was the offender. "Jerk."

The job opening was a possibility at least. Something to present to Simon and the boys during dinner, after she finally admitted she was out of work. Again. The timing couldn't be worse either, what with Kevin headed for college in August. School tuition, it was another form of domestic terrorism.

The overnight delivery was waiting for Ester on the front doorstep. She carried the cardboard box into the kitchen and sliced the tape open with her car key. She removed the top layer of bubble wrap, revealing the giraffe mask. Its coloring was too orange. The gunman's mask was more brown. But it was close enough.

She folded the delivery box flat and placed it and the bubble wrap in the recycling bin. She carried the mask upstairs to her bedroom, not looking at it. She lay down on her back on her bed, taking deep breaths. She pressed the mask to her face and pulled its elastic cord over her head. She rested her clasped hands on her stomach, feeling herself rise and fall.

Her face turned hot and damp behind the mask. Her recycled breath quickened and climbed. Her ears filled with the growing sound of the outside world entering her and her insides leaving her. Her eyelashes batted the back of the plastic face, their scratches the same grating noise as the gunman's lashes had made. Through the eyeholes, she was seeing the world the way he had. She tried to picture how she and Crystal had looked to him. Tried to understand how he had made so little of them, of Crystal, he could do what he did.

She shot up, gasping and pulling off the mask. She swung her legs off the bed and curled her hands around the edge of the mattress. She pressed her feet to the floor, but the hardwood wasn't enough to keep her tethered. She was back inside the store, seeing Superman look up from the linoleum tiles. His gaze more sad than tender, she realized. Like he was thinking, *This is how humans are.*

Nice Shock

Ester printed out the job application form and completed it by hand, adding her signature with a flourish. She'd hated her name growing up. Back then *The Scarlet Letter* was included on most high school and college syllabi, and people regularly connected her to its heroine. When the novel was assigned to her ninth-grade English class, her fellow students teased her mercilessly and nicknamed her Scarlet. She pleaded with her parents, wanting to legally change her name. She would have swayed Dad too, she knew it, but Mom remained adamant.

"That name's my gift to you. I was thrilled you were a girl, I'd have gone for a fourth child if you weren't, so thanks for that. You shot right out of me too, and didn't cry. You roared. I had to give you a powerful name. Regardless, there was no way you were going to be called anything ordinary. My maiden name was Mary Smith. Believe me, you don't ever want to suffer that tedium."

"You named your sons Tim and Rod," Ester said.

"That's different. Men get to stand out whatever they're called."

"But *Ester*, really? Prynn wasn't unusual enough?"

"The near-namesake gets you noticed."

"Who wants that kind of attention? It's not just those who've read the book either, most everyone makes remarks."

"Because your name's remarkable, see?"

"It's stupid."

"You're named after a famous heroine and should embrace it."

"Have you *read* the novel?"

"Have you thought about how you might be your own kind of heroine?"

"That's not pressure." Ester and Mom laughed, but something in Ester's stomach started to twist, and had never really relaxed since.

Mom died three months later, at age fifty-two, from a massive stroke. Ester then swore that no one, nothing, would ever take away her Mom-given name, least of all herself.

Ester timed her arrival at Blazers for eleven fifteen, when the breakfast service would be finished and the lunch service had yet to start. Inside the minivan, she rechecked her reflection in the visor mirror, relatively pleased with her dewy complexion and largely frizz-free hair. She'd inherited her smooth skin, thick mane, and large lips from Mom. They had both also once boasted chiseled cheekbones. She pushed her face closer to the mirror. Two puffy wads of skin drooped over her eyelids. When had they appeared? She poked and lifted the wads. When she released them, they instantly collapsed. She slapped the visor closed. Furtive, she scanned the parking lot and reached into her bra, scooping and lifting each sweaty breast in turn. She tugged her navy-and-white blocked dress away from her stomach and pulled the navy blazer tighter across her front, so it looked like it could close. She froze. In the rearview mirror, she was wearing the giraffe mask.

Inside Blazers, Ester approached the crusty-looking man behind the podium, knowing even before she heard his terse voice that he was the one she'd spoken with on the phone. She also knew from the website that he wasn't the hiring manager. That task fell to a woman. He delayed several long seconds before looking up from the desktop screen he was poking with his trigger finger. "The restaurant is closed until noon."

She glanced sideways at the long bar, its TVs casting her back to Capitanis and her knitted face trapped inside multiple supersized screens. "I'm here for drinks."

His brow crimped with disapproval. "Take a seat anywhere you like."

She crossed to the bar, shaky on stiletto heels. It didn't help her balance any that she could sense Mr. Personality tracking her. A loud clatter of metal sounded, making her flinch. She traced the noise to the rear of the restaurant and the two servers dismantling a row of chafing trays. The few customers dotted about seemed immune to the disturbance, and also parked in place, as if they'd nowhere else to go. She wished it was Capitanis hiring and not this dated hotel restaurant. She reminded herself that whatever hope she had of getting this job, there was no way Capitanis would employ someone like her to be the face of their upscale, award-winning restaurant.

She reached the end of the bar farthest from the four men sitting separately and nursing drinks. She considered climbing onto a barstool and playing at a customer in case Mr. Personality was still watching her. The bartender abandoned the dishwasher he was emptying and greeted her with a bleached grin and a beer coaster.

"What can I get you?" His southern drawl and flaxen hair added to his appeal, but his recessed chin, how it blurred into his neck, stopped him from being outright attractive.

"I was hoping to speak with Allie."

"Let me see if she's around." He moved midway down the bar and reached beneath the counter, bringing a black walkie-talkie into view. Ester presumed the gadget was called something hipper nowadays. "Can I say what this is about?"

She spoke low but firm. "The hostess position."

He summoned Allie. Her staticky response promised she'd be right there.

Allie was Ester's height and likely also in her early forties. She appeared to be a yoga disciple, her toned body a temple of bones, angles, and dips. She offered her hand, and on contact Ester experienced a shock, similar to the zap from a dodgy electrical outlet, only pleasant.

"Nice to meet you," Ester said.

"Likewise. What can I do for you?" Allie said.

Ester held out her application form, the pages quivering midair. "I thought I'd drop this off in person, if that's okay, and take the opportunity to introduce myself."

"Oh, all right. Very good." Allie scanned the form. "Ester Prynn. Someone's a Hawthorne fan."

"My mom. I've forgiven her, mostly, but introductions can be a bit of a production."

"You also rhyme."

"Yeah, I heard that."

"It's a great name."

"Thanks. Besides my mom, you might be the only person to have told me that."

"Really?" Allie said with intensity.

Ester, puce, thought maybe Allie was gay. "Thankfully not that many people read the novel anymore, and the movie has been pretty much forgotten."

"Demi Moore, right?"

"Not that forgotten then," Ester said.

They laughed.

"I admit I only read the SparkNotes in college," Allie said.

"I probably wouldn't have read it either if it wasn't for the whole namesake thing, and I can't say I recommend it. The prose is as dense as cement. As for the ending, it's a major, confusing letdown."

"Glad I dodged it then." Allie gestured to the row of green pleather booths along the wall. "Let's sit."

Seated together, Ester had to stop herself from complimenting Allie's woodsy perfume. She rattled off her college server experience and embellished her hostess record. She also talked up her spotty admin and sales jobs and cited her excellent people and organizational skills. "I'd give the job my all."

"I don't doubt it." Allie presented the hotel and restaurant as a boutique, family-owned business intent on staff treating customers and each other like one of their own. "A home away from home. Of course it's something we can always improve on."

Cue Mr. Personality, Ester thought.

Allie described the daytime trade as mostly hotel guests for breakfast; tourists and corporate types for lunch; and a mix of both groups for dinner and drinks, along with locals and in particular sports fans. She also listed the job's pay and benefits, which were decent.

"I've got several interviews set up over the next couple of days, but I should be able to get back to you by Friday. How does that sound?"

"Sounds great, thank you. I really appreciate your time and this impromptu interview."

"Of course."

Ester struggled out of the cushioned booth, acting a total klutz. Allie walked her to the front of the restaurant. Mr. Personality's wide-set eyes raked Ester like she was a bad oyster he'd swallowed. So much for the happy family ethos.

"Thanks again, it was so nice to meet you." Ester pumped Allie's arm, oddly thinking of shaking a flower by its stem.

"Same. We'll talk soon," Allie said.

Outside, Ester floated to the minivan and onto the driver's seat. She pulled her door closed and the strange enchantment dissipated. She sat in its afterglow, elated, confused.

Night Out

Ester, Rachel, and Donna sat perched on barstools around a high-top table, annihilating flatbread topped with prosciutto and mushrooms and debating the merits of the Portuguese red blend, which they were drinking way too fast.

"Just the right amount of jam," Ester observed, smacking her lips. She'd resisted the night out, wary of the cost, the effort of getting ready, and more talk of the holdup, but she was glad now that Rachel and Donna had refused to let her flake. If she'd stayed home, she would have likely pickled herself with TV, junk food, and cheap booze, especially after Allie not phoning as promised. She obviously didn't get the job, but the courtesy of a call would have been nice.

"How are you, really?" Rachel said.

"I'm all right. It's so much worse for Crystal."

"Any news on the gunman?" Donna said.

"Not yet."

"Crime's gotten out of control, especially in the city, and don't get me started on their homeless crisis. I mean, who would want to live in San Francisco anymore?" Rachel said.

"I wouldn't go that far," Ester said, drawing laughter.

"Yeah, okay," Rachel said.

"People are desperate, that's the problem," Donna said.

"The country's gone to hell," Rachel said.

"The whole world has," Donna said.

"Cheers!" Ester said, raising her glass.

"Yes! Sorry! We're supposed to be giving you a good time." Rachel steered the conversation to current movies. The three turned uproarious discussing the creepy final scene in *The Favourite* where Emma Stone as the lady's maid performs cunnilingus on Olivia Colman as Queen Anne while the two are surrounded by tens of rapidly multiplying rabbits.

"You have to watch *Fleabag*, it's brilliant, and Olivia Colman's character in that is hysterical," Ester said.

"I love Susie in *The Marvelous Mrs. Maisel*, she's played by Alex what's her name? That's a dream sidekick role right there," Donna said, to hearty agreement.

The conversation turned from celebrities to local figures as they speculated on the real reason Principal Campbell had resigned from Rayland High. They also covered which kids wanted to get into which high schools and colleges, couples in various forms of jeopardy, and how Charlie Neville's telltale skin was turning mustardy. A striking young couple entered the wine bar, looking like they'd stepped out of an edgy clothing catalog.

Rachel drew her shoulders toward her ears. "Every time that door opens, the draft cuts through me."

"We can ask to move," Ester said, looking around for a free table.

"It's okay," Rachel said, pulling on her jacket.

"This is the wettest, coldest March I can remember here," Donna said.

"People need to stop saying climate change, it's a catastrophe," Rachel said.

"And we're back," Ester said, triggering more laughter.

"Right, right. No depressing talk allowed," Rachel said.

Two bottles of red wine later, they were ticklish with dopamine and falling about laughing.

Their buttoned-up server appeared with knots in his forehead. "Ladies, I need you to keep the noise down."

"Ridiculous," Rachel said when he moved off. "We weren't that loud."

"We kinda were," Ester said.

"She's not wrong," Donna said.

"Howler monkeys are quieter," Ester said.

"This is why we love you," Donna said.

Rachel raised her glass. "To Ester, we're so glad you're okay."

The three clinked glasses.

"You're not actually supposed to do that," Rachel said.

"Not clink glasses? Really?" Donna said.

"Yeah, I read that someplace. Bad etiquette, or bad luck, one or the other," Rachel said.

Ester insisted they clink glasses again, to undo the faux pas.

"I don't think clinking, then unclinking, is a thing," Donna said.

Ester wasn't taking any chances.

Ester returned from the restroom and shared a photo on her phone of the flier on the back of the stall door, announcing the start of a local women's choir. She'd loved to sing as a girl, in the back of the car and around the house mostly, but she'd also performed in school recitals and talent shows. People said she'd gotten her voice from her mom, but Mom's voice was sweeter, more melodic. Nowadays, Ester only ever sang in the shower and alone in the car and had forgotten that when she was little she'd dreamt of becoming a pop star.

Rachel, squinting, enlarged the flier on the screen.

"You need to give in and get yourself a pair of reading glasses," Donna said.

"Never." Rachel passed Ester's phone over to Donna.

"Let's join," Ester said, thinking how much her mom would give to sing one more song, to do one more anything.

"No thanks," Rachel said.

"Really? I think it'd be a lot of fun," Ester said.

"You've heard me sing 'Happy Birthday,' right? I have to be the only person on earth who can mess that up," Rachel said.

"It's a hard pass from me too," Donna said, returning Ester's phone. "I swear I have PTSD from taking choir in school *and* at church all those years. My mom refused to accept that the first two verses of the national anthem were all I was ever going to be able to sing well, that and the chorus of 'All by Myself.'"

"Come on, let's at least check out the first meeting. What else do you have to do on a Tuesday night?" Ester said.

"The flier could be more welcoming," Donna said. "Make a point of inviting minorities."

"All the more reason for you to join," Ester said.

"I'm not going to be the token Black person, thanks very much," Donna said.

Ester continued to plead, but Donna and Rachel wouldn't be persuaded. "Fine, I'll go on my own."

"Next you'll be donning orthopedic shoes and a 'Can I speak to the manager?' hairstyle," Rachel said.

"How very dare you," Ester said laughing, but her enthusiasm for the choir was already dimming.

Another wave of cold air gusted through the open doorway. It didn't seem to reach the catalog couple, now sitting at the bar and leaning close together, absorbed, lustful. They looked like an ad in a glossy magazine, selling what we wanted to own.

In-N-Out

Ester remained pinned to the mattress on her side, her hand pressed to her throbbing head. She, Rachel, and Donna had drunk a bottle of red wine each. Her stomach roiled at the thought, and she gritted her teeth against the urge to vomit. At least the room had stopped spinning and she'd stopped sweating. During the night, inside the damp, tilting dark, she'd worried her galloping heart was going to burst.

Simon emerged from the bathroom. "You alive in there?"

She opened one eye. "Just about."

"That bad?"

"Worse."

"How much did you drink?"

"Lethal proportions." A phantom gun annoyed her temple and a chill scaled her back. She glanced at the clock on her nightstand and groaned aloud. She never slept in and hated that she'd wasted half the day already.

Simon finished drying himself and tossed the towel across the room. "Dammit."

He'd obviously missed the laundry basket and hadn't fared well on the basketball court earlier either. Saturday mornings, he played hoops religiously with his buddies, and she could always read the tiny, sour signals whenever he'd underperformed. *Sour.* She was thrown back to the sharp smell rising off the gunman.

Downstairs, shouting erupted between Kevin and Jason, a fight about Jason leaving "effed up" comments on Kevin's social media posts.

"Make them stop," Ester said.

Simon moved to the open doorway. "Hey, you two, cut it out."

They did not.

"Great." She rolled onto her back, releasing a swarm of white floaters in front of her eyes. "Oh God."

"Boys! Your mom is dying up here," Simon shouted.

"Can you not?" she said, annoyed.

"Can I get you anything?"

"A glass of water would be nice.

And In-N-Out," she added.

"Does that mean I'm getting dressed?"

"Yes."

"Yes?" He lunged toward her.

"Yes, you're getting dressed."

Downstairs, the front door slammed closed, one or other of the boys storming off. "Do you really want In-N-Out, or are you going to complain afterward that I shouldn't have—"

"Yes, I really want it," she said.

"Just to be clear, we're still talking about fast food?"

"You're exhausting."

"I know how I'd like to exhaust you." The front door slammed again, a second son departing.

"Go get me fries, a cheeseburger, and a strawberry shake."

"We have the house to ourselves," he said.

"You'd get more from a corpse."

"I'm going to try to not think about that."

"Me too," she said, her mood diving.

"Onions, or no?"

"No thanks."

"You're going to hate yourself after you eat it."

"Go already."

"Yes, ma'am."

"That's more like it."

"Last chance." He stood with his gray-haired torso thrust forward, his muscular legs planted apart, and his hands on his expansive hips. A signature Superman pose, only naked.

Ester's ringing phone pulled her from a fitful nap. She rolled over, sending up a fresh burst of white spots, and answered groggily. "Cheeseburger, no onions, fries—"

"I'm ferrying them to you as we speak," Simon said.

"To what then do I owe the pain?"

"I met Larry and his dad while I was in line."

"Larry?"

"Yeah, the kid from Jason's class, with the lisp."

"Harry. And it's not a lisp."

"What is it?"

"I don't know exactly. He has trouble enunciating."

"Anyway, his dad was telling me that the twenty-four-hour gas station on Cabrillo was robbed last night. They're saying it's the same guy."

"Are they sure?" Ester's heart resumed its nocturnal racing, and her skin returned to clammy. Whenever the vital organ did this, skittering like a small animal, she worried she was going to die young like Mom.

"Same MO, I guess, a handgun and an animal mask."

She reared up on the bed. "I'm going to take a shower. How much time do I have?"

"I'll be home in fifteen. Are you okay?"

"Yeah. Yeah." She hung up and held her phone to her pounding chest.

When she stood up, her head felt too light. She drained the glass of water Simon had delivered, the last of its ice hitting her face. In the closet mirror, the wine stains on her crusty lips looked like dried blood. She opened the sliding door and rummaged inside the storage container stuffed with summer clothes that no longer fit.

Her frantic hands found the giraffe mask. She lifted it to her face and secured it with the taut elastic cord. Her irises appeared more blue than green in the glass door. The gunman's were chips of a pale winter sky. His caustic smell refound her, and a squirt of bile scalded the back of her throat. She pulled the mask off, snapping its elastic in two.

In the kitchen, she placed the mask in the sink and aimed the gas lighter's yellow-blue flame. The giraffe's chin caught fire, and the burn scaled its plastic face. Licking. Melting. The disfigured mask struggled and collapsed. Disappeared. She realized this was why she'd purchased it. Why she'd allowed it into her home.

Overflowing

Ester rechecked her phone. There was still no word from Allie regarding the hostess job. If she didn't hear anything by Monday afternoon she would follow up, but the outcome seemed inked. The milkshake inside her curdled. She rushed to the kitchen sink, gagging, retching. The assault passed and she returned to the island, grateful to have the house to herself.

She'd never felt this sickened, or listless, at least not from alcohol poisoning. Just replying to Rachel's and Donna's texts required bodybuilder effort. The pair were undergoing similar toxic torture and vows of never again and a flurry of emojis with green faces and medical masks followed. Ester texted Crystal, checking in. News of the second holdup would be so much more triggering for her. She returned her attention to her laptop and reattempted a search through the job listings, but it was like she, and not the screen, was scrolling downward.

Her phone pinged with a text and photo from Crystal. *torpedo misses u*. The goldfish stared out from Ester's screen, a frontal close-up that colored him more salmon than gold and exaggerated his black eyes and open mouth, a look that screamed alarm.

She hesitated, unsure if she was fit to drive with such a hellacious hangover. The ominous feeling pushed her out of the house.

Ester marched past Rich's truck and into the store. What's the worst he could do? Crystal's eyes widened on seeing her and darted to the restroom in the back corner, its door ajar. Ester nodded, acknowledging she understood Rich's whereabouts. A twentyish customer with long matted hair scanned the candy shelves, while Dan Charles eyed the snacks, the wiry man's beige coat in serious need of dry cleaning. Lydia Greeslie zeroed in on the produce section. The woman's face was forever squashed, and her fingernails perpetually chipped and dirty. It was her one saving grace, working in the garden center and helping the world to breathe a little better.

"You should come back later," Crystal said. "The toilet overflowed again, and Rich is in there trying to subdue it."

Ester pressed her hand to her queasy stomach. "There's a visual I don't need."

"You okay?" Crystal said.

"Self-inflicted wine wounds."

Behind Crystal, Torpedo flitted back and forth inside his bowl like he was racing something.

"What did Rich have to say about our little friend?" Ester said.

"He likes him, if you can believe it. Of course I didn't tell him he came from you."

"And Torpedo misses me?" Ester said wryly.

"I was trying to be cute. I didn't mean to make you come running."

"He looked spooked in the photo and I thought maybe he was catching your mood after the second holdup."

Crystal lifted her phone and tapped Torpedo's photo, enlarging it. "Wow. I can totally see that."

The scrawny youth appeared next to Ester and placed an assortment of candy and chewing gum on the counter. Ester inhaled the waft of weed. She'd never smoked it but liked its earthy smell. Crystal rang him up. He refused a bag and exited the store, his bounty clutched to his chest like a kid at Halloween.

Crystal crossed her arms over her breasts, her hands disappearing inside her pits. "Two armed robberies in a week and he's still out there, it's scary."

"I hear you."

"At least he didn't hurt anyone this time."

Dan stepped forward, Lydia close on his heels. He placed several packets of roasted peanuts on the counter and demanded a bottle of scotch. The peaty alcohol's phantom smell plugged Ester's nose, making her shudder. She would never, ever, drink that much again.

Lydia lifted her chin. "That's a lot of nuts."

Dan remained dour and pulled his wallet from his back trousers pocket.

"Another of your poker nights, is it?" Lydia said.

Crystal handed Dan his change and bagged his items.

"It might surprise you to know that I'm a bit of a shark myself," Lydia said.

"I'm sure you are," Dan said heavily. He placed the brown paper bag under his arm and moved off.

Lydia sniffed. "It doesn't cost anything to be civil."

The only response was the store bell as Dan let himself out.

"I didn't expect to see you here, Ester Prynn." Lydia always used Ester's full name. "I heard Rich fired you."

"I quit, actually."

"Lucky you. Some of us don't have that luxury, do we, Crystal?"

"That's me, lucky." Ester furious-smiled so hard she could feel her teeth coming out of her face.

"Shocking about the gas station also getting robbed last night," Lydia said. "Horrible to think someone like that is still among us."

"Tell me about it," Crystal said, scratching her forehead at the pink, shiny edge of her wound.

Crystal didn't say anything further until Lydia exited the store. "He'd never strike here again, would he?"

The restroom door banged against the far wall, startling Ester and Crystal. Rich emerged with the mop and bucket and barreled toward the back door. He snared Ester in his periphery and rushed at her, sloshing water from the bucket and holding the mop like a spear. "Get out of here, you, and don't ever come back. I mean it. Go on, go."

"I'll catch you later," Ester told Crystal, and mock-sauntered to the door.

"No one walks out on me! No one," Rich said, furious, shaky.

Right as Ester reached the minivan, her phone rang. The caller ID read Blazers, sending a jolt through her. "Hello?"

"Hi, Ester? Ester Prynn?"

"Allie, yes, hi."

"How are you?"

"Good. I'm good, thanks. And you?"

"I'm sorry I didn't get back to you sooner. We had several strong applicants, and the final decision wasn't only up to me." Ester braced herself for the worst. "But I'm pleased to say we'd like to offer you the position, if you're still available?"

"Really?"

"Really."

"That's fantastic, thank you."

"Congratulations."

"Thank you so much."

"We'd like you to start next Thursday at three, if that works? That'll give you a couple of hours to settle in and train on the reservations system and seating chart before we begin the dinner service at five."

"Sounds great. I'll be there."

"Excellent. I'm about to email you various employment forms, they should be self-explanatory, but let me know if you have any questions. It would be really helpful if you could complete and return those ASAP."

"Of course, no problem."

"Wonderful. See you Thursday."

"Yes, see you Thursday. Thanks again."

Ester coasted home. She'd hoped hard and yet hadn't dared believe she would actually get the job. There had to be younger and better-qualified applicants, but Allie, and whoever else, had chosen her. She doubted Mr. Personality had cast a vote in her favor. But not even the thought of having to work alongside him could cool the fizz in her veins. Wait until she told Simon and the boys, and Rachel and Donna. Her dad. She imagined Dad's delighted response, as if he were still himself.

She accelerated past the robbed gas station.

Almost home, she remembered she'd forgotten to tell Crystal about the new choir.

Sing, I

The closer the minivan drew to the high school and the inaugural choir meeting, the more Ester buzzed with a blend of dread and excitement. Mostly, she was curious about who was behind the choir and who else would be there. She wondered if she would have to undergo an audition in front of everyone. What if she failed it? She turned into the school parking lot, encouraged by the number of vehicles. It was unlikely all their passengers were there for the choir—there were constant, various happenings at the school—but it suggested she wouldn't be the only one to show up to the gym.

She quick-marched across the chilly parking lot, fresh anxiety snapping. She wasn't that great a singer and had no idea what she was getting herself into. Was she an alto, soprano, or something else? The only thing she felt sure of was that she was going to mortify herself. Annoyance bubbled up. This would be so much easier if Rachel, Donna, or Crystal had agreed to join her. She reminded herself she could leave anytime she wanted. No one was holding a gun to her head.

She entered the school behind another woman, who held the door open. Ester, thanking her, stepped into the building. The tailored, sixtyish stranger wavered in the lobby, seeming lost.

"Are you here for the choir?" Ester said.

"Yes," she said, brightening.

"The gym's this way."

"Are you one of the organizers?"

"No, I'm just checking it out." She offered her hand. "Ester."

"Sue Wang." Her hand was small and cold, her squeeze pleasant. "I've never been in a choir, have you?"

"Not since middle school." Ester would have happily joined her high school's a cappella group, but by then the relentless teasing over her name had made her want to hide, not put herself in front of people.

"The flier said no experience necessary," Sue said, patting her salt-and-pepper updo like it was a pet.

"I'm sure we won't be the only novices." Ester returned the favor and held the gym door open for Sue.

About two dozen women dotted the large space. Ester recognized several locals, mostly fellow school parents, but there were also a few welcome strangers. To her dismay, she spotted Lydia Greeslie sitting on a bleacher, completing paperwork on a clipboard.

A striking woman, reminiscent of Nina Simone, commanded a card table to the right of the gym. She stood up, showing off her multicolored headwrap, matching maxi dress, and regal height. "Everyone, as soon as you're done with the membership forms, please return them to me and we'll get started. If you haven't already picked up the welcome brochure, please do so. It tells you a little bit about me and my mission for our choir. You should know whom you're entrusting your voices to and the exciting things I anticipate us doing together."

"This is a lot," Sue said, stopping short. Behind her, the gym door opened and Allie appeared.

Allie made straight for Ester, a big smile cutting her face. "Small world."

"Around here, yes," Ester said, sure her smile exceeded Allie's.

"Looks like there's paperwork to complete," Allie said.

"I was just getting to that," Ester said.

They fell into step together, and reached the card table laden with stationery and sundries, including a suggestion box bedazzled with multicolored crystals.

"Hello, welcome. I'm Monica Briggs, your choir founder and director." Monica's exuberant handshake caused her gold hoop earrings to sway. Ester thought of Donna, who would be impressed that a Black woman was at the helm.

Ester and Allie reciprocated the energetic introduction and moved off to complete the forms. She realized Sue had left the gym and felt bad for the older woman. Like everyone else, something had brought Sue here. Ester supposed something stronger had caused her to take off.

Monica called the meeting to order and invited everyone to take their seats on the bleachers. Ester and Allie sat down next to each other, their thighs brushing together. Ester's stomach quickened, as if with new life.

Monica began with an eloquent introduction and followed with an overview of the kind of songs they would perform together—classical and contemporary with flavors of jazz, soul, and folk.

"I was afraid she was going to say rap," someone said, to suppressed snickers.

Ester stiffened. Allie, glowering, scanned the bleachers. Monica continued, seeming not to have heard the slight. "I see our group as a sisterhood celebrating the joy and power of raising our voices together as one."

Someone behind Ester said, "She's very new age."

"Next we'll be chanting om."

"First order of business, let's decide on our name," Monica said.

Allie's arm shot up. "What about Lunar Ladies?"

"Great," Monica said.

More suggestions followed, slow and orderly at first, but the freshly minted choir soon devolved into shouts and good-natured booing.

"Rule the World."

"California Crooners."

"That's the winner right there!"

"Lark."

"Absolutely not."

"Coven."

"What are we, witches?"

"Yes, please." Laughter rippled through the group.

"True Song."

"For Your Supper." The name drew affirmations and applause.

Ester had been working up the courage to share a suggestion for some time and at last blurted out, "Sing, I."

Dubious laughter sounded.

"As in eyeballs or the pronoun?"

The laughter climbed.

"Settle down, people," Monica said.

Ester almost let the moment pass. "As in the pronoun." Her voice sounded croaky, like it did first thing in the morning, before coffee lubed the hoarseness. "I don't know about anyone else, but too much of my life has been about others—pleasing them, disappointing them, looking after them, recovering from them—"

Uneasy, knowing affirmations and laughter sounded.

"Somewhere along the way I lost my I." She faltered, not sure how to explain herself better, but circling something she felt deeply. Allie's presence made her want to articulate it, and to impress. "Sing, I is a salute, and a commitment to putting ourselves and our voices front and center."

"Damn."

"I love that."

Allie started the applause, and it multiplied and climbed. Ester's face heated.

"We'd have to give that spiel every time for people to understand the name," Lydia Greeslie said.

"What about the Nightingales?" she continued.

"Birdsong."

"Gal Vox." The suggestion set off more affirmations and applause.

Monica patted the air with her palms. "All right, how about this?" She checked her notes. "We've got one, two . . . four strong contenders already—Lunar Ladies, For Your Supper, Sing, I, and Gal Vox. I think we should vote on those four, otherwise we're going to be here all night. What do we think?"

The group voiced consensus. Four rounds of showing hands followed, with the majority voting for Sing, I, and For Your Supper coming in a close second. The group clapped and cheered.

Allie's warm breath glanced Ester's ear. "Well done."

Ester couldn't account for what Allie's praise, and the closeness of their bodies, was doing to her. It was like an oar stirring her insides. She glanced down, astonished that she was able to remain still while her unseen parts churned.

Monica talked them through vocal warm-ups and invited them to stand. She played a piano track from her phone and they practiced singing the scales together on repeat, climbing up and down the notes to an eight count.

After a dubious start, the group's pitch and harmonies strengthened. Monica handed out song sheets, reassuring them they would mostly learn by ear and didn't need to be able to read music. "For tonight, we're also not going to worry too much about technique or your voice parts. We'll start into all that at our next meeting. This is just a runthrough for fun and to end tonight with our voices raised together in song. Yes?"

"Yes," they chorused.

Accompanied by the backing track from *The Sound of Music*, the group delivered an off-key but earnest performance of "Do-Re-Mi." Ester's voice, weak and hesitant at first, built with the song, Allie's velvety tones, and the choir's collective force.

Above the school parking lot, there were so many stars it was like Ester was seeing double. "That was fun."

"So much fun," Allie said.

"You've a beautiful voice."

"I don't know about that, but I do love to sing," Allie said.

Ester arrived at her minivan, embarrassed by its mominess. "This is me."

"I'll see you on Thursday."

"Three o'clock," Ester said.

"Three o'clock it is."

"Thanks again for the opportunity."

"We're delighted to have you."

"You're okay for getting home?"

"Yep. I'm parked right over there." Allie flapped her arm, indicating the street. "Sing, I, it's a great name, congrats again."

"Thanks. I really liked Lunar Ladies too."

"Basic, next to yours," Allie said.

"I would never put you and basic together."

"Why thank you."

Heat returned to Ester's face. She shouldn't have said that, not least because Allie was now her boss. "See ya."

She rushed into her vehicle and was recovering on the driver's seat when her phone rang. It was Jason, wanting her to pick up glue sticks for his science diorama.

"See, you do need me," she said, playing, prodding. He ended the call.

She pulled out of the parking lot and turned left instead of right so she could drive past Allie. She tapped the horn softly as Allie dropped into her yellow Beetle. Allie returned the beep. Ester kept checking the rearview and driving in the wrong direction until Allie's car disappeared. Only then did the unmoored sensations stop, like inside she'd been running in circles.

On the highway, strong winds picked up. Ester maintained a tight grip on the steering wheel, her knuckles yellow and popping. Another blustery gale blasted the minivan, so strong she worried she would veer out of her lane. She checked the other vehicles, reassured that they were holding steady. Still she drove faster, eager to get out of the hostile elements. The winds kept coming at her, whipping the pleasure from a wonderful night.

Later, she would tell Jason she'd gone through a storm for him and his glue sticks, and it would stun her how his face opened in surprise, in thanks, like something behind it had unlocked.

Numb Fish

Ester arrived at Blazers fifteen minutes early for her first shift, feeling nervous but bolstered by Allie's belief in her, and by her pinstripe skirt suit paired with the canary yellow top for a pop of color.

Sal, the chinless bartender from the day of her interview, informed her Allie wasn't at work.

The floor seemed to disappear from under Ester. "Is everything all right? She said she'd be here to train me."

"As far as I know everything's fine. Shifts change on the regular." He tapped the counter, like knocking. "I'll let Bob know you're here."

She nodded, trying to hold onto her composure and hoping Bob wasn't Mr. Personality.

He was.

Bob, his nose like a chunk of poppy seed bagel, issued the barest welcome and marched her back to the front of the restaurant. He stood too close to her behind the hostess podium and rushed through a demonstration of the reservations system and its seating chart and pagers. Whenever she asked a question, he clucked his tongue, sending darts of irritation through her. He similarly hurried through a tour of the restaurant and kitchen and glossed over introductions to her coworkers.

Chef Lucinda's nicotine-stained smile was contagious. "Now you know where I am, don't ever go hungry."

"I won't, thank you," Ester said.

For Bob, Lucinda's expression remained as biting as frost.

Right at five o'clock, Ester guided her first party of the night to their table. The jovial family of six hailed from Columbus, Ohio, and they were enjoying an RV adventure along the West Coast. The grandmother, her doughy face oozing mischief, said it was her first road trip. She cracked a laugh. "Still enjoying firsts, at my age."

"Never too late," Ester said, making a mental note.

The six opened their menus like they were eagerly awaited books.

The rest of the busy shift passed with only minor glitches and minimal stress. Throughout, staff and customers alike buzzed with talk of the *Bachelor* finale playing from the big-screen TVs. The show culminated in a shocking nonproposal of marriage and ended with the highly anticipated reveal of who the next bachelor-ette would be.

Ester had never gotten caught up in the #BachelorNation frenzy. The show and its various spinoffs seemed rife with sexism and cringing fantasy. Yet several marriages and offspring had come out of it, and those relationships seemed to be sticking, so what did she know. Her thoughts returned to Allie, wondering again about her absence and hoping she was okay.

At the end of her shift, Bob said not unkindly, "You survived then?"

"Yes, thanks. See you tomorrow."

"I can't wait."

And there endeth not unkindly.

The house spilled dark. Ester had thought Simon might have waited up for her, it being her first shift and all. She kicked off her shoes in the entryway, hissing in pain as her crushed feet flattened on the hardwood. She'd endured standing for almost nine hours straight in those heels, utter implements of torture.

She hobbled to the kitchen, the wall clock winding toward midnight. She was bone-weary and yet strangely wired, her brain in overdrive. She poured herself a generous glass of cabernet, heaped water crackers and brie cheese onto a plate, and added a square of dark chocolate bumpy with almonds.

In the living room, she scrolled through the newly released TV shows on offer, the light from the mute, close-captioned screen coloring the room blue-gray. The first episode of *Russian Doll* pulled her right in. Imagine having to relive the night you died on repeat until you got your relationships right.

As Nadia dies again on-screen, Marcus's long-ago wheezing filled Ester's head. She'd witnessed several of his asthma attacks during the three years they'd dated in college, and after a couple of puffs of his inhaler he was always fine. Which made his death all the more senseless and tragic. The old fear stirred inside her, stippling her skin with goose bumps. What if he could have gotten to his inhaler in time but chose not to? He'd moved to Chicago two weeks after graduating from college and four weeks after they'd broken up because she'd cheated on him.

Marcus materialized in front of her, slapping his chest in the same way he had the last time she saw him. "You wrecked this."

She rushed the glass of wine to her head.

Inside Golden Leaves' back dayroom, Ester prattled on to Dad about Blazers, the choir, Kevin's high SAT scores, and his stealth soccer goal that clinched yet another win for his school. She had less to say about Jason's surliness and his growing obsession with video games or Simon's same old, same old. She considered mentioning the holdup and some of what had followed. Her mind filled with the giraffe mask inside her kitchen sink, melting, the flames flickering.

Dad fidgeted in his chair, seeming to want to stretch. She fussed with his pillows. He quieted, and she placed her hand over his, covering his sinewy blue veins. He grunted and his arm flew up, throwing off her grip. She swallowed. Of late, he was increasingly intolerant of touch, making him ever more unreachable.

He did allow her to fix his limp white hair. A caregiver had combed it forward again. He'd worn it parted to the right. She would leave another note to remind staff. Despite the discomfiture of his papery scalp stretched tight over his skull, she hummed softly as she worked, doing her best by the tune of that Garth Brooks song he liked, "The Dance." Finished, she praised and admired him.

At the end of her visit, he cried. The nurses and caregivers had assured her that his tears, and agitation, didn't mean anything. They claimed he was beyond emotion. But how could they tell? It made her think of those who insisted fish can't feel their captors hook, drag, suffocate, and batter them to death. How does anyone else ever know what we do and don't suffer in silence?

Tiny Countless Acts

Ester crossed the hotel parking lot, reduced to short and dowdy in her flat black shoes. But needs must. Her feet and shins were still aching from the previous night, and there was no way she would be able to withstand another shift in heels. To compensate, she'd intensified her efforts with her hair and makeup, and armored herself in an ivory dress patterned with black bowler hats that clung to her curves and allowed the tops of her breasts to breathe.

She entered Blazers and released the heavy door behind her. The sight of Allie standing at the hostess podium also sent something inside her swinging. She tried to breeze forward with poise, but it was a total trudge in flats. Her blush raged, heat even in her ears. She wasn't only a mess of awkwardness and embarrassment, she was both pleased to see Allie and still nursing disappointment at her absence the previous night.

"I see we didn't scare you away," Allie said.

"Not yet," Ester said, struggling to match Allie's light mood.

"Let's hope we keep it that way."

Ester's thin veneer cracked. "Is everything all right? You said you'd be here yesterday, to train me."

"Yeah, I'm so sorry about that. Bob needed to swap shifts. I heard you did great, well done."

"Thank you."

Allie closed her leather-bound planner and clutched it to her chest. "I'll let you get to it. Shout if you need anything."

"I will, thanks."

As Allie walked away, Ester pushed down the urge to shout.

Ester was hours into her shift when a stocky, square-jawed customer dropped to one knee in the waiting area, tied his shoelace, and swapped his pager with that of a family of four sitting on the bench to the right of the podium. Ester told herself she must be mistaken, but a short while later he and his guest presented themselves at the podium with the stolen, buzzing pager.

"This isn't yours," Ester said, still in disbelief that he would go to such lengths to cut in line.

"Excuse me?"

"I saw you take this pager from those guests right there."

"What are you, crazy? I did no such thing."

His blonde companion tugged his arm. "Let's just go."

"We're not going anywhere."

Ester processed the pager, lifted menus from the podium's rack, and approached the family of four—the dad's center part boyish and the mom and her two daughters sporting matching overbites. "Welcome to Blazers. If you'd like to follow me to your table."

The five moved through the restaurant. The deceitful customer called after her, "We were next."

Staff and diners looked over. Ester seated the family in a prime booth. "Enjoy your dinner."

She returned to her station, relieved to find the couple gone. She collected their original pager from the bench seat and sterilized it with an antibacterial towelette. She also disinfected her hands, wiping, wiping.

During closing the following night, Sal invited Ester to join him and a group of staffers going to the Late Bar. "We go most Saturdays."

She was tempted; she'd never been to the popular karaoke bar, but she'd worked three nights in a row and could barely keep upright. Plus, Kevin had a soccer game in the city at nine in the morning and she was on snack duty for the entire team. "Maybe next time, thanks."

She lingered in the coatroom, and the restroom, hoping she might bump into Allie. If Allie was going to the Late Bar, maybe Ester could muster the energy. She arrived at Allie's office, finding its door ajar and a thin column of light shining through like an invitation. She hesitated, her hand raised and her head straining to poke through the opening.

She retraced her steps, crossing back through the restaurant. The lingering waft of roasted herbs and meats hung in the air. She thought about the many meals diners had eaten during her shift, and the number of hands the food had passed through from beginning to consumption. How people are connected in a myriad of ways we don't consider all that much.

Outside, Ester hurried across the dark parking lot, clutching her keys in her fist. Behind her, a heavy tread drew close. At the minivan, she fumbled getting her key into the lock. The shadow grew inside the van's white paint.

She spun around. "Oh, it's you."

Her fright receding, she struggled to remember the dishwasher's name. He continued to the driver's side of the battered Honda parked next to her, looking vaguely alarmed.

"I'm Ester, the new hostess."

He pulled his driver's side door open.

"Are you going to the Late Bar?"

"They don't ask me."

"I'm sorry." As he dropped into his car, she added, "They didn't invite me either."

Throughout the drive home, she berated herself for the stupid lie. Was that supposed to make him feel better?

Alejandro, she remembered. His name was Alejandro.

David Bowie joined her in the minivan. She sang along to "Let's Dance," half daring to believe her tone and control had improved after only one choir practice. Not because of anything she'd learned, it was too soon for that, but thanks to the swell in her confidence and spirits.

In her driveway, she remained behind the steering wheel, too tired to move, and listened to pop and rock songs while watching the headlights shine on the front of her house, two glowing tunnels leading through and beyond.

I'll Take Widow, Please

Ester, Rachel, and Donna started out on the coastal trail, giving thanks that the cold, wet spell had passed. Ester silently admired the lake-like sky and welcomed the warm, salty breeze. The drift of fresh horse dung returned her to her Montana childhood. She saw the herd of wild horses rove the expansive brown-green range beneath Pryor Mountain, their hooves rumbling and their powerful bodies rippling.

"How did Kevin's game go?" Donna said.

Ester recounted how, early in the second half, Kevin intercepted the ball from a swift cross kick and scored the first goal of the match. His next goal, he headed the ball deep into the back of the net. The team went on to win 3-0 and Kevin beamed the entire ride home, despite his banging headache.

"Ouch," Rachel said.

Ester silently wished Jason had attended the game, to support his big brother, and to get him out of the house. He was becoming more of a recluse and getting too attached to video games, and violent ones at that. Simon had quipped that next Jason would be torturing animals. The comment incensed her. Contrite, Simon promised to talk to Jason and to do more with the boy, anything to get him outside, and out of himself.

Rachel shared how a basketball had slammed her full in the face in fifth grade, almost knocking her unconscious. She never played the sport again. "Worst pain I've ever felt, besides Liza tearing out of me."

They segued to their childbirth stories, retelling them in all their gory. Donna admitted that even after sixteen years she continued to harbor resentment against Gary for leaving her alone for most of her first labor. The hospital had induced her, and she'd labored for forty-plus hours before Tilly finally crowned. Throughout, Donna was drugged up, vomiting black, and shitting herself. "As if that wasn't awful enough, the nurse almost burst my bladder with the catheter."

While Donna labored for that biblical length of time, concerned the baby was stuck and convinced she would rip wide open, Gary had returned to work to put out a figurative dumpster fire. He arrived back at the hospital right as Donna started pushing. "He's never apologized or so much as pretended to feel guilty."

"I hate it when they don't even pretend," Rachel said with humor.

"You know what I mean," Donna said.

"You felt abandoned," Ester said.

"Exactly," Donna said.

Arms of sunlight shone through the gaps in the branches. In the openings between the tree trunks, Ester caught partial views of the stunning beachfront properties below, and in the distance tens of black-sheathed surfers rode the huge white waves. She felt an ache for her dad. What he would give to summit those breaking waves again, like traveling on a majestic nautical beast.

All these years later and it still amazed her that less than six months after Mom died, Dad moved from Billings, Montana, to Modesto, California, uprooting Ester and leaving her two older brothers behind. Tim had opted to remain in his classes at the local state college and to assume responsibility for their home, and for Rod, who was still in high school. Ester had no memory of Dad insisting her brothers also move to the Bay Area or of her brothers wanting her to stay home with them.

At first, Dad rented a rundown two-bedroom apartment on the outskirts of Modesto and Ester attended the local high school with its firmly rooted cohorts of jocks and nerds. She'd hoped the move to California was temporary, since Dad seemed as miserable as she was, but he soon purchased a townhouse in Half Moon Bay, swapping horses for surfboards and riding the highest waves he could catch.

Donna's talk of busyness pulled Ester back to the trail. "Everything's rush, rush, rush. I wish life would slow down."

Ester urged her and Rachel to reconsider joining the choir. "It's a lot of fun, the antidote we all need."

"Like I said, choirs have scarred me for life, and I want less to do, not more. Sorry," Donna said.

"Same," Rachel said. "I can barely keep up with my home and work calendars as it is, never mind adding something else to the mix. I'm tired all the time." She launched into a rant about Robbie's snoring, and how he wakes up every morning refreshed and oblivious to her enforced insomnia. "I swear for those first ten minutes each day I hate the man."

Ester envied them having such strong feelings toward their husbands. She and Simon mostly took each other for granted, and while she loved him, she didn't think she was in love anymore.

The three reached the peak of the trail, flanked by towering trees dotted with blue herons and red-winged blackbirds. The glittering ocean and white-sanded beach stretched out below them. Ester contemplated the sheer drop, a long way to fall.

She couldn't decide if she should stay with Simon after the boys left for college, or if she should leave. She was afraid of making a terrible mistake either way. What if staying meant missing out on her best life? What if leaving meant searing regret and winding up alone? It would be so much easier if Simon wasn't a good man. Or if fate decided for her and he died.

"You okay?" Rachel asked.

Ester started guiltily, and deflected with the stolen pager incident.

In the lull after the laughter, Rachel said, "At least Blazers is a step in the right direction. I'm so glad you left that store."

The comment clipped at Ester.

"It's going well?" Donna said.

"Yes, thanks. My manager, Allie, she's great." Ester did and did not want them to notice the tremble in her voice.

"Anyone's better than Rich, right?" Donna said.

"For sure," Ester said, relieved and disappointed they hadn't picked up on anything.

Donna complained about her mounting welfare caseload, saying it was impossible. She would need ten of her to help that many families. Rachel's clients were furious about the tanking stock market, as if it were her fault. The conversation turned to St. Patrick's Day and soda bread recipes. Two white butterflies winged their way across the women's path, drawing fresh delight. Then Ester remembered their lifespan averages two weeks.

The three friends reached the mica-studded strand populated with visitors alongside a smattering of locals and dogs—the shoreline scene so blue-beautiful, it seemed more cinematic than real. At the edge of the ocean, the trio removed their shoes and socks, rolled up their leggings, and stepped into the cold, sparkling water. The tide tugged Ester's calves, as if wanting her to go deeper. She imagined wading out to an orange boat with a white sail and climbing in. She watched herself grow small against the horizon.

"We have paradise right on our doorstep," Rachel said.

"We sure do," Donna said.

Ester closed her eyes and turned her face up to the sun. She would stop squandering her many blessings and be grateful for everything she had, including Simon. She would emerge from the Pacific with her pining left on the seafloor.

Catastrophe

By the end of Blazers' breakfast service the entire lower half of Ester's body was throbbing with pain. Her shift wasn't over until four o'clock either, and then there was dinner with Simon at Sale del Mare at seven. She'd returned home from work the previous night to find a card and a bouquet of pink roses on the kitchen island, a preemptive strike from Simon for their eighteenth wedding anniversary. She'd forgotten the occasion entirely. Saved by the internet, she booked his favorite local restaurant online.

On waking up, she announced their dinner plans and initiated sex. Throughout, he kept asking her to tell him what she wanted. She hated that.

"Excuse me?" The deep voice belonged to a thirtyish man with green-gold eyes that caused Ester's heart to palpitate. "Sorry, I didn't mean to startle you."

"My fault," Ester said. His eyes channeled Marcus, as did how well he filled out his fitted white T-shirt and blue suit jacket. He was taller than Marcus, though, and lighter skinned.

"I know I'm late, my day got off to a rough start, but I'm hoping I can still grab breakfast? I'd much prefer to eat here than at the airport."

"I'm afraid the buffet's been cleared away already, but let's get you seated and I'll see what we can do."

His whole face smiled.

In the kitchen, damp wisps of Lucinda's hair had escaped her chef's hat and attached themselves to her cheeks like tentacles. "Not a chance, sorry."

"Can you give him something from the lunch menu?" Ester couldn't begin to explain how much she needed to see this man filled and his day turned around.

Lucinda wiped the sweat from her brow with the back of her tattooed arm. "If he wants to wait an hour. Plus he'll have to pay. There's no substitutions for the comp breakfast."

"I doubt he can wait, he's headed to the airport. There must be something we can give him. Please?"

"Sorry, I don't make the rules."

Ester moved to the row of steel chafing dishes on the long table against the wall. She lifted the lids, pleased to find they still contained the leftovers. She loaded a plate, and carried the lot to the microwave.

"Give it here," Lucinda said wearily. "Most of that will reheat better in the air fryer."

"You're the best, thank you."

Ester returned to the tardy guest with a plate of buttered toast, the full American breakfast, and a pot of fresh, steaming coffee. He thanked her and introduced himself. She liked the name Will, and liked it for him. They chatted about the weather, the Warriors, soaring Bay Area real estate values, and how people in Will's hometown of San Antonio were also getting priced out of the housing market. His phone's ringtone went off, bringing "Locked Out of Heaven" into the restaurant. He declined the call.

He and Ester gushed over Bruno Mars and hailed his a cappella. "Have you seen him on James Corden's *Carpool Karaoke*? He's brilliant," Ester said.

"No. Was that recently?" Will said.

"It's from a couple of years back, at least, but it's so good. You have to watch it."

"I will, for sure."

Ester urged him to also watch *Carpool Karaoke*'s latest episode with the Jonas Brothers, who were reuniting. "I laughed so hard I spit red wine on my son's phone. You can imagine how that went over."

Bob appeared at the hostess podium and curled his pointer finger, beckoning. Ester approached him, picturing herself in slinky heels and not her self-sabotaging flats.

"I'm writing you up," he said. "Do you know how many health and safety standards you violated by reheating leftovers?"

She tried to appear unruffled. "I thought our first priority was making the customer happy?"

"We could get fined, even closed down, by the Health Department, not to mention the risk of food poisoning and our getting sued."

She swallowed her anger. "I'm sorry. It won't happen again."

"Oh, I know it won't." He strode off, leaving her panicked. She couldn't lose this job.

On Will's way out, he offered her a twenty-dollar bill. She protested, but he insisted. He exited, and she was twenty-one again, standing on the sidewalk, clutching a cold coffee cup with both hands like it could still give heat, and watching Marcus walk away for the last time.

That evening, Ester begged off going out to dinner as promised and suggested she and Simon celebrate their wedding anniversary at home with a fancy bottle of wine, their favorite Thai takeout, and some great TV. To her relief, he easily agreed.

The food arrived, wafting coconut and lemongrass. Ester unpacked the containers of blue rice, battered calamari, veggie yellow curry, and crispy tiger prawns in a mango glaze, her mouth watering.

Kevin and Jason carried their meals past the dining room.

"You can join us, you know," she said.

The boys continued upstairs. She also decided against the dining table and entered the living room. Simon dropped down next to her on the couch. They ate quickly from their laps, murmuring appreciation for the rich, spicy flavors, and drinking the fruity cabernet with equal abandon.

Two episodes into the third season of *Catastrophe*, Simon said, "That's just not believable. It's got to be believable."

She ignored his familiar complaint, biting back annoyance. What wasn't realistic about infidelity, unemployment, having to downsize your home, the stress of parenting, and the glow fading from a marriage?

His sighing and restlessness climbed with the third episode's arc. "It's so obviously *written*."

"Well *yeah*," Ester said.

"Nobody goes on like that."

"I'm enjoying it, okay? It's clever and funny, and it's moving."

"Sorry. I thought it was *our* anniversary."

She offered him the remote control. "Do you want to watch something else?"

"That's a trick question."

"It's really not."

"Okay. How about *Peaky Blinders*?"

"You know that's too violent for me," she said.

"See?"

They watched *Catastrophe* through episode 4 and decided to call it a night.

"So much for comedy," Simon said.

"It was. Ish." Ester powered off the TV. In twenty-five minutes, episode 4 had slapped her with scenes depicting violent trauma, Sharon's fraught relationship with her brother, her dad's worsening dementia, and her fear of aging.

ETHEL ROHAN

In bed, Ester yielded to Simon's reach, on account of their anniversary. Her unwillingness, distaste even, felt as huge as Rob's secret in *Catastrophe*. Rob was abusing alcohol again, and only bad would come of it.

Amazing

Several more women attended the second choir meeting, increasing Sing, I's membership to over thirty singers. Ester spotted the older woman who had ducked out of the first meeting and, delighted, made her way over. "Hey, you came back. It's Sue, right?"

"Yes. I thought if I don't try, I'll never know."

"You're going to love it."

"That's great to hear, thank you." Sue waved to someone beyond Ester. "I invited moral support," she said, and excused herself.

Ester wished again that Donna and Rachel had joined the choir with her. She gravitated to her same spot on the bleachers, followed by Allie. Allie's blond hair, which she usually wore in a sleek bun, fanned her shoulders and framed her heart-shaped face. Her eyes made Ester think of gleaming, oceanic marble.

Allie hadn't appeared quite as appealing at work the previous Sunday when she'd pulled Ester aside and cautioned her regarding the reheated leftovers. "There are serious liability issues."

Ester dismissed the memory and imagined Allie and her sitting together someplace besides the school gym—on barstools or a picnic blanket. She would maybe confide in Allie, saying how Will had evoked her dead ex from college.

Kate Moore sat down on the bleacher in front of Ester and Allie, her bald head hennaed in laurel leaves and lotus flowers.

"It looks fabulous," Ester said. Others echoed the compliment. Kate's subsequent delight belied her brutal cervical cancer diagnosis.

The freckled redhead Ester had noticed at the last meeting because of her cute pixie haircut and cuter white boots, was rocking a pair of red suede sneakers with high wedge heels. Ester remembered finding red roller skates in Mom's closet after she died, new and still in their box. People presumed the skates were a gift from Mom to Ester, but Ester often wondered. They wore the same shoe size, so maybe Mom had bought the skates for herself. Perhaps she wanted to try something new, something fast and exciting.

The redhead caught Ester staring and raised her leg, allowing her sneaker to hover midair. "I can hook you up if you like."

"Yes, please," Ester said, doubting she could afford them.

"Gwen." She extended her hand, her nail polish also a bold red. Ester introduced Allie.

"I want in on the shoes too," Allie said.

The three exchanged phone numbers, and Gwen texted a link to the New York store. "Free shipping, free returns."

Phyllis Sheen, her sweater's neckline dotted with pearls, lamented the death of local businesses due to online shopping and the "mogul who shall not be named." Several eager heads turned in their direction, and the conversation would have continued had Monica not called the meeting to order.

"To begin, I'd like each of us to introduce ourselves and share an interesting personal fact—"

A volley of groans interrupted Monica.

"Shoot me now," Gayle Simmons said, to laughter.

The gunman's rough, plastic lips rammed Ester's mouth. His pistol dented her temple.

Monica snapped her fingers, and the gathering quieted. "This is going to be great, trust me. Extra points for inspiring us, and extra-extra points for shocking us." More laughter rolled through the group. "Please also tell us what you hope to gain from our choir. I'll start us off. I'm Monica Briggs. Many years ago, and for a very brief time, I was a backup singer for Celine Dion—" Impressed sounds went up. "I'm pretty sure she doesn't remember me." More laughter. "What I'd like to get out of this choir is a sisterhood where we raise each other up right along with our voices." Applause and foot stomping erupted.

Member after member introduced herself, sharing stories of army tours, learning differences, throat polyps, illnesses and disabilities, civil rights activism, a pilot's license, a pierced labia, and a tattoo with a typo.

"Warrior, with only two r's, and it's right here on my wrist for everyone to see," Hildy Hampton said to great hilarity. She performed a spin on the spot in her wheelchair. Ester tried to remember the details of Hildy's long-ago accident. It happened during spring break, Ester was pretty sure, after Hildy dived off a bridge into a rushing river. The teen hit a rock, breaking her neck and severing her spine.

It drew closer and closer to Ester's turn to introduce herself. Despite proposing and defending the choir's name at their first meeting, she hated speaking in public, and couldn't think of a single interesting fact about herself to share. By the time Allie started talking, Ester was rigid with dread.

"I'm Allie Rogers. In my early twenties I spent three weeks in Peru, herding goats in the Andes. I can still smell them." Fresh laughter sounded. "I'm here because I love a good sing-along, and lately I've been feeling kind of lonely. I want more interests and people in my life."

"I feel that," someone said. Several murmured in agreement. Allie's loneliness stunned Ester. How could someone as magnetic as her feel disconnected?

Ester realized everyone was waiting for her to speak. "I'm Ester. Ester Prynn. For those of you familiar with *The Scarlet Letter*, you'll appreciate the roastings I've endured over the years." She paused for the laughter to quiet and to collect herself. "I'm here because I loved singing as a girl and I somehow forgot that. I want to get back to more of the things that used to bring me joy, and maybe find new areas of happiness too."

After the applause, Monica asked, "And your interesting fact?"

"I . . ." Ester couldn't land on a response.

"Should we come back to you?" Monica said. Ester nodded, her face ablaze.

The new member next to Ester said, "Hi, I'm Sandy—"

Ester spoke in a burst. "A couple of weeks back my coworker and I were held up at gunpoint. I watched the robber crack my coworker's head open—"

Gasps sounded.

"He also held the gun to my face, and . . . and he kissed me. No matter how hard I try to block it out, I can still feel his gun, his mouth, on me. Can still see and hear him strike my coworker."

The group voiced sympathy and consolation. Allie gripped Ester's hand in both of hers.

"Are you okay?" Monica said.

"Yeah, sorry." Ester wiped a renegade tear.

"Please don't apologize," Monica said.

Someone squeezed Ester's shoulder, and another woman patted the top of her arm. Allie didn't break her hold on Ester's hand until every woman present had spoken, and the group clapped its hardest and loudest.

"You're all amazing," Monica said. "Let me hear you say it."

"We're amazing."

"Louder," Monica said.

"We're amazing."

"Last time, with all we've got," Monica said.

"We're amazing." The refrain spread over the huge, high gym, a rally cry.

Monica led the group through vocal warm-ups, and the Beatles' "Let It Be." There were several talented singers among their members, and the group already sounded more harmonized and soulful than at the first meeting. Ester knew from *Carpool Karaoke* that the song was about Paul McCartney's dead mother appearing to him in a dream and offering words of comfort. She wondered what Mom's ghost would say to her. Marcus's too.

Ester and Allie exited the school amid a stream of choir members and continued to the parking lot together. "I wouldn't ever have guessed you were a goat farmer."

Allie chuckled. "It was a tie between telling everyone about my shepherding days or that I'm pansexual. I decided being pan shouldn't be considered an interesting fact. Being straight isn't."

"Pan?"

"Men, women, nonbinary. I'm all in."

"Oh. I didn't realize."

"You seem shocked."

"No, I . . . I thought maybe you were just gay."

"Just gay. You make it sound outright unimpressive."

Ester laughed nervously. "Yeah, no. Sorry. I'm going to stop talking now."

"What was my tell?"

"What?"

"You said you thought I was queer. My sexuality's no secret, but I didn't think it was obvious either."

"I don't know really." Ester could never admit that Allie exuded sex appeal and was causing havoc to her wiring.

Allie faced her. "I don't want to brush over what you said back there. I'm really sorry any of that happened."

"I'm sorry I didn't include the store on my résumé. It was too raw."

"It's fine, don't worry about it."

Even as Ester ordered herself to keep it together, her face crumpled.

"Come here." Allie hugged her.

Ester broke from the embrace, conscious of onlookers. Allie glanced at the dispersing women, seeming to register Ester's discomfort. "Let's go to your van."

From the front passenger seat, Allie said, "I'm here for you."

Ester didn't know where to look. The space felt too enclosed, too conspicuous. "Thanks, that's very kind, but I'm okay, really."

"I don't think you are," Allie said softly.

Ester's hand rushed to her mouth, dulling a keening sound.

"Hey, it's okay." Allie placed her hand on Ester's shoulder, rocking her a little, as if trying to dislodge what was clogged.

"I'm sorry, I'm not usually such a mess."

"You're not a mess."

"You wouldn't say that if you knew about this crazy thing I did after the holdup."

"Try me."

"It's kind of gross."

"I can handle it, I've dewormed goats."

Ester laugh-cried. "I ordered a giraffe mask online, the closest I could find to the one the gunman was wearing. When it arrived I lay down on my bed and put it on. I imagined the gunman seeing my coworker Crystal and me through its eyeholes." Her voice cracked and she faced her driver's side window.

They sat in silence until she managed to haul out more. "I burned the mask in my kitchen sink and watched it vanish. But it wasn't enough. I keep seeing the gunman and his mask, keep feeling him, and the gun, digging into me. Meanwhile Crystal, who was actually, horribly assaulted, is back at work already and being an absolute trooper."

"Your feelings are completely understandable, and valid."

Another cluster of chattering women pushed through the school's main doors. Ester jerked backward, putting distance between herself and Allie. "I should go."

"It's your minivan, so technically I'm the one who needs to go."

"Right. Right. Okay then, goodnight, and thank you."

As Allie exited the minivan, she paused in the doorway. "Take care of yourself."

Ester nodded, unable to speak. She'd shown too much of herself and wouldn't allow that to happen again.

Good News

Ester marched to the bottom of the stairs for the second time. "If I have to go up there, you'll be sorry." Jason's floorboards creaked in response. "Good call!"

She returned to the kitchen and to Simon and Kevin reading their phones and eating cereal like it was a synchronized sport. She'd tried banning phones during meals, but they kept reappearing. Her family didn't see the irony of the internet connecting them with continents of humanity while keeping them absent around actual people. Which brought her back to Allie saying she'd joined the choir because she felt lonely. That still surprised her. But not nearly as much as their exchange inside the minivan, and the tingling sensations that shot through her body when Allie touched her shoulder, rocking her, loosening her.

Jason plodded in and plopped himself down next to his dad and brother at the island. It also bothered her that her husband and sons sat on the same barstools day after day. Whenever she suggested they shift seats, the three looked at her like she'd proposed something ludicrous. Jason also fell to mindless eating and doomscrolling. Inside his resting insolent face, he looked ever paler and thinner, and those darkening mauve shadows beneath his eyes were especially worrisome. She felt a surge of guilt over their fight the previous night.

She'd returned home from Blazers shortly after midnight to find the telltale crack of bluish light beneath his bedroom door. She barged into the room and disconnected his headset from his desktop. Rapid gunfire and agonized screams tore the air. Her and Jason's shouts also grew louder.

"You spend more time playing those disturbing games than you do anything else," she said.

"They're the only thing around here that doesn't suck."

She confiscated the headset and his controller. He tried to grab them back, and a tug-of-war ensued. She twisted and elbowed, and soon exited his room shaken but victorious. He slammed the door closed behind her.

As he rushed down the last of his cereal, she tried to say something conciliatory or at least some benign comment that wouldn't give him cause to roll his eyes and utter that disgusted guttural sound he'd weaponized. Everything she said of late angered him. "You never listen," he accused. He also berated her for not remembering his friends' names or other information he'd supposedly shared with her, but which she swore he'd never told her—like that he suddenly hated mustard and used to love history, although he now dismissed all of his school subjects as pointless.

The landline rang, its trill alien in the era of cell phones. The four ignored it. Almost all the calls on the house phone were from telemarketers. She should get rid of the line; it would be one less bill to pay every month. Yet living in fire and earthquake territory, it seemed prudent to keep it. The caller ID's robotic voice announced the call was from Golden Leaves.

Ester rushed across the room and lifted the receiver. "Hello?"

"Ester?"

"Yes?"

"This is Nurse Judith from—"

"Hi Judith, is Dad okay?"

"He's developed pneumonia, I'm afraid, and passed a difficult night—"

"I thought you were about to say he passed away."

"No, no, sorry, my bad. But he is very weak. You should come in as soon as you can."

Simon appeared next to Ester and rubbed her back. "Is he still there or at the hospital?" she said.

"He's here. Dr. Tracey advised against transferring him. We can give him all the care he needs."

"Do you think . . . Is this it?" Ester said. Simon drew her into his chest and kissed the top of her head.

"It's difficult to say. He might rally, he might not," Judith said.

"I have two brothers who live in Montana. Do you think they need to be here?"

"It really could go either way, but if it were my dad, I'd make the trip."

Ester thanked Judith and hung up. Simon hugged her, his chin on her head. "What do you need?"

She needed to call Blazers and let them know she wouldn't be at work.

Of course Bob answered the phone.

Ester phoned Tim en route to the nursing home. As soon as she started speaking, tears sprang up. She twisted the skin at the hollow of her throat to make them stop.

"Keep me posted," Tim said.

She phoned Rod. He also wasn't in any rush to book a flight. "What's his doctor's number? I'll give him a call."

She arrived at Golden Leaves and announced herself through the intercom, still fuming over her brothers' ambivalence. She pushed open the buzzing door and stepped inside.

Stella rushed down the corridor toward her. "He's taken a turn. Hurry."

Ester raced after her, and into Dad's room. Judith and the nurse's aide, Greg, stood on either side of Dad's bed, Judith forcing a thin tube down Dad's throat while Greg tried to pin Dad's shoulders to the white pillows. Dad thrashed on the mattress, gurgling and choking.

"What's going on?" Ester said.

"We're suctioning him, so he doesn't drown in his own fluids," Greg said.

"Can you wait outside, please? We'll have him feeling much better in just a sec," Judith said, sounding stressed. Stella reached for Ester's shoulders to steer her away.

Ester moved to the foot of the bed. "Dad, it's me, Ester. Try to relax, okay? Nurse Judith is going to drain your lungs so you can breathe easier." She knew her efforts were likely useless, Dad didn't know or understand her, but she hoped a soothing voice might at least offer him some comfort.

Dad stilled. She'd barely finished congratulating herself when she realized he'd passed out. The suction machine whirred to life. Brown-yellow fluid flowed from Dad's lungs and through the tube into the white plastic container. Ester fought the urge to retch.

Judith finally powered off the machine and removed the tube. She wiped the thick dribbles from Dad's lips and chin. Still unconscious, he drew a long, whistling inhale. Judith checked his pulse. "It's thready. The next twelve hours are critical."

She and Greg stepped away from the bed. Ester moved next to Dad and brushed his damp white hair back from his face, his head conical. Eggy. She pulled her hands clear, remembering his newfound intolerance for touch.

She remained by his side throughout the morning, her hands itching to return to him but knowing that's not what he would want. Not anymore. She alternated talking, singing, reciting poetry, and bearing silent witness.

She and Simon texted back and forth. Tim and Rod had each texted once, asking for an update. She wondered how they would feel if their children responded in the same way to their likely imminent deaths. She appreciated that they had their own abandonment issues, and it had to be so much worse to be deserted by your father than by your brothers, but he was still their dad, and before losing Mom had broken him, he'd been a good one.

She placed a damp washcloth on Dad's fevered brow. His breathing remained labored, and his congested lungs crackled. She considered the three plump pillows beneath his head. Animals were euthanized for less. He started to wheeze, like Crystal, like Marcus. A coughing jag racked his body. Gasping, his eyes opened wide, showing their blood-threaded whites, and his legs pumped up and down on the mattress, as if he were trying to outrun himself.

Ester reached for the red panic button above his bed, flashing back to the store's alarm on the morning of the robbery. Dad arched his back, as though trying to open his lungs wide. She hesitated, seeing herself suffocating him, then drove her thumb into the call button.

Simon and the boys visited in the early evening, bearing magazines, drinks, snacks, and Indian takeout. Ester urged them to leave and eat dinner at home. She didn't want Dad to smell the tantalizing drift of spices and food that might torment him with hunger. They left in a hurry, Simon promising to return if she needed him.

Within the hour, Rachel and Donna also stopped by, adding to Ester's supply of drinks and snacks. The three sipped red wine and binged on chocolate and chatter. Amid the disease and decay and sugar, everything seemed heightened and surreal, and Ester's laughter turned hysterical. She finished, breathless. "Sorry. God. What is wrong with me?"

"It's called grief," Donna said gently.

"You should go home and get some rest; you look exhausted," Rachel said.

"I will, in a bit."

Rachel and Donna said their goodbyes to Ester, and to Dad, and made her swear she wouldn't be far behind them.

"They'll call you if there's any change," Rachel said.

Rachel's words remained in her wake. Ester ached for change.

Golden Leaves dimmed and quieted to night mode. Every so often the odd cough, moan, or babble sounded along the corridor or from deeper inside the building. A man called mournfully for his mother. On and on he cried out. Why wasn't anyone on staff responding? Ester considered leaving Dad and going to comfort the distraught man, but she worried Dad might choke on himself in her absence. The wailing man's noises eventually stopped. Ester's heart continued to thump.

The night nurse, Wanda, entered the room, dragging a jangly medical cart.

"Is that man okay?" Ester said.

"Who?" Wanda said, moving to Dad.

"The man crying out for his mother."

"Oh, Alan. He does that. Lots of them do."

A sensation in Ester's chest, like ligaments knotting. "Has someone helped him?"

"I've just left him. He's fine."

Wanda checked Dad's vitals. "His pulse is a little stronger." She seemed to feel the need to add, "That's encouraging."

Ester should let Tim and Rod know, but she couldn't bring herself to contact them. If they cared enough, they would reach out to her.

"Can I get you anything?" Wanda asked.

"I'm okay, thank you." Ester reached for her water bottle and chugged, rinsing more than drinking.

Ester's head dropped forward, startling her awake. She blinked inside the murky room and swiped at the drool leaking from her mouth, her ears alert to Dad's strained breathing.

"Hey."

Ester's head jerked to her right, finding the chair next to her occupied. In the slats of moonlight pushing through the window blinds, Allie looked as faint as her whisper. Ester grasped blearily at her phone in her pocket, wondering what time it was, and if Allie was real.

"How'd you get in here?"

"The night manager and I go way back, and a chicken potpie holds untold powers of persuasion. I'm sorry I woke you. I was on my way home from work and thought I'd check in." Allie lifted her chin, indicating the fat white bag on Dad's bedside locker, amid the clutter of drinks and foodstuff. "I brought water and snacks, but see you're all set."

"Thank you," Ester said.

"How is he?"

"Hanging on. For now."

"I should let you get back to sleep." Allie half rose from the chair.

"Stay, please." Ester hated that her eyes were brimming.

Allie hugged her, and Ester pressed her brow to the side of Allie's neck, catching traces of something herby. Allie stroked the side of Ester's head. She smelled of rosemary, Ester realized, of comfort.

Ester awoke to the sound of grunting. She glanced at the empty chair next to her. Allie had stayed for a couple of hours, and they'd talked about all sorts of things—what might lie beyond death, how to milk a goat, and was it okay to raise children to believe in the Easter Bunny and the tooth fairy? What about Santa Claus?

Dad's only movement was his shallow, bubbly breathing. The gray light beyond the window confirmed he'd made it to dawn and well past those critical twelve hours. She straightened on the chair, her back and shoulders stiff. The grunting resumed. It took her a second to make sense of the apparition in the dim doorway.

Joan rolled into the room, her noises climbing. She bucked on her wheelchair, shaking a roll of toilet paper at Ester. Ester struggled to her feet and accepted the questionable offering. Joan's bumpy finger stabbed the air, indicating the toilet paper, and next Dad. It registered that she wanted to gift Dad with one of her most prized possessions. Ester placed the toilet paper on the bed beneath Dad's hand, noting the base of his fingernails were no longer black-blue. Joan's smile was like the sun coming out from behind a cloud.

"Thank you," Ester said, overcome with a softening that could sink her.

In the full gloom of morning, Dr. Tracey examined Dad, the fifty-ish medic squat and paunchy, his hair more strawberry than blond.

His broad brow pleated with surprise, almost admiration. "He's one for the books."

Judith spoke up next to him. "Your dad has the strength of a bear, and a grizzly at that."

She and Dr. Tracey waited for Ester's response with bright, expectant expressions, as though they'd delivered good news.

Don't Know Much

Sal and several other staff members filed out of Blazers, bound for the Late Bar. Allie appeared next to Ester. "Are you joining us?"

Ester was exhausted, and wary. She wanted Allie and her to be a blossoming friendship, and she wanted them to be something else. Something that scared her. She should go home. But she flashed back to Dad almost drowning in his own fluids, and her head in the crook of Allie's neck next to Dad's bed. "Why not?"

In the front doorway, she remembered Alejandro. "I'll be right back."

She headed to the kitchen, finding it empty, and crossed the restaurant toward the coatroom. She rounded the corner as Alejandro emerged from the restroom. When she invited him to the Late Bar, he seemed more spooked than pleased. "Come on, it'll be fun. It's my first time too."

"I not know anyone there."

"Of course you will, there's several of us going."

He stepped around her. She spoke to his narrow back. "Why don't you invite some friends? They could meet us there?"

His grimace eased. "Maybe my girlfriend."

"Great. We've ordered rideshares."

He pulled his phone from his back pocket. "Let me check."

Ester, Allie, Bob, and Alejandro shared one car, while Sal and the rest of the staff climbed into two other vehicles.

"Race you!" Sal shouted to no one in particular before disappearing into the sky-blue Prius.

Inside the Corolla, Bob occupied the front passenger seat. In the back, Allie sat close enough to Ester for their heat to commingle while Alejandro sat pressed against the door, his hand holding onto the roof handle like he needed its support. Ester suspected he was wearing the earbuds for the same reason.

Ester, seated by the other door, leaned forward. "So your girlfriend's joining us?"

Alejandro nodded, looking like a rabbit in the headlights.

"What's his name?" Bob said, nodding at the laminated dog photo hanging from the rearview.

"Bruce," their driver said.

Ester's attention drifted from Junse Chen's ID on the dashboard to his broad build and prominent cheekbones, his thoughtful gaze. *She was most definitely straight.*

"German shepherd, they're a big dog, lots of energy," Bob said.

"Great breed, highly intelligent," Junse said. The dog's photo swayed with the motion of the car, as if the conversation had brought him to life.

"I'd love a dog, but it wouldn't be fair. My apartment's too small and there's no garden. It'd be stuck indoors on its own way too much," Bob said.

"That's a shame," Junse said.

"Never met a dog I didn't like," Bob said. As for people . . ."

Ester wondered who, what, had ruined humans for him.

The four entered the too-loud bar and squeezed their way through the tight throng of revelers. Already Ester could taste the icy relief of a salty, limey margarita. A rainbow of strobe lights lasered the air, and thin silver beams flashed from a disco ball above the karaoke stage. Below the huge sparkling orb, a willowy man crooned A-ha's "Take On Me," his falsetto impressive.

Allie collected twenty dollars from each of them for the drink kitty and pushed through the crowd to the bar. Alejandro read his phone, and Bob people-watched. Ester pretended to be engrossed in the Elvis wannabe onstage, the rhinestone-shirted man flaying "Love Me Tender."

Allie worked her way back through the crowd, a drinks tray raised high. She arrived jostled but with minor spillage. Bob, his dripping martini in hand, ventured deeper into the crush of customers. Ester, Allie, and Alejandro lifted their glasses, saying "salud." She winced on tasting the potent margarita, more alcohol in it than in her Great-Uncle Earl at the end, and he'd died of cirrhosis. She said as much aloud, making Allie laugh hard. Alejandro, not seeming to have understood, gulped his beer. Allie said something to him, but her words were muted by the music and singing, the violent chatter.

Alejandro's pockmarked face flickered delight. A young woman brushed past Ester, reaching for him. They hugged, and Alejandro introduced Jacinta. Her wide smile threw her button nose and small eyes off-balance in a captivating way.

Allie, Alejandro, and Jacinta chatted together in Spanish. Ester, risking another mouthful of tequila, returned her attention to the stage. A fat, attractive woman had arrived at the chorus of Aretha Franklin's "Chain of Fools" and was doing the Queen of Soul proud.

"Are you planning on singing?" Allie asked.

"The tequila's not that strong," Ester said.

"How about a duet? I'm game if you are."

"I don't think I know any."

Allie picked up a thick songbook from the ledge next to them, and she and Ester pored over the playlist, their heads close together. They decided on "Don't Know Much," and Allie set about filling out the signup slip.

Bob reappeared, waving his empty glass at Allie. "Time for round two, banker." He eyed the signup slip. "Not more Annie Lennox, I beg you."

"I keep telling you, you don't know what's good for you. But no, no Goddess Annie tonight."

"I'll brace myself regardless," Bob said.

"Better double brace yourself, we're doing a duet," Allie said, nodding at Ester. Ester's pulse quickened. She'd been running the love song's lyrics in her head and regretting the choice.

"Aren't you two getting cozy," Bob said, turning Ester's stomach cold.

"You can join us if you like," Allie said.

"You don't want that," Bob said.

"I'm sure we don't," Allie said, winking at Ester.

Bob eyed them suspiciously. Ester's panic surged. Allie held up the folded signup slip. "I'll drop this off and get the drinks."

"That's okay," Ester said, lowering her glass to the ledge. "I think I'm going to go."

"Wait. What happened?" Allie said.

"I'm sorry." Ester turned to leave. A reedy blonde blocked her path, the young woman swaying and her face gaunt, her upper lip curled. Ester made to move around her.

"You're Kevin's mom." The girl's sharp features and silver eyebrow bar looked familiar, but Ester couldn't place her. "I'm Kim. My little brother Stevie is on the soccer team. I recognize you from the games."

Something beyond Ester distracted Kim, but before Ester could make her escape, Kim's sticky eyes found her again. "Fancy meeting you here."

Ester gestured vaguely. "There's a few of us here from Blazers Restaurant."

"Yeah, I heard you got the hostess job. I applied too, but no joy. Obviously." Her subzero gaze swept Bob before returning to Ester. "You must have a ton of experience, or something."

"Excuse me," Ester said, hurrying off.

Allie called after her but didn't follow her outside. *Good*, Ester thought, trying to breathe in the moonlight. It was almost funny. Kim thought she'd fucked her way into Blazers with Bob. She hadn't considered there might be something between Ester and Allie. *Which there isn't*, Ester informed the night air. She was married, and straight, for Christ's sake, and wouldn't ever be unfaithful to Simon. At twenty-one, she'd vowed to never cheat on anyone ever again. Once was once too often. Once was maybe fatal.

Home Invasion

Ester arrived home in the late afternoon to an empty house, having survived her third shift working alongside Allie since her abrupt exit from the Late Bar. While their interactions remained polite and professional, the cooling between them was palpable. She told herself that was for the best.

She removed a bar of chocolate from the fridge and rushed a hard square into her mouth. She reopened the temperamental appliance, wondering what to make for dinner. She pushed the door closed. She had worked around food all day long and was tired of having to think about it. They could order takeout. She scanned the untidy kitchen, her mind running through the rest of the house. There were so many chores she should do, not least tending to the various mounds of laundry upstairs and down in the garage, which seemed to mate and multiply by the day. She should also go see Dad while it was still daylight and not leave it until later, when she would be even more drained and would have to drive in the dark.

Instead, she flopped down on the couch with the remote control and the remainder of the chocolate bar. She scrolled through the staggering number of show choices, deciding on a new dramedy, *Good Girls*. During the first sassy, high-stakes episode, she sat up straight on the couch, straining to hear. The sound of distant tiny explosions made her question if she'd placed a bag of popcorn in the microwave. Then she realized.

She tiptoed upstairs and paused outside Jason's bedroom door, her ear cocked to the *rat-a-tat-tat* of warfare. He'd obviously searched her bedroom and reclaimed his game controller, but wasn't able to find his headset, which she'd hidden in her bathroom. She pushed the door open, finding him transfixed at his desk in his school uniform, his thumbs working the game controller with alarming speed and dexterity.

She said his name, but his attention remained on the screen. She crossed the darkened room, opened the curtains, and raised the window to the max, letting in much-needed air. His room reeked of sweat, stale food, stinky feet, and something yeasty she didn't want to speculate on. She returned to him, his cluttered desk a litter of soda cans, candy wrappers, an empty bag of family-size potato chips, and a ketchup-streaked dinner plate. If that wasn't evidence enough that he'd ditched school and stayed home all day long to game, the catatonic look on his face was a frightening giveaway.

"Jason!" she said, slinging the word. He continued to ignore her. She grabbed the controller. He held on, forcing her to wrest it from him. The victory was short-lived. He lunged at her, his look murderous. She drew back, dropping the controller. He hesitated, seeming confused by her fear and his strange new power, and snatched the controller up from the floor.

"That's it. You just played your last video game," Ester said.

The argument escalated and they were practically breathing fire on each other when the front door closed.

"Hello?" Kevin called out, as if unsure he'd entered the right house.

Moments later, he appeared in the bedroom doorway. "Jason, cool it."

"Shut up, you. This is none of your business."

"Calm down, would ya?" Kevin said.

"You're not my dad."

"Your dad will be home soon enough and then you'll be sorry," Ester said.

"Get out of my room!" The heels of Jason's hands slammed her collarbones, sending her stumbling backward. He seemed as stunned as she was by his aggression.

Kevin pushed Jason down onto his chair. "What the hell?" He turned to Ester, his furious look softening. "Are you okay?"

She loomed over Jason. "I am your mother, and you will never touch or speak to me like that again, is that clear?" His hateful look almost doubled her over. "Are we clear?"

"Yes." The word was a dagger.

"As long as you're under this roof, you're banned from gaming," she said, lifting the controller from his desk.

"No!" He sounded like she was about to take a screw gun to him.

"I hate you!" he said as she moved out of the room.

She turned around in the hallway, dropped the controller onto the hardwood, and stomped on it with both feet. Jason screamed, his face like a mask about to rip open.

"Um, Mom, I have a friend downstairs," Kevin said.

She stepped off the little heap of shattered plastic beneath her sensible shoes and, taking a deep breath, smoothed the skirt of her dress with both hands. "Well then, let's go say hi."

"You're the worst!" Jason slammed his bedroom door closed.

The teenage girl sat forward on the living room couch, as if readying to make a run for it. Ester followed Kevin into the room, struggling to maintain her feigned composure. How had things gotten so bad between her and her baby boy?

"Mom, this is Mena," Kevin said with a hint of awe.

"Pleased to meet you, Mena. I'm sorry about the sound effects. Son number two is a work in progress. Kevin, on the other hand, is our perfected model."

Mena chuckled. "I can't argue with that, Mrs. Davis. You did well on this particular prototype."

Kevin, cursed with Ester's blushing gene, turned maroon.

"My last name's Prynn, actually, but please call me Ester."

"Ester Prynne?" Mena said, seeming unsure if they were still joking around or not.

"I was hoping the name recognition might have died out by your generation," Ester said.

Mena's delicate hand covered her grin. "Is that really your name?"

"Yes, except I've no 'e' at the end of Prynn."

Mena laughed. Ester's expression jumped to chilling.

"You should probably leave," Kevin said deadpan.

Mena looked stricken. Ester and Kevin laughed. Mena's hand pressed her chest. "I thought you were serious."

Simon arrived home and entered the living room, taking in the merriment. "What am I missing?"

Kevin introduced Mena.

"Nice to meet you," Simon said.

Ester invited Mena to stay for dinner. "That's if pizza and salad are okay?"

"Sounds great," Mena said.

Kevin smiled down at her on the couch. Ester needed to look away from their glow.

Ester stood at the kitchen sink, singing to herself while washing a head of romaine. Simon shouted from the living room. "For the pizzas, are you good with a medium vegetarian and large garlic chicken?"

She called back, "Make it a large veggie and a medium chicken."

"I'll get two large."

"Don't do—" She let it go, and set about chopping the lettuce. She considered appealing to Jason a final time but decided to let him sulk in his room and go without dinner if that's what he wanted. She rubbed her right collarbone, which was still smarting.

She would have staked her life on the certainty that he would never raise a hand to her. As soon as Mena left, she and Simon would give him the lecture of his life.

Crystal texted, her message stemming the chorus of "Let It Be" in Ester's throat. The gunman had committed a home invasion in El Granada and seriously injured the homeowner, an elderly woman. Crystal learned of this third robbery from the police, who had scheduled her to appear at the San Mateo Sheriff's Office at nine the next morning to view a photo lineup. *have u heard from them?!*

Ester was typing her response when the call came in. The police sergeant asked her to appear at the sheriff's office at nine fifteen the next morning. If she preferred, officers could come to her house.

She volunteered to come into the station, not wanting photos of suspects, and possibly the gunman, inside her home. "The only thing is, I'm working in the morning, and I'm fairly new to the job. Would it be possible for me to stop by during my lunch break?"

The officer insisted. "The sooner the better."

She agreed, and he thanked her before hanging up. She pressed the side of her phone to her lips, silently praying that the gunman's latest victim would pull through. She tried to not imagine what he'd done to her.

A Fix

Ester entered the San Mateo County Sheriff's Office unsettled and bleary-eyed. She'd slept fitfully, suffering flashbacks of the holdup, flash forwards to this lineup, and reel after reel of further catastrophic scenes. In one, the gunman robbed Rich's store a second time and pistol-whipped her to unrecognizable. In another, she identified the gunman, and his case went to trial, but he was given parole and later attacked her in her home, beating her to a pulp. Nothing she told herself could stop the gruesome images or lessen how real they seemed.

She pushed herself toward the reception desk. The bearded, portly officer instructed her to wait on the wooden bench opposite him. Seated, she checked the time on her phone. 9:08. Crystal was likely looking at the photo lineup right then. They had chatted on the phone the previous night and decided not to travel together to the station. It might muddy their states of mind, and later in court their shared commute might complicate any positive ID one or both of them made. They laughed tinnily at themselves, saying they were likely overthinking it, and drawing on too many TV crime shows, but they agreed it was better to be cautious rather than sorry.

Ester waited on the hard bench. At 9:15 she started to worry the parties concerned had forgotten about her. She tried to meet the desk officer's small eyes above that manicured beard, but to no avail. She rechecked online for any update on the gunman's latest victim, Josephina Wolas. The most current news cycle didn't include anything they hadn't already reported on repeat. Ms. Wolas, "a spinster" and retired dental hygienist, remained in critical condition. Hospital machines beeped in Ester's head. Right as her heart rate reached a reckless speed, a stringy officer with a surprisingly pudgy face appeared along the corridor.

Sergeant Halloran introduced himself, and she followed him down the drab corridor, into a bare, musty room with peeling beige paint and two grimy windows. A laminated table with two gray chairs occupied the center of the room. Halloran dropped onto the seat facing the door and gestured to the chair opposite. "Please."

She sank onto the plastic, feeling strangely guilty, as though she were under investigation. Halloran offered water, coffee. She doubted she could hold a drink steady. "I'm okay, thank you."

Halloran jutted his chin forward, indicating the recording device at the end of the table. "Our conversation will be recorded, that's routine and shouldn't concern you any, all righty?"

She nodded, her lips sucked in. He pressed record, and outlined how the photo lineup and her role as witness would unfold. She watched his mustache move as he spoke, unable to look away from its calisthenics.

"Ma'am, do you have any questions? Concerns?"

"Not so far, thank you. I am a little worried about how helpful I can be. The gunman was wearing a mask and a hoodie and had no distinct features that I could see. I can't even tell you the color of his hair."

"That's okay. You're under no obligation to ID anyone. Just do your best."

She tried to look encouraged, and competent. He pushed a sheet of paper across the table and asked her to review and sign an admonishment statement. The document's name struck her as odd and intimidating. Ironically, it sought to relieve her of any sense of fear or pressure, and it went on to demand her complete confidentiality. Far from reassured, she signed her name at the bottom of the page, the scratch of the pen's nib loud in her ears.

"Okay, here we go." Halloran opened the second brown manila folder on the table and placed a sheet with six headshots in front of her.

She studied the two rows of suspects, the weight of the task pressing. They were six average, middle-aged white men with mostly meaty builds. Two were bald, and the rest were a mix of dark-haired, sandy, and salt-and-pepper. Two sported beards, one was stubbled, two were shadowed, and one was clean-shaven. She kept coming back to the men's eyes, their lips. Sweat pooled under her arms and between her legs. Her entire body felt overheated, hotter than human temperature should climb. She worried Halloran could smell her perspiration and hear how fast and heavy she was breathing.

"There's no rush. Take your time." He shifted on his chair, sending up creaking sounds.

She searched each man's face and torso, wishing she could see their full-length photos. The gunman bore a pear-shaped potbelly that he carried low. She needed to see their hands too. If they were large and veiny. Needed to tell if there was a certain forward lean to their stance, like someone about to pounce.

It was useless. She knew nothing with certainty. Everything had happened so fast, and the gun, mask, and kiss had made more of an impression than the robber himself. "I'm sorry, I can't be sure, but I don't think it's any of these men."

"That's fine," Halloran said, but she heard his disappointment.

She took another sweep of the six men. Suspect number three looked almost amused across the eyes, and number four's gaze and chin seemed combative. Number two looked dazed, and his lips were slightly crooked. "No, I'm sorry."

"I want to thank you for coming in, ma'am."

"If I saw them in person, I might be able to tell more."

"Those physical lineups are mostly an East Coast, big city thing, where they're booking tens of perps a day."

"I'm really sorry I can't help."

"That's that then," he said, underscoring that she hadn't performed as hoped. He hesitated, as if weighing something. He lifted his right arm like it was suddenly heavy, and placed his hand flat on the photo sheet. His trigger finger tapped on suspect five. She swallowed uselessly, her mouth and throat so dry they hurt. Her eyes darted to the recording machine. Halloran's tight expression held a warning. She rushed to standing.

He pushed another sheet of paper across the table, one that stated she'd failed to make a positive ID. She signed and dated on the dotted line, her handwriting barely legible. He began returning the paperwork to their respective folders.

"I have a question." She couldn't keep the tremble out of her voice.

Fear crossed his puffy face. "O-kay. Just bear in mind, ma'am, we're still being recorded."

"Can you tell me how the latest victim, Ms. Wolas, is doing? I mean, beyond what the media is saying."

"I'm sorry, I can't tell you anything outside of what's public knowledge, which is that she's critical. I will say if you pray, pray for her."

Ester felt the color leave her face. He addressed the recording machine, officially ending the interview, and turned it off.

"I read he wore an animal mask this time too." For some reason, Ester pictured the gunman with a tiger's face.

"He doesn't need one. I saw that old woman in the hospital, he is an animal."

When Ester spoke, her voice seemed to come from a distance. "Why do you think he hurts some and not others?"

"Why do any of them do what they do?" He moved past her and opened the door. On her way out, he handed her his business card. "Call me if anything new comes to mind."

She hurried along the corridor, hoping he'd remained in the room and wasn't trailing her.

"Ester!" Crystal jumped up from the bench seat Ester had occupied minutes earlier. "How'd it go? Did you ID him?"

Ester glanced over her shoulder, relieved to not see Halloran, and ushered Crystal toward the exit, conscious of the desk duty officer and the other uniforms milling about. She and Crystal had signed confidentiality oaths.

"What's going on?" Crystal said.

"Let's get out of here," Ester said.

Crystal's chaotic kitchen was almost impressive in its various pileups of dirty dishes, wares, clothes, and toys. There was also a colorful scatter of mail and takeout menus. Ester dropped onto a chair at the messy table, thinking it mirrored her insides.

Next to the stacked sink, Crystal mounted a step stool and reached into a cabinet. "Got it," she said, her hand latched onto a half-empty bottle of brandy. From another cabinet, she removed two short glasses, more suited to breakfast juice than alcohol.

"It's ten o'clock in the morning," Ester said.

"It's almost ten thirty."

"In that case."

Crystal poured, and they touched glasses. Ester said, "I found out recently that clinking dates back to medieval times, to supposedly drive out evil spirits. Did you know that?"

"Let's do it again," Crystal said. They did, the sound less clink and more crack.

The brandy fumes kept snatching Ester's breath, and it took her several attempts before she could follow Crystal's lead and down the generous measure in one swallow. Crystal's fingers worried the scar at her hairline, the indentations from the knit of stitches still visible. The angry wound itself had calmed, its edges faded to an almost pretty pink.

"You okay?" Ester said.

"If he's caught—"

"When he's caught."

"We'll have to testify in court right in front of him. That's going to be so much worse than today."

"Let's not go there until we have to."

"Meanwhile, he's still out there." Crystal poured them a second brandy. "He has to be a local, right?"

"It seems that way."

"The thoughts of him lurking and watching, deciding on his next prey. It'd scare you out of your mind." Crystal also drained the second brandy in a single swig.

"Whoa, take it easy."

Crystal's hands covered her face. "If it had to happen, I wish he'd hurt me more."

"Oh my God, why would you say that?"

Crystal's hands dropped so swiftly, it was as if an invisible force had yanked on her wrists. "At least then I might have gotten some kind of settlement deal. As it is, I'm just left with the trauma, three kids, a dead-end if not deadly job, a tumor of bills, and this worsening sensation in my chest like weasels fighting. I don't see any way out, and I don't see how anything's ever going to get any better."

"How can I help?"

"You can't. No one can." Crystal raised the brandy bottle midair in a question.

Ester's hand covered her glass. "I'm done."

Crystal poured herself a third drink.

"I really wish you'd join the choir, it would help take your mind off things."

Crystal laughed harshly. "Yeah, a choir. That's exactly what I need."

"I'm serious. It's a great group of women, mostly, and singing the songs, well, you lose yourself in them."

"I want the kind of lost where I can't be found."

"Don't say that," Ester said.

"There's something else . . . I recognized one of the suspects."

"What? Who?"

"Suspect number two—"

Ester recalled his empty eyes and lopsided lips.

"His name's Mark. Mark Fanelli. He and I went to Brisbane High together and dated for most of junior year. He was my first serious boyfriend. Serious for me, at least. He didn't care." She scoffed. "Fits the pattern."

It took Ester a moment to recall the pattern. Crystal's ex-husband had left her and their two kids for another woman, and the father of her third child walked out on them while Crystal was still pregnant. Neither dad was paying a cent in child support. "You deserve nothing but the best."

Crystal snorted. "Do I?"

"Yes. Absolutely."

"Anyway. Mark. He was, like, sixteen and a hell of a baker of all things. A total artist about it too—the slick icing and fancy writing and decorations. His specialty was these fabulous buttercream flowers begging to be eaten. The insides delivered too. Perfectly even layers of golden sponge cake with sugary, silky fillings. I can still taste them."

The flash of pleasure on Crystal's face turned to pain. "Mark got into drugs and started dealing. Then a rich kid in the city OD'd on some of his stuff and the police, prosecutors, whatever, tried to get him for manslaughter, but he got away with something less, I can't remember what exactly. I guess he's been in and out of prison ever since. When I saw his photo this morning, it was like he was looking at me and not the other way around. Like he still had control of me." She tipped her head to the ceiling. "God, he was a total bully." She looked back at Ester, her eyes full. "If I'd done everything he wanted me to, I likely would have OD'd as well or ended up in prison right along with him."

"But none of that happened. You didn't give in to him. You're so strong, you've no idea."

Crystal raised her glass and eyed the amber liquid tenderly. "Not as strong as my little BFF right here."

"Should I be worried?" The question came out sterner than Ester had intended.

Crystal pushed the brandy bottle aside. "I know when to stop."

"Something weird also happened during my lineup."

"Oh yeah?"

"The police officer tapped his finger on suspect five, trying to get me to pick him out."

"Jesus. What did you do?"

"I was too freaked out to do or say anything."

"I'm trying to remember number five. They all looked much the same."

"They must think he's the gunman," Ester said.

"He wasn't, though. I'm pretty sure none of them were."

"Me too. Maybe if we could have smelled them."

Crystal guffawed. "What?"

"The gunman gave off this strange, acidic smell. Didn't you notice?"

"Yeah, now that you mention it. What the hell was that?"

"I wish I knew. It made me think of my grandma's air conditioning. It used to blast this weird stink through her whole house. Makes me queasy thinking about it."

"Well, now you've got me feeling ill too," Crystal said.

"Sorry. I really am no help."

"No, you're not," Crystal said, and they laughed, sounding nothing like themselves.

Soul Star

Inside his office, Principal Howe instructed Ester, Simon, and Jason to take a seat. The moment cast Ester back to Sergeant Halloran and that claustrophobic, ailing interview room. Seated, Jason bounced his right leg and rubbed his bangs between his thumb and fingers, his demeanor sullen, resistant. In grave tones, the crease-faced principal informed Ester and Simon that Jason had repeatedly skipped school in the past month, for a total of seven days.

Simon issued embarrassing shocked noises. Principal Howe continued undeterred, saying Jason had also forged notes supposedly from Ester that excused his absences due to strep throat, and next the flu. During recess, a zealous parent on yard duty overheard him bragging to his classmates about his truancy and record-shattering video game scores.

Great, Ester thought. Her thirteen-year-old son was a gaming addict, a blowhard, *and* an idiot. She sat seething and worrying. Prior to puberty and gaming, Jason had given them little to no trouble. In fact, he was so timid and obedient she had worried there might be something wrong with him. And now here they were, her fears for him coming to fruition, but far from how she had expected.

Principal Howe pressed his hands to his chin, prayerlike. "Have there been any changes or difficulties of late, socially, or at home?"

Ester recalled her reflection in her closet mirror, when the giraffe mask was wearing her.

"No, none," Simon said. "At least not that we're aware of. Jason?"

Jason's right leg bounced higher, and he rubbed his bangs faster with the full of his palm, escalating the sound of friction. The gunman pushed his face close to Ester's, his eyelashes batting the giraffe mask. *Scratching. Scratching.* Her scalp started to itch.

"Have you anything to say for yourself, young man?" Principal Howe said.

Jason remained mute. Ester's temper rocketed. "Jason, your dad and Principal Howe asked you a question."

The look he gave her. Lethal snakebites release less venom.

On the drive home, she and Jason argued back and forth while Simon tried his best to referee.

Ester entered the school gym with Crystal in tow, still not recovered from the quarrel with Jason. Or the argument that followed with Simon, over how severely they should discipline their second son. Simon shared nothing close to her outrage and concern. "I'm not saying boys will be boys, but—" She'd stopped and schooled him right there.

The maw of dread in her stomach tightened as she and Crystal moved deeper into the gym. If Crystal hadn't agreed to try out tonight's meeting, Ester might have stayed home, given the day she'd had. This was also the first choir practice since her rushing out of the Late Bar, and she didn't expect things to go any better here with Allie than they had at work.

More than once she'd played out in her head what might have happened if she'd stayed at the bar. She pictured Allie and her singing starry-eyed together onstage in front of a rapturous audience, and afterward hugging each other and taking deep, delighted bows.

But when they exited the stage, Bob stood waiting with his phone raised. "That was quite a performance, which I recorded in full."

Even imagining that moment, and Bob's sneer, caused Ester's ears to ring.

She located Allie, standing in a small circle next to the singer who'd crushed "Chain of Fools" at the Late Bar. Monica would be pleased to have a singer of her caliber, and another Black woman, in the group. Donna had said how weird it gets, and how often it happens, being the only Black person in the room. Ester felt stupid and shallow for never having considered that, especially when she'd dated Marcus for so long. She moved to the cluster of women standing farthest from Allie and introduced Crystal. The women extended a warm welcome, and the fright in Crystal's face eased, if only a little.

Monica called the meeting to order, her dress and box jacket patterned with splashes that recalled the color of the sky at sunrise. Her glasses matched the outfit's ethereal shades, and her necklace, a chunky turquoise affair, hugged her shiny décolletage. Ester wanted to get herself some of that bold put togetherness. She and Crystal moved to a nearby bleacher. Allie sat down on a faraway row next to the soul singer. Ester hadn't thought her mood could sink any lower.

Monica drew the women's attention to the bedazzled suggestion box on the card table, and next to it the stacks of colored index cards. "Before you leave tonight please take some time to write down your thoughts on where you see us going as a choir. I'd like you to think about such things as possible venues for future choral performances, both local and beyond. Also let me know if you're interested in competing in regional and national contests at some point. St. Patrick's Cathedral in New York City, for one, has a fabulous competitive program that amateur choirs can video audition to participate in."

"Carnegie Hall, here we come!" Frannie Jones shouted, raising laughter.

"Hey, Carnegie Hall is possible. They showcase choirs from all over the world, why not us someday?" Monica said.

Ester imagined traveling with the choir to New York City. She'd never been. She pictured seeing the Statue of Liberty in person, and the Empire State Building. Beyond taking in the skyscrapers, she would also walk the city's bridges, tour the 9/11 memorial and museum, and stroll through the heart of Central Park—maybe catch an Off-Broadway show, if she could get a cheap ticket.

"There's a wonderful open-air concert series in Napa Valley," Lydia said.

"Great idea," Monica said, typing into her phone.

"We could audition for *America's Got Talent*," the soul singer said, eliciting more amusement. She and Allie high-fived.

Annoyance gave Ester the courage to speak. "Aren't we getting ahead of ourselves? Travel is expensive, and it means time away from work and family. We're also a new choir just starting out. We're not going to be ready to perform, let alone compete, on a professional stage anytime soon."

"Totally," Crystal muttered.

Tessa Thompson, a jewelry maker, raised her hand, her fingers heavy with rings. "A lot of us were drawn to this group because it's local and free." Sounds of unanimity went up.

Eleanor Allison, her spine stooped and her neck sunk deep in her shoulders, rattled her steel walker. "I'm game to go anywhere."

"You tell 'em, Eleanor."

"We'd all go anywhere if we could."

"That's right."

"You're getting paid to be here, we're not."

That last comment dropped like a brick, and Ester felt bad for Monica, who'd rightly received a state grant to found and direct the choir.

Monica raised her hands. "Okay. Okay. How about this? Let's think of the suggestion box as a wish list without limits, and let's see what we come up with. That way we can at least explore what a dream path forward looks like, and who knows how far we might go together with that kind of blueprint, yeah?"

Cheers and applause followed, restoring the group's elevated mood. Ester couldn't pull herself from the doldrums.

"If we do decide to travel we could fundraise to cover our expenses," Frannie said.

"That's what I was thinking," Monica said. "I'm also going to apply for sponsorships and various other grants. It's worth a shot. And if any of you can help me with that, please let me know."

"We could set up a GoFundMe."

"What about a good old-fashioned bake sale?"

"A car wash."

"We could have a giant yard sale here at the school."

A debate ensued over whether the school would allow the choir to fundraise on-site for a nonschool event. The consensus was that they would not.

"We could record a CD and sell it online and in hard copies," Sue Wang said.

"That's a brilliant idea," Monica said, typing on her phone.

Kate Moore raised her hand, the hennaed laurel leaves and lotus flowers on her scalp fading. "Our first performances could be local community outreach, to help us gain experience and do good while we're at it. That wouldn't cost us anything besides gas, and we could carpool to cut down on that expense, and emissions."

"I love that idea."

"I love this group."

Kate continued, "To start, we could perform at my chemo center in San Mateo. Patients often have to sit alone for hours during treatments, and we'd love to be entertained."

A loud chorus of support went up, followed by suggestions for performances at the Children's Hospital in Oakland, and the

General Hospital in San Francisco, which cared for some of the Bay Area's most injured and marginalized. Monica pointed out the time, thanked everyone for their enthusiasm and creative responses, and urged them to still go ahead and complete suggestion slips. Ester planned to add Golden Leaves to the outreach schedule.

Monica led them through head relaxation exercises, posture corrections, and vocal warm-ups. During a rehearsal of "Let It Be," their voices rose like pure prayer.

Monica circulated the sheet music for "Fall" by Chloe x Halle. The sibling singers were so young and contemporary Ester wouldn't ordinarily have heard of them but for months last year Kevin had played the song on repeat.

The choir's first efforts at "Fall" elicited self-conscious laughter. After several attempts, the song and harmonies started to come together. Early in the practice, Crystal had sung under her breath. By the end of the meeting she was singing aloud—shaky, pitchy—but getting heard.

As the gym emptied, Monica pulled Ester aside. "I thought of you when I heard about that terrible home robbery. How are you doing?"

Behind Monica, Allie was exiting the gym with the soul singer. Ester said, "I can't stop thinking about the elderly victim, Ms. Wolas. It doesn't look like she's going to make it."

"I read that, it's appalling," Monica said. "What dies in us that we can do these things to each other?"

"I know." Ester nodded at Crystal pacing back and forth by the gym doors. "Crystal's the one he pistol-whipped during the holdup at the store."

"How awful. I didn't realize that. I'm so glad she's joined us."

"Me too. It'll be good for her."

"For all of us. I couldn't be more excited and hopeful for everything that's to come," Monica said.

Ester couldn't hold onto her smile. "I should go, I'm Crystal's ride."

"Go, go," Monica said, her face furrowed with concern, "and take care of yourselves."

In the minivan, Crystal insisted on talking over Sam Smith's serenade. "I get us performing for local patients and old people, but this traveling to Napa Valley, and New York City for Pete's sake—"

Ester wished Crystal would stay quiet and allow her to listen unhindered to Sam Smith sing about magic and us giving and getting everything.

"There's no way I'm ever going to compete in front of judges or sing any place fancy or faraway."

"That's fine, that's your choice," Ester said.

"Where's the choice if contests freak me out and I can't afford to travel anywhere?" Crystal riffed about blanking onstage in the fifth grade during a spelling bee competition, and about having zero options in life. "I'm totally cornered."

Ester willed her to please shut up. Crystal did not.

What We're Going to Do with You

Ester hovered next to Jason at the kitchen island, the boy riding high on the acceptance he'd received moments earlier from Holy Redeemer High School. His fingers flew over the laptop's keyboard anew, logging into the portal to St. Francis's placement results. He scanned the loaded page. "Come on."

"What?"

"The link isn't live yet." He refreshed the page.

Ester tried to keep her voice light. "You're going to break the keyboard."

They'd known about his confirmed enrollment at Rayland public high school for several weeks and that's where his admissions journey should have ended. But back in the fall he'd insisted on also applying to Holy Redeemer and St. Francis. The latter, considered the more elite and competitive of the two parochial schools, was where he claimed all his friends were going.

Ester and Simon couldn't afford either school and had urged him to be glad of Rayland, but he'd pleaded and raged on and on with Ironman stamina. It sliced Ester that he seemed to need the bragging rights that one or both acceptances would bring. Most heart hitting, he also appeared to need to know he was worthy of admission.

At the eleventh hour, she and Simon reluctantly ponied up the application fees for both schools, on the firm understanding that Jason's attending either school was financially impossible. Some deluded part of her had dared hope that by the time the placement results came around maybe they would have won the lottery, or Simon would have received a miraculous promotion with a huge raise and generous benefits. Anything, something, so that they could grant Jason his burning wish.

He stabbed the laptop's Return key. "Come on."

Her stomach tilted. They should never have let him apply to either parochial school.

"Why's it tak— wait, it's loading."

"Relax, sweetheart, whatever—"

He shot off the barstool, knocking it to the floor. "I got in!"

"Congratulations, that's great. Good for you."

His frantic attention returned to the screen. She righted the barstool, her apprehension climbing.

"And I got financial aid!"

"How much?"

"I'm checking . . . Five thousand dollars!"

"Is that per semester?"

"Um." He scanned the screen. "It's per year, and we have to reapply each spring." He grabbed his phone, typing furiously.

"What are you doing?"

"Duh. I'm telling my friends."

"Telling them what exactly?"

"What do you think?"

"I want to be sure we're on the same page here. You're making me nervous."

He held his arms out from his sides, appealing. "Mom. You've been standing right here. I've got my pick of all three schools."

"And that's amazing, but you remember what we agreed to, correct? You applied to St. Francis and Holy Redeemer for the satisfaction and the supposed glory of getting in, but you're going to Rayland."

"Supposed glor— You wouldn't say that if it was Kevin who got in."

"That's not true."

"I'm not going to Rayland. I'm going to St. Francis."

"You can't."

"Why not?"

"You know why not."

"You're working at Blazers now and making way more money than you were at the store—"

"Way more is a stretch, and I'd need to hold down three jobs to afford Holy Redeemer or St. Francis. Even if you got that puny financial aid for all four years, an education at St. Francis would still cost eighty thousand dollars. At least."

"You'd find a way to make it work for Kevin!"

"You need to be careful about the stories you tell yourself."

"You can't tell me that Kevin isn't your favorite."

"He's easier, that's for sure."

Jason's features widened, as if something had crashed into the back of his face.

"Don't look at me like that. You know what I mean."

"Yeah, I do."

"Please, I don't want us to fight."

"It's not fair! How come all the other kids can afford to go wherever they want?"

"That's not true either. A ton of kids you know are going to Rayland."

"Yeah, the losers and rejects."

"That's a terrible thing to say."

His shouts and protests continued. She tried to calm him. His breathlessness ratcheted up to hyperventilating. Every time she reached for him, he escaped her. She followed him around the kitchen, consoling.

He charged upstairs and into his room. She reached the door before he could close it and shouldered her way inside. He dropped onto his bed, crying and punching the mattress. She'd never seen him this upset or agitated. Nothing she said was reaching him.

"Please get out. Please leave me alone." He sounded like he was in terminal pain.

Fear tightened its hands around her neck. "Okay, I'll leave, but first I need you to promise me you're not going to do anything."

He froze in the fetal position and looked at her hard. "What do you mean?"

She forced out the words, afraid she was putting ideas in his head, but more afraid of ignoring the depths of his distress. "I'm worried you're going to hurt yourself."

"I would never do that, Mom." He said it so softly, so stunned, her throat filled.

"Okay good. Then I'll leave you alone like you asked, but I'm downstairs if you need me, okay? I know you're hurting, I do, but I promise it'll pass."

It was something her mother often said, and something that wasn't always true.

Sunday morning, Rachel set a brisk pace along the dirt trail, as if trying to outstride the fog. Ester struggled to keep up, her mood and body dragging. Donna, equally cardio-challenged, complained of pain in her left hip.

"Congrats again to Jason, he must be thrilled," Rachel said.

"I wouldn't say that exactly," Ester said.

"Uh oh," Donna said.

"He got his hopes up that St. Francis was an actual option."

"And it isn't?" Rachel said.

"No, there's no way," Ester said, fighting a stab of envy that Rachel and Robbie could afford to send their three girls to Holy Redeemer, or anywhere else they wanted to go.

"That's hard," Donna said.

"I'm kicking myself for ever letting him apply, but I swear that kid's backtalk could wear down the IRS," Ester said.

"I'm sorry, and I'm going to steal that line," Donna said.

"Me too, on both counts," Rachel said.

"It is what it is. He's going to love it at Rayland, he just doesn't know it yet. I can totally see him thriving in their robotics club and woodworking classes," Ester said.

"Well, you know Tilly and Henri are very happy there," Donna said.

"They all land where they're supposed to," Rachel said.

"They do," Donna said.

That also seemed like something that wasn't always true, but Ester said nothing.

Rachel, maintaining her brisk pace, broke into a breathy mono-logue about the April Fools' prank she planned to play on her family. She was going to pretend that an international property management company had headhunted her for a job too good to refuse, one that required their family of five to relocate to Hong Kong.

Ester hated April Fools'. Too often the supposed joke backfired, and life doled out enough chaos without us willfully orchestrating it.

"Careful, they might love the idea," Donna said.

"Yeah, I can think of worse fates," Ester said.

"Are you kidding me? Robbie and the girls are total homebod-ies. They're going to lose their snot," Rachel said.

Donna turned the conversation to the fast approach of May and the end of the school year. Talk of graduation ceremonies and par-ties, and caterers and cakes, veered into a discussion of sugar and inflammation. Donna admitted that despite the science, and her clickety hip and swollen knees, she didn't think she could ever give up chocolate.

"Me neither," Ester said.

Rachel swore by apple cider vinegar for curbing appetite and balancing blood sugar levels. Ester offered the odd comment, wanting to appear interested and agreeable, but her head was full of the growing trouble with Jason. Following Friday's meltdown over St. Francis, he'd stayed out long past his curfew and hadn't arrived home until after midnight. He and Simon squared up to each other in the living room, and at one point she thought they were going to come to blows. Ever since, Jason refused to speak with them. He'd gotten another controller and headset someplace and was back to gaming until all hours at night.

"I don't know what we're going to do with you," Simon had said as Jason stomped up to bed in the early hours of Saturday morning. It sounded like a threat and a plea.

A large gray dog darted from the woods, startling Ester back to the trail. The husky's owner appeared moments later, a blocky middle-aged man with hay-colored hair and a spritely step. He was suitably dressed in Gore-Tex against the lurk of rain in the overcast sky, whereas the three women weren't so prudent in their Lycra and polyester layers. He ignored them as he passed by, his look stony. In his wake, Rachel complained about inconsiderate owners who allowed their dogs to roam off leash.

Ester believed well-behaved dogs had as much right to the trail as people did, but she wasn't in the mood to get into it. She only wanted to savor the trees like protectors on both sides of her and the white-crested waves climbing and crashing in the distance, the ocean a giant green spill. In the metallic sky, the loud, thick smatter of crows seemed both ominous and a feat of magic. The soft dirt beneath the women recorded their footprints, leaving impressions of their past selves. The thought buoyed Ester. With every step forward, they were each changed by time and place. They were starting over.

Ester arrived home, rolling her shoulders and rubbing her hands together. The morning's chill had invaded her bones. She called out, receiving no response, and moved upstairs to check on Jason. His room was empty. She called his name and looked into the bathroom. She returned downstairs and scanned the back garden and garage. So much for his being grounded. She phoned him, but he didn't pick up. She would set Simon on him later. She didn't have the energy to deal with him.

In the kitchen, in a fit of self-indulgence, she decided on a long, hot bubble bath with add-ons. She removed a bar of dark chocolate and the bottle of champagne from the fridge, which had gone unpopped for too long. On closing the fridge, the appliance issued its clanking noises, as if scolding her.

"Rude," she said.

Upstairs, she filled the bathtub with steaming water and an entire five-pound bag of lavender-infused bath salts. As the water rose, she changed into her robe and started in on the champagne and chocolate, the meld of fizz and silk in her mouth divine. Rachel and Donna's conversation earlier about sugar and inflammation came to mind, as did the link between inflammation and dementia, but right then she didn't care. *Everything in moderation-ish.* She placed her phone, the champagne and chocolate, and various hair and face products on a chair next to the bathtub. Hissing, she immersed herself in the hot water, its temperature bordering on masochism.

Taking her sweet time, she lathered herself in sandalwood-scented soap. Clean, pinked, she loaded the loofah with the oatmeal scrub and repeated a circular caress of her entire body, polishing herself to rosy. Throughout, Ben Platt crooned from her phone, another young, contemporary singer-songwriter Kevin had introduced her to. She savored a second glass of champagne and two more chocolate segments. Buzzed to an exquisite degree, she applied a green tea brightening mask to her face and neck.

She reclined in the tub, sending the water level up to her collarbones, and pressed her shoulders and feet against the enamel. Drowsy, she closed her eyes and inhaled the fragrant cocktail of rose and lavender and wood, promising to pamper herself like this more often, sans the champagne. That would be dicey decadence on the regular.

The clay mask hardened and tightened. She seemed to be shrinking along with her face. She sat up straight, uneasiness lapping her edges along with the water. Suspect five from the photo lineup appeared in the bathtub opposite her, causing her severe heart cramp. She could only manage shallow breaths. Anything deeper caused her clenched heart to border on stopping. She ordered the misfiring organ to right itself. Naked, furry, suspect five raised his dripping hand and pulled a giraffe mask down over his face.

She plunged her head into the bathwater and stayed under to past the point of pain, until her lungs were hammering her chest like fists. She burst from the water, gasping and finding herself alone. Her fingers cleared the rivulets of melted mask from her eyes while streaks of green dripped onto her chest and leaked downward. She scrubbed herself, ridding her skin of all traces of the mask, and welcomed back her steady heartbeat.

She needed to get out of the bathtub and away from suspect five's phantom linger, but she was light-headed and fighting white dots. It wasn't only that she'd drunk too much too fast and steeped herself in too-hot water for too long. Dread was also keeping her soldered to the tub. Beyond this solid oval space lay the aftermath of the holdup, the gunman's escalating robberies, and the press of Jason, Dad, Simon, Allie, and Halloran. Pinned to the enamel, she was also relieved of the sense of urgency gathering inside her of late. A tornado-like build that demanded she take off running and keep going until she couldn't anymore.

Maybe Sergeant Halloran was right. Maybe suspect five was the gunman. But obviously the gas station clerk had also failed to ID him. She needed to stop second-guessing herself. Three eyewitnesses couldn't all be wrong, and who knew Halloran's true agenda. She wondered how many other witnesses he'd tried to influence, and how many suspects were wrongly ID'd and possibly convicted as a result. She was angry with herself for not speaking up in the moment, and for her continued silence since. She should, would, report him.

She expected the righteous decision to make her feel better. It didn't. From her phone, Ben Platt crooned "Grow as We Go." If she played the song for Simon, would he get it? Could they grow together and stop drifting apart? Her head reeled. She needed to take herself to bed. She unplugged the drain and tucked her knees to her chest, watching the water sink.

Her phone rang. She reached for it on the chair and declined the call. She wasn't up for talking with Crystal or anyone else.

Crystal rang again. Ester answered, concerned. Crystal sounded distraught, smothered. "What is it? What's wrong?"

Crystal continued to splutter, her words garbled. It took Ester several awful seconds to understand who had died. "Jesus. I thought something had happened to one of your kids."

Crystal, sniffling, recounted endearing details from Torpedo's all too brief life, her emotional eulogy interrupted twice by customers. Ester, shivering, shriveled, resubmerged as much of herself as possible in the disappearing water. The tap dripped onto her right foot like a single column of rain.

Crystal blew her nose. "I'm sorry, I know I'm being ridiculous, but he was great company, and as silly as it sounds, I felt safer with him here."

"You're not being ridiculous. That's why I got him for you. I'm going to head back to the pet store right now and get you another goldfish."

"Thanks, but I don't think I want to risk it. Not if it's not going to last."

"Okay then, I'll head straight to you." The last of the purple-tinged water streaked with green circled the drain and glugged as it exited.

"You don't have to," Crystal said.

Ester's cold skin had tightened and pimpled. "I want to."

She dried and dressed herself, and moved downstairs and into the garage. After a harried search, she retrieved one of the boys' old baseball bats. The bat would at least give Crystal some sense of protection. She could name it Torpedo Two.

Essential Body Part

Ester reached into her closet, hoping for a moment of wizardry, like pulling a rabbit from a hat. She'd already tried on four different outfits, none of which worked. She'd known about this dinner to celebrate Robbie's fiftieth birthday for weeks, and yet here she was on the night scrambling for something to wear. She didn't imagine Monica, fashionista and choir director extraordinaire, ever floundered like this. Or Allie. Allie possessed a relaxed confidence and chic image, as if she were perpetually fresh off a preppy fashion runway.

Ester arrived at her red satin top and pulled it from the hanger, drawn to the supposed color of champions. Inside the closet mirror, the top's scooped neckline allowed a kiss of cleavage to peek out, while the black flared trousers thinned and lengthened her legs and the sexy red stilettos added glamour. She peered at her face, checking for rogue hairs. The lines around her eyes and mouth were deepening, and the two brown spots like tea stains on her left cheek and temple were darkening. She was getting older faster.

Simon materialized behind her and pressed his cool lips to the side of her neck. His kissing her soft spots used to open her up like a tulip. She twisted out of his hold. "We're going to be late."

"Always an excuse."

She pecked the hard line of his mouth. "Later, okay?"

"Yeah, yeah." He crossed the room and lifted his wallet and phone from the dresser.

She was following him out of the bedroom when Crystal phoned. Her stomach sank. "Hang on. I need to take this."

"I thought we were in a hurry."

She hated how he sulked whenever he didn't get sex, and how he often set himself up for failure, wanting it at impossible times. "Crystal, hi."

"You're not going to believe this," Crystal said, upbeat.

"Try me."

"The car will be here in three," Simon said, reading his phone and moving downstairs.

"Rich appeared in the store this evening with not one but two goldfish, and in an actual aquarium, a small one, but still. And get this, he reckoned Torpedo died from loneliness."

"I'd say that's deep, and good for him, but this is Rich we're talking about."

"I know, right? Then he announces both goldfish are female—"

"About the only way he can get two women."

"Seriously." Crystal's laughter cooled. "You should have heard him go on about how to identify a goldfish's sex, like all of a sudden he's an expert."

"I bet that's the only sex he's ever aced."

"Stop, you're going to make me pee myself."

Ester had almost peed herself during the holdup. "Listen, if that's it, I've really got to run."

"No, wait. I saved the best part for last."

"Oh yeah?"

"I named one of the goldfish Es after you, not that I can ever tell Rich that, and the other one is Gish. Only now I can't tell them apart."

"I'm honored, I think."

"Rich must have hit his head or something," Crystal said.

"Now would be a great time to ask for a raise."

"Right? That would be a true test of his new nature."

"I'm serious, strike now, while he's completely dependent on you."

"Hmm, good point. Because you know he'll find someone desperate enough soon enough. He hates covering shifts," Crystal said.

"There you go then."

"I'll think about it."

"I'm telling you, do it."

"Okay, I will."

"ASAP."

"Yes, ma'am."

"Car's here," Simon called from the bottom of the stairs.

"I hope this pair lasts a lot longer than Torpedo did," Crystal said.

"I'm sure they will."

"One more thing. I Sharpied a skull and crossbones on Torpedo Two and stashed it beneath the counter."

"Perfect. Well done." Ester hoped Crystal would never have cause to use the decorated baseball bat, at least not as a weapon.

Ester eyed Donna's fat filet mignon, half wishing she'd ordered that instead of the king salmon. She started into her meal, the glimmer of regret evaporating. Her salmon was grilled to lemony, flaky deliciousness. The roasted asparagus and creamy potato gratin also tasted scrumptious, while the fruity cabernet with its undertone of black currant was almost as decadent as their surroundings.

The storybook restaurant, tucked inside an alleyway in San Francisco's trendy SoMa neighborhood, was an oasis of fine furnishings, tangerine lighting, abstract oil paintings, and flickering candlelight. Equally mood enhancing was Rachel and Robbie's generosity in paying for the extravagant dinner, especially when their four guests could never reciprocate in kind. The tenor among the six friends was as exalted as the venue and meal, one outdoing the next with wit and anecdotes, their laughter raucous.

Simon mentioned he was called for jury duty. "Like clockwork, every twelve months."

"Better than getting audited, which is my annual penance the past few years," Gary said.

"Have you served on a jury before?" Donna asked.

"No, but I would like to, at least once," Simon said.

"It's a pain," Robbie said.

"Depends on the case," Rachel said.

"How'd you get away without serving for this long, if they keep calling you?" Gary said.

"Work deadlines, mostly. One time I knew the arresting officer, that's a conflict of interest, and last time I answered *yes* when the prosecutor asked if I believed that police racially profile. That'll get you sent packing every time," Simon said.

"Which they do," Donna said.

"Totally. I didn't intend it as an excuse, I meant it," Simon said.

Gary recounted how years back he'd served as a juror in a bank robbery trial. The defendant wore pantyhose over his head during the holdup, but the nylon leg was so laddered his face was visible in the security footage. While Gary went on, the fugitive gunman lurked in the wings of Ester's mind, but she refused to allow him onstage.

"And he still pleaded not guilty," Gary finished.

The six howled. Ester smiled across the table at Simon. They needed more nights out like this, more fun. To be interesting, and interested. He grinned back, his sheen alluring. She wanted to taste his salt.

Somewhere in the lull between dinner and the ceremonial arrival of the fiery birthday cake, Donna asked about Jason. "Are things any better?"

Ester's high mood deflated. "He's still licking his wounds over St. Francis, and still has another couple of days of detention to complete for his truancy. On top of that, he broke his curfew last weekend, a first."

"Eighth grade is a tough year. You can't wait to finish elementary school, but you've also got this mess of feelings about high school and growing up in general," Donna said.

"We've tried to get him to see the school counselor, but he won't go. He thinks it's a punishment, that we're saying he's damaged and in need of fixing," Ester said.

"We need to come up with consequences that actually work," Simon said.

"Like what? We confiscated his gaming accessories, yet again, and tried grounding him, but he refuses to stay home," Ester said.

"If we grounded Tilly or Henri there's no way they'd set foot outside," Donna said.

"What are we supposed to do? Lock him in his room? Physically restrain him?" Ester said.

"You could take away his phone, TV, pocket money, all of his privileges," Rachel said.

"Our girls would prefer to have an arm amputated than to have their phones taken away," Robbie said.

"That's the whole point. It's got to hurt," Rachel said.

"Crack down now or pay later," Gary said.

"When do you ever crack down on our kids?" Donna said.

"When do we ever have to?" Gary said.

His words landed with a thump and Ester sat bristling. She hoped they might move on from the topic, she'd been looking forward to this fancy dinner for ages, but Robbie had to weigh in again. "Taking his phone away will get through to him for sure. It's practically an essential body part, even for me, a grown adult."

"You, a grown adult? That's debatable," Gary said, inciting bursts of laughter from everyone but Ester.

Robbie segued to basketball and the Warriors' current funk. A lively chat ensued until Gary turned somber. "Dad losing interest in the NBA, that was the first indication there was something seriously wrong. We thought it might be depression, or dementia. Never imagined it would turn out to be an inoperable brain tumor."

Donna placed her hand over Gary's on the table, her lips pressed tight. Like passing a baton, the group took turns sharing updates on their parents and stepparents. Simon was the only one of the six who was both an only child and adult orphan, although Ester could essentially claim the latter too. His dad died shortly after Jason was born, from a fall while hiking in the Santa Cruz Mountains. His mom had died when he was nine, in a car crash. It was what bonded her and Simon from the beginning, their mother wounds.

Luckily, before it came around to her turn to speak, staff circled the table, and their server placed the chocolate cake and its thicket of burning candles in front of Robbie. The group sang "Happy Birthday" while Rachel, tone-deaf and self-conscious, mimed along. Delighted exclamations and applause followed. Robbie closed his eyes, issued a wish, and extinguished the flames with two blasts of boozy breath. Ester cast her own silent ask.

On the drive home, Ester remembered that years back someone broke into Rachel's car. The robber smashed the front passenger window and pilfered CDs and spare change, the only items of value. Rachel described sitting into the vehicle for the first time after the incident. Shattered glass dotted the front seats and floor, as if the ceiling had rained diamonds. Rachel shivered on finding the crushed cigarette butt in the coffee holder and spotting the ashes on the floor on her driver's side, smudged underfoot. It took her weeks to get over the thought of a stranger, a thief, loitering inside her car, in her driver's seat, in what had been a private, safe space. One in which she ferried herself and her three daughters to and fro. "I got that car professionally cleaned, twice, and I could still feel him inside it."

Simon climbed into bed, naked and erect. Ester begged off her earlier promise, her arousal during dinner extinguished. She was too tired, too tipsy, too full. "I'm syrup."

"All the better to drink you." He dipped his head.

She rolled free. "No way, not happening."

"What about me? What about my needs?"

When she didn't respond he turned his back to her and tugged the covers, bundling himself. Within seconds, he was snoring. *How was that possible?* She lay awake for a long time, praying for clarity, for answers. Only her body responded, in its tightness, its heaviness.

Scratchers

Ester headed to the store before work to check in on Crystal and the two new goldfish. En route, she was almost past the site of the gunman's second holdup when she swerved the minivan and turned into the gas station, barely missing its curb. She parked next to the clerk's kiosk and waited for the surge of adrenaline to abate. Her jumpiness eased somewhat, and she exited the van.

She approached the sixtyish man behind the kiosk's Plexiglas, feeling like she was inside her throbbing pulse and not the other way around. She'd experienced the same strange, consuming sensation on emailing the police chief earlier in the week to report Sergeant Halloran for attempted coercion, and to which she had yet to receive a reply.

She reached the clerk, his swollen thyroid like the bloat in a frog's neck. She stood mortified and mute, her trapped words ramming each other like bumper cars.

"Ma'am?"

"Can I get some gum, please?"

"What kind?"

"Um, Fruit Stripe."

He lasered the packet of gum with the barcode scanner. "That it?"

"I'll take a couple of Scratchers as well."

"What's calling to you?"

She eyed the carousel of choices, wondering how many times a day he said those words, and for how many others the question knocked them sideways.

She pointed to the black and silver two-dollar Scratchers. "I'll take those."

"Two, you said?"

She nodded. He set about scanning the Scratchers. She spoke in a rush. "I was working at the convenience store Rich Goods the day it was robbed. Were you on duty for the holdup here?"

"Yeah, I was."

"Those masks, right?"

"I'll never look at a hippo the same way again."

"He ruined giraffes for me and my coworker Crystal. My ex-coworker, I should say. I quit."

"Well for some," he said, harkening back to Lydia Greeslie's jab.

"Now I'm serving my time at Blazers Restaurant."

He ignored the attempted quip and totaled her purchases. She paid, and he placed her change and goods on the slot tray between them. She regretted her choice of gum as soon as her hand closed around its wrapper patterned with zebra faces. "I'm sorry it happened to you too."

His bulging thyroid climbed and sank. "Same. I can't understand how they haven't caught him already? It's not like he's casting his net very far. Or maybe he is, and we don't know it. You'd think the more he does it, and so soon together, the quicker he'd get caught."

"I hear you. Hopefully the police are closing in on him."

"Hopefully."

"I'm guessing the sheriff's office also called you in for the photo lineup?" she said.

"Yeah. We're not supposed to talk about that."

"Right, sorry. It's just . . ."

"What?" he said.

"Did you meet with a Sergeant Halloran?"

"Halloran, yeah. Why?"

"He pressured me to ID one of the suspects. I wondered if maybe he'd done the same to you?"

"Can't say he did. Can't say we should be talking about this either," he said.

"Right. It's just I can't stop second-guessing myself. What if I got it wrong, and Halloran's right?"

"The gunman wasn't in that lineup, no doubt in my mind."

"Thanks for telling me that. I didn't think so either."

"Now if that's all?" He cocked his bulbous chin, indicating the couple of customers in line behind her. She hadn't realized anyone was waiting.

"Thank you. Thanks so much." She turned to leave, and turned back to him, placing the two Scratchers in the slot tray. "For you. Good luck."

His face bloomed with surprise, lifting the hard edges off him. "Hey, thanks, lady."

He called after her. "If I win big, I'll split it fifty-fifty with ya."

She waved, smiling. She'd read someplace that the people who make it hardest to reach them are the ones who need connection the most.

Back in the minivan, she texted Jason. *I love you.* She added, deleted, and readded the red heart emoji. She knew better than to wait for a reply.

Ester entered Rich's store, finding mustardy Charlie Neville at the counter, accepting his change from Crystal and squirreling a fifth of whiskey into his inside jacket pocket. He grunted a greeting at Ester as he exited, a jellied, hunted look to his eyes. Up until last year he'd taught math at the boys' elementary school, but alcoholism had forced him into early retirement. His wife, Lucy, was a member of Sing, I, her voice a standout, although more crow than thrush. It had to eat at her, watching her husband pickle himself.

Ester admired the lighted aquarium on the shelf behind the counter, situated right on Torpedo's former site. The fishes' foot-long abode was decorated with white sand, red rocks, green trees, and bright-pink coral. Rich really must have hit his head. More than once.

"Watch this." Crystal lowered herself to eye level with the fish and started singing "Let It Be," her mellow voice sweeter and more confident than her halting, warbling efforts at her first choir meeting. "You see that? They're dancing."

She resumed singing. Ester watched, taken aback. It did seem like Crystal's voice was propelling the goldfish. The agile pair cut the clear water, flitting back and forth, and diving and rising. One appeared to pull off a pirouette.

"Incredible." Ester clapped.

"I showed Rich, and he flipped out. He even called the papers and news stations, trying to get them back here to cover it. He pitched it as a feel-good story following the holdup. Who is he, and what has he done with the real Rich?"

"You and your dancing goldfish could go viral."

"Cue the big time," Crystal said.

"We can dream."

"The pet store guy gave Rich this whole lesson on how to identify their sex. It's pretty interesting. Not that I told Rich that. Males have these white marks on their faces called breeding stars—"

Ester checked the time on her phone. She needed to get to work.

"—breeding, as in making babies, not, you know, inhale, exhale. Isn't that cool? Another telltale sign is that the males chase the females to mate. Go figure. Then there's body shape. Females are fatter, basically. There's also something about a part of the fin, whether it's an innie or an outie."

The store bell rang, announcing an emaciated teen with long blond dreadlocks. She headed straight for the wall of glass freezers and stopped in front of the rows of ice cream. Ester considered telling Crystal about her encounter with the gas station clerk.

Crystal's demeanor turned giddier. "I can't believe I'm saying this."

"Okay, I'll play. Saying what?"

"Rich asked me out."

"Shut up."

"Yep." Crystal twisted her torso from side to side, coquettish.

"Why do you look distressingly pleased with yourself?"

"It's hilarious, and kinda flattering."

"Please. Rich is a creep."

"I don't know. I'm starting to see a different side to him," Crystal said.

"You can't be serious?"

"Take the fun out of it, why don't you?"

"Tell me you told him where to bury it," Ester said.

"No one's noticed me like that in a very long time."

"What did you tell him?"

"I said I'd think about it."

"I'm sorry. I can't see what there's to think about."

"Easy for you to say. You're not hurting for anything."

Ester resisted the urge to fire back. She had her struggles, but Crystal had things far worse. "I have to fly. I'm going to be late for work."

"Don't let me stop you." Crystal's attention jumped to the straggly teen, now working her way up the bread and cookies aisle. "Word of advice," she said, crossing the store and easing the pint of ice cream from the crook of the girl's branch arm. "Always get your frozen goods last."

"See ya," Ester said on her way out.

"See ya," Crystal said, her tone as cold as the tub of ice cream she was returning to the freezer.

The Big Date

Kevin and Mena arrived at Blazers, his lurching stride unmistakable. He was growing into a handsome, sturdy young man, a mirror of his dad. Ester powered on her hostess smile and readied the right mix of fawning. It was Mena's birthday, and her and Kevin's first formal dinner date. Ever. Kevin had forewarned Ester to treat them like VIPs but to not embarrass him.

"Hi, we have a seven o'clock reservation." Kevin's irises betrayed tiny explosions of mischief and nervousness. Mena smiled conspiratorially, her charcoal mini dress drawing out the gray in her eyes and her high ponytail accentuating her cheekbones.

Ester hugged her. "Happy birthday, sweetheart."

She collected two menus and escorted the pair to the middle prime booth. Allie had approved their seating earlier in the week and instructed Ester to comp their drinks and dessert. Ester thanked her profusely and wished the conversation had lasted longer.

"Wow, thank you," Mena said, sliding onto the bench seat.

"Be sure to save room for dessert," Ester said, winking at Kevin. He rolled his eyes.

Their server, Maria, appeared. Ester still wasn't over Maria's claim that, when she was a toddler, her mother used to wedge a broken matchstick between her top front teeth every night so she would have Madonna's signature gap. Which she did.

"I hear we're celebrating?" Maria said.

"It's Mena's birthday," Kevin said.

"Happy birthday, Mena. Are we seventeen? Eighteen?" Maria said.

"Seventeen," Mena said, crimson.

"Enjoy," Ester said.

"I'll take good care of them," Maria said.

"I know you will, thanks," Ester said.

Allie approached her as she returned to the front of house. "I see the happy couple has arrived. They could be the poster for first love."

"They've got it bad, all right, although Mena's not as obvious about it as Kevin."

"It's intense at that age, especially for their generation. They've got infinite fake lives and staged love coming at them constantly on social media."

"I know, I worry," Ester said.

"Not that I'm saying we had it easy. No one does. I fell hard at sixteen, and I'm not sure I've ever loved or ached that much since," Allie said.

Sal waved Allie over to the bar, leaving Ester alone with thoughts of love and ache and Marcus. She would never forgive herself for cheating on him—and with a random guy at a party. She had vague memories of feeling reckless and defiant that night. She and Marcus had been dating for almost three years by then, and she didn't see how the relationship could continue after he graduated from college. They were too young and the choices too many to continue to commit to monogamy.

There was also a whole wide world beyond Half Moon Bay that she was determined to explore. Marcus insisted he would wait out the year until she also graduated and then they could go anywhere she wanted, but she'd burned with the need to set out on her own. Why didn't she just break up with him? Why, for that forgettable one-night stand, did she have to betray him? It was further unforgivable—after her being so hellbent on freedom and adventure—that she'd never managed to break away from Half Moon Bay. But Marcus's death had leveled her, and only months later she would meet Simon at the Mavericks surf competition, where they were both sandy, beer-buzzed spectators. He turned out to be solid when she was a puddle, and two years later they'd gotten pregnant and married.

A party of six appeared at the podium. On learning there was an hour-long wait, they asked to speak to the manager. Allie easily smoothed over the situation and bowed out. Ester paused in the midst of taking down the party's details. "I'm sorry, I'll just be a sec."

She moved after Allie. "Are we okay?"

Allie seemed to be working up to something bigger but all she said was, "Why wouldn't we be?"

"I wasn't sure. I mean, after that night in the Late Bar."

"Yeah, no, we're good."

"Great. I'm so glad." Ester hooked her thumb toward the waiting group. "I better get back."

"That's probably a good idea." Allie's smile could melt wax.

When it came time for Kevin and Mena's dessert, staff gathered in front of their booth and sang "Happy Birthday" while the sparkler topping the cupcake fired multicolored flames. Several diners joined in on the song and the applause. Kevin kissed Mena. The soft way he looked at her afterward, Ester wanted to reach into his chest and cup her hands around his young heart. Like Marcus's, it was going to get wrecked.

Ester exited Blazers among the babbling group headed to the Late Bar and climbed into the rideshare, relieved to have cleared the air with Allie. That past nonsense, her imagined lesbian leanings, she was done with all that.

As before, she, Allie, and Alejandro occupied the back seat. It was Bob's night off and this time Sal sat up front. He and the driver, Rudy, discussed legalized cannabis and growers' complaints that government regulations were crippling them financially.

Alejandro pulled out an earbud. "All the people in prison for cannabis, why they not free now?"

The men and Allie agreed, talking over Miley Cyrus filling the car with "Party in the USA." Ester was still thinking about her other life, the one where Mom and Marcus didn't die and she'd gotten away from Half Moon Bay when she was young.

Allie's fingertips glanced the side of Ester's knee. "You're quiet?"

Ester pulled her leg aside, glancing at Alejandro.

"Sorry." Allie curled her hand closed on her thigh, as if crushing something.

Inside the Late Bar, Sal acted as banker for the group and he and Alejandro disappeared to get the round of drinks. Ester and Allie watched the quintet of inebriated women onstage, screeching "I Will Survive."

Ester broke the silence, which was practically vibrating. "They should have one of those hooks, to pull them offstage."

Allie dipped her head. "What?"

"I said they should—"

The second group from Blazers arrived, Maria among them. "Too cute," she said of Kevin and Mena. "What I'd give to be their age again. I'd do a whole lot differently, I tell you, and I'd have way more fun doing it." She cackled, the Madonnaesque gap between her teeth like a black hole.

Ester didn't trust herself to respond. We can't go backward. Can't redo the past. So why go on about it? Sal and Alejandro returned from the bar. Ester drank deep. The crush of sweaty, shiny people was overwhelming, as was the thumping noise and the invasive strobe lighting. She wondered where everyone had come from.

During her third Moscow mule, she imagined the swell of patrons was a huge cast of actors shipped in from elsewhere and playing characters in a frenzied scene from a TV drama. Meanwhile, outside, the sleepy town of Half Moon Bay was watching the show while eating salty, buttery popcorn and drinking cold, dripping beers—the viewers enthralled by their town's various fictions playing out on their screens to background karaoke performances that ranged from cringing to spine-tingling.

Allie climbed the stage and performed Tina Turner's "Private Dancer." The provocative lyrics and Allie's velvety voice and sensual movements brought the crowd to a near-silent standstill. At the song's end, the audience raised ear-splitting praise and appreciation. Allie stood smiling, luminous.

Ester pushed through the throng to the restrooms and locked herself inside the end stall. So much for swearing off Allie's effect on her. A woman entered and occupied another stall. A second woman arrived. Ester waited until both women exited the restroom before she emerged from the stall. She moved to the sink and checked her reflection while washing her hands. She reassured herself no one would know the erratic state of her insides by looking at her.

She was pulling a paper towel from the dispenser when Allie appeared in the doorway. Allie acted startled and seemed about to duck out.

"Wait, please," Ester said.

Allie stepped into the restroom, the door slapping closed behind her. Ester crossed the short distance between them and pressed her lips to Allie's. She walked Allie backward, pinning her to the restroom door and kissing her deeper. Desire surged from her toes and out the top of her head, like a firework. She slid her hand down Allie's neck and caressed her breast. Allie moaned into Ester's mouth. The door cracked open, pushing against Allie.

"What the fuck?" a woman said. She scowled at Allie and Ester before stumbling into a stall.

Panic swept through Ester. She spoke low, conscious of the other woman. "I'm sorry. I shouldn't have."

She hurried from the restroom and plowed back through the blockade of revelers. She pushed past her coworkers, her head down, and continued toward the exit. She thought maybe Maria called after her. Marjorie, the soul singer and new Sing, I member Allie was friendly with, appeared in the crowd, waving and grinning.

Ester glanced back in the doorway, catching Marjorie and Allie's tight hug. She burst into the night and its shock of silence, emptiness.

Serial Killer

Ester searched the house and the garage for the bottle of plant food. The task felt urgent—the money tree plant was dying and she didn't like things to get away from her. Not the plant or its elixir. She rifled through the kitchen drawers a second time, her right thumb throbbing. Earlier, she'd sunk her teeth into a slab-hard protein bar with such force she'd managed to bite her thumb to the point of bleeding.

She returned to the living room and texted Simon. He didn't reply for several long minutes. *Plant food? That's random. I have no idea.* She didn't know why she'd bothered. He and the boys never knew where anything was. She tossed the phone onto the couch. "Hardly random." He obviously hadn't noticed the neglected plant. If she didn't look after it, no one would. She followed the phone onto the couch and talked her temper down. What was she so worked up about? She could pick up more plant food the next time she was out. She returned to the dwindling plant and plucked its brown leaves, chiding herself over its decline.

She resisted the urge to saturate the plant's parched soil and consulted the internet for the best course of recovery. Site after site recommended icing versus watering indoor plants. The ice cubes' slow melt allowed the soil to absorb the water more thoroughly and avoided excess moisture pooling at the bottom of the pot, which rotted the roots. She returned to the kitchen, placed the dead leaves in the compost bin, and filled a glass full of ice cubes. Back in the living room, she placed the ice on the soil and packed it around the plant's braided trunk. "Come on, come back to us."

The piano tune from an old TV commercial for Miracle-Gro filled her head. The ad's depressed, befuddled character couldn't figure out how to save his houseplant, and at the end of the ad there was a caption next to the product's logo that read . . . *it's no secret*. She wasn't sure anything could revive this plant. That day at the garden center weeks back, Simon had said this would happen. No one in the family could claim green thumbs. But she'd read that plants make all sorts of positive differences to a home, and she insisted on acquiring one.

Lydia Greeslie recommended the money tree. "It's practically invincible."

Simon said to Ester, "Even you can't kill it."

The supposed joke catapulted her back to Mom, collapsed at the bottom of the garage stairs. Dad had insisted Mom died instantly and didn't suffer, but that night Ester overheard mourners speculating over how long Mom might have lain alone on the cold, hard concrete, calling for help while her brain bled out.

Ester had never admitted to anyone that she hadn't found Mom immediately after returning home from school. She entered the house that afternoon and dropped her backpack in the hallway, next to the mess of shoes surrounding the coatrack. She called out to Mom and didn't think much of the responding silence. She preheated the oven, removed the ham and pineapple pizza from the freezer, and placed it on the middle rack. Minutes later, tendrils rising from the splotches of burned cheese on the bottom of the oven set off the smoke alarm. She waved a tea towel under the alarm to stop its piercing wail.

She watched TV in the living room, scarfing down a cold can of cola and almost the entire pizza. She picked the cubes of pineapple from the last slice and pushed them into her mouth all at once. Tart-sweet juice spilled over her tongue, and her taste buds fizzed. A good hour passed while she remained oblivious to the horror that lay below her in the garage. Ever after, she would wonder how she hadn't sensed anything ominous. How she hadn't known Mom was in fatal peril.

She at last entered the garage to get the mail, hopeful of a letter from her school pen pal in Guadalajara. At the top of the stairs, she flipped on the light and spotted Mom on the ground. She rushed down the steps and dropped to her knees. Mom's face felt warm, and she looked like she was only in a deep sleep. Ester had never before checked someone's pulse or breathing. She couldn't tell if she was doing it wrong, or if there was in fact no life current. She also didn't know CPR but worked on Mom's chest anyway. What was that song you were supposed to pump your hands in time to? She couldn't remember. She kept working Mom's chest to the beat of *wake up wake up wake up.*

She abandoned her efforts, terrified she was wasting precious time, and raced back upstairs to call 911. Throughout, she felt like a spirit hovering above the house, watching everything play out far below her. She returned to Mom's side, crying and pleading, saying *no,* saying *please,* saying *Mom Mom Mom.* It wouldn't be until hours later, while Dad was on the phone to the funeral director, that she would start to wonder if Mom was still alive when she'd returned home from school and while she'd delayed upstairs, watching TV on loud while stuffing herself. Since then, even the sight of pineapple made her gag. She similarly avoided thoughts of her setting off the smoke alarm, and how its beseeching blast and her thudding footsteps might have been the last sounds Mom heard.

Aromas of roast chicken, sausage stuffing, and root vegetables wafted from the oven. Ester stood at the stovetop, stirring the gravy and trying to ignore the pulsing pain in her teeth-indented thumb. She was struggling to mash the potatoes with her left hand when Crystal texted. *told u!   new cashier starts tomorrow   hope she's faster learner than u BAHAHAHAHA*

Ester smiled to herself, glad that Crystal was over her huff. There was no possible realm where her going on a date with Rich was a good idea. Ester typed a rushed response *Whats she like?*

havent met her yet will let u know tomo

Ester replied with a thumbs up emoji and returned her phone to the counter. She transferred the mashed potatoes and other fixings into heated serving dishes and arranged the stuffing and carved chicken on a platter. She ferried the last of the steaming fare into the dining room, calling to Simon and the boys, "Come and get it."

The words turned midair and dived at her like wasps, shattering her homey delusion. No meal could make up for her betraying Simon and kissing, desiring, Allie. Its every morsel was coated in her guilt and shame, and she was feeding it to her family.

Kevin and Jason joined her at the table. While the three plated up, Simon delayed in the kitchen. Without fail, every time dinner was ready, he found something to futz with and always arrived at the table last. Whenever she mentioned his odd delay tactics, he denied the infuriating habit.

He appeared with a pint glass of water.

She nodded at the sweat-beaded glass jug on the table. "I already brought the water."

"Oh well. Won't go to waste."

She couldn't tell if he was being pleasant or patronizing. She piled a little of each dish onto her fork and moaned as the flavors hit.

"Mmm. Did you make this stuffing?" Simon said, his mouth full. He seemed to doubt she was capable.

"How was school?" she said, her jaw tight.

"It was school." Jason gave her that look, like he couldn't deal with how dumb she was.

"Are you sure you went?" Kevin said.

"Shut up, golden boy," Jason said.

"That's me," Kevin said.

"Asshole," Jason said.

"Hey, that's enough," Ester said.

"Can we be civilized, please? Your mother went to a lot of trouble," Simon said.

"How was your day?" Ester said into the intermission.

"Good," Simon said. "What about you? Did you find the plant food?"

She shook her head, annoyed that he'd reminded her.

"Plant food?" Kevin said.

"It doesn't matter," Ester said.

"Any update on that poor woman?" Simon said.

"Ms. Wolas. She's still critical," Ester said.

The four fell silent, apart from cutting and chewing and swallowing. Ester's appetite left her. She doubted other families found it this hard to talk to each other. Doubted they felt like they were playing roles and rehearsing words from a script.

She tried again. "So that's it? No one has any news from their day?"

"I fixed a major bug in a portfolio program for one of our biggest investment clients," Simon said.

"Nice," Kevin said.

"Nice," Jason said, mimicking his brother in a nasally voice.

"What has gotten into you?" Ester said.

"How's that girl? You still seeing her?" Simon said.

"Mena, yeah," Kevin said.

"That's it, Mena." Simon sounded pleased with himself. "What about you, champ? Any person of interest?"

Jason's face burned.

Kevin scoffed. "What girl would date him?"

"Don't be cruel, Kevin." Ester eyed Jason and spoke lightly. "Maybe he's not interested in girls."

Jason shot to his feet, his hateful look spooking her. "Maybe, like always, you don't know what you're talking about."

"Sit down, and do not raise your voice to me," Ester said.

"You heard your mother. Sit down, son," Simon said.

"I'm done."

"You'll sit back down until dinner is over and then you'll help your brother clear the table and stack the dishwasher. You two do nothing around here," Simon said.

Ester tried to not join in the ensuing uproar, but her frustration poured out. "It's true. You two never help out with chores, and I'm constantly picking up after both of you. I do everything around here on top of working full-time, and I'm sick of it. I'm not Wonder Woman, and I can't keep going like this. I'm beyond shattered."

Simon sat nodding solemnly. "You're not much help either," she said.

Jason moved to the door. "Get back here," Simon said.

"Let him go," Ester said.

"Why would you say that?" Simon said, as soon as Jason exited.

"What?" she said.

"About him not being into girls."

"Because maybe he's not."

Simon and Kevin exchanged a confused look. "Do you know something we don't?" Simon said.

"You can't presume everyone's straight." She carried her leftovers into the kitchen, fresh blood blooming on the Band-Aid on her bitten thumb.

Simon and Kevin cleaned up after dinner. Ester watched TV in the living room, remembering another commercial from her childhood, about cheese. The catchy jingle promised that the whipped spread added spectacular zest to food. Mom used to tease her about how much of it she consumed, saying that if she wasn't careful, she would turn orange. Ester never did explain to Mom or anyone else that she didn't particularly like the topping, with its nothing taste and elastic texture. No, she was after the ad's singsong guarantee that the cheese added personality to everything it touched.

Get Ready

The seagulls' screeching mirrored Ester's mood. They sounded like they were flying directly above the minivan, an unseen, hostile escort. If she wasn't one of the choir's designated carpool drivers, and if their first outreach performance wasn't in support of Kate's cancer treatment center, she would have made her excuses and stayed home rather than face into more mirrors of illness and death. In last night's dream, Death's mouth covered hers, inhaling her breath, emptying her lungs.

Even on waking, the dream chased her and herded her into Marcus's sparsely furnished apartment in Chicago, where, beyond his bedroom window, the sun was sinking to invisible. Below, the dark rush of vehicles and people traveling the maze of South Side streets were clueless to his life leaving him—his erratic breath as confused and terrified as waves abandoned by the moon's magnetic force.

The day Marcus died, Sylvie Lutz showed up at Ester's front door, her damp face a telegram of tragedy. While Sylvie broke the bombshell, Ester could see her reflection in her best friend's black-rimmed glasses. It was like watching herself in a horror movie on two tiny, smudged screens.

Sylvie had long since emigrated to Australia, moving first to Perth and later settling in Melbourne, her husband's hometown. Far enough away and long enough ago that she and Ester had lost contact. Ester silently wished her former best friend well. Unlike Ester, Sylvie had fulfilled the promises and prophecies of their youth and escaped Half Moon Bay—and America entirely.

Ester's attention landed on the self-inflicted bite on her thumb. Next to the fading wound, the skin on the back of her hand was awfully wrinkled. She checked her left hand, which was similarly crepey. She opened the center console and blindly searched for hand cream, finding none. She slammed the console's lid closed. At least she had outrun the seagulls.

She pulled up alongside Gwen Freeman's driveway. Bubbly Gwen and her seemingly endless assortment of fabulous footwear lived in a sunny yellow house fronted by mature trees and beds of colorful flowers. Ester texted to say she'd arrived, and waited, mentally rehearsing an upbeat greeting and face-splitting smile.

Gwen emerged from the fairy-tale house and strutted to the minivan with a fashion model's flair. In a lesser being, her navy sneakers would induce vertigo. With each step, the wedge heels lit up in a psychedelic green.

"What?" Gwen said saucily on opening the front passenger door.

"You're too much," Ester said, amused.

"We're bringing the light today, aren't we? That's the whole point, right?"

"That we are," Ester said, her mood lifting.

Ester picked up Crystal at her house. Crystal shrieked so hard on seeing Gwen's special effects shoes, Gwen insisted she try them on. Like a wondrous child, Crystal repeatedly stomped her feet on the back floor of the minivan, lighting up the shoes like blinking signs and sending the three women into fits of laughter.

"How's Lily settling in?" Ester asked when she'd recovered her breath. "She's my replacement at the store," she added, for Gwen's benefit.

"Good, I think. I only worked that first shift with her," Crystal said.

"The one where she kept chewing and popping gum," Ester said, smirking.

"Don't remind me. It was like she was slap boxing it."

"Is she from here?" Gwen asked.

"She moved here from Phoenix a couple of weeks back, inherited her aunt's house up on Elm Road," Crystal said.

"Nice," Gwen said.

"Not for her aunt," Ester said lightly.

"True," Gwen said. "Did we know her?"

"I didn't, anyway," Crystal said.

"Me neither," Ester said.

"Her name's escaping me. Suzanne something, I think. Sorry," Crystal said.

"No worries. I was just curious," Gwen said. "Your new coworker, Lily you said? She should join Sing, I."

Ester and Crystal found each other in the rearview. "Yeah, maybe," Crystal said.

"What?" Gwen said.

Ester and Crystal met again in the mirror. "I guess it's not a secret," Crystal said.

"What's not?" Gwen said.

"Lily's transgender," Crystal said.

"And?" Gwen said.

"I'm not sure everyone at choir would be cool with her joining us," Crystal said.

"So we exclude her because of a few bigots?" Gwen said.

"The school might also take issue," Crystal said.

"The school? You mean because of the restroom fracas? That whole thing's ridiculous," Gwen said.

"I agree," Ester said.

"You don't have to convince me. I'm just trying to protect Lily," Crystal said.

Ester remembered Crystal's eldest child identified as nonbinary. "At least ask her? Let her decide what she wants to do."

"Sure, I can ask," Crystal said.

"What else can we solve?" Gwen said jovially.

They arrived at Marjorie's pink apartment building located deep inside Montara. Ester had learned her full name from the carpool signup and didn't think *Marjorie Frank* suited the soul singer one iota, but who was she to judge anyone's name.

The chemical smell of Marjorie's hairspray was potent enough to be a fifth passenger in the van. Ester pointedly cracked the window open. Marjorie appeared heedless. She, Gwen, and Crystal struck up an animated conversation about the latest episode in the final season of *Game of Thrones*. Ester had never watched the epic TV show, despite its global, rabid following. By all accounts the series was brilliant—its own captivating world and compelling cast of characters, in particular its warrior women leaders. But Ester refused to engage with what some critics said was still ultimately the glorification of rape, violence, and patriarchy. Marjorie's big laugh cut the air, her glittered, attractive face thrown back. Ester adjusted the rearview, disappearing Marjorie.

She picked up Kate last. On this occasion, Kate would sing for her fellow chemo patients instead of undergoing treatment alongside them. "I had my dose of liquid assassin earlier in the week."

"How are you feeling?" Crystal said.

"I'm as good as it's going to get for right now," Kate said. Her fellow passengers murmured encouragement and support.

"What do we want to hear?" Ester said, reopening the middle console and flicking through the CDs, her gaze jumping between them and the road.

Marjorie raised her phone midair. "I've got a playlist to live for right here. Takes us all the way back to the Temptations and brings us right up to Bey. This is the real reason they say once you go Black, you can't go back."

Ester saw Marcus's smiling face.

"Bring it," Kate said, shimmying her shoulders. The Temptations' dulcet voices offered up "Get Ready." The five women sang along, making it sound less like a love song and more like a fight song.

During the opening notes to Beyoncé's duet with Ed Sheeran, and while the minivan passed the distant view of the Farallon Islands and their shark-infested waters, Marjorie said, "This is Allie's and my fav."

The blush surged from Ester's chest and into her face. The previous day marked one week since she'd kissed Allie in the Late Bar restroom. Her chest and stomach no longer squeezed at the recollection, but there was still a prickly heat to the memory and she was relieved that Allie was working today and wouldn't be at the chemo clinic. Her first time to see Allie after the kiss was the previous Monday, inside Blazers' coatroom.

She couldn't look at Allie straight. "Saturday night, that was a mistake, I'm sorry." She lifted her chin. "It wasn't professional, or right."

Allie's expression clouded. "If you feel I acted in any way inappropriately and want to file a report with HR—"

"Of course I'm not going to file a report. That was all on me."

"If you change your mind—"

"I won't." Ester pretended to search her purse. Allie exited. Ester pushed her face deep into her jacket hanging from a hook.

The medical center's staff and patients offered the choir a warm welcome. After a flurry of introductions, the singers lined up in their respective rows and Monica conducted them through Chloe x Halle's "Fall."

It was only while singing to these patients hooked up to toxic IVs for hours each week, sometimes each day, that Ester fully appreciated how hopeful and powerful the song's lyrics were. How beautifully the choir sang together. On the chorus, Marjorie's effortless, heartfelt solo was almost too stirring. At the song's end, the staff and patients clapped and cheered, as did the spectators crammed into the doorway and spilling over into the corridor.

During the choir's performance of an abbreviated version of Leonard Cohen's "Hallelujah," Ester was struck by how sick some patients looked, and how radiant others. She wondered who among them would survive and who would not. Something told her that the shiniest ones were those closest to death. She hoped she was wrong and that every patient present would recover. Hoped, like the lyrics from "Fall," that luck, faith, mercy—whatever it is that sustains us—was on their side.

The choir ended the brief recital with "Let It Be," their most practiced and polished song. Under Monica's expert direction, their voices climbed to the final chorus. Ester imagined their closing refrain wrapping around the patients like giant wings, a gossamer shield between this world and the next.

To Be Themselves

Simon phoned Ester midafternoon to say he'd been excused from jury duty.

"How'd you get out of it?" she said.

"The defense didn't seem to think I could be impartial in a drunk-driving manslaughter case when my mother died in a car crash."

"They brought that up in front of everyone?"

"Yep. They ask everyone lots of personal stuff."

"How are you feeling?"

"I wouldn't have minded serving, I think it'd be interesting."

"That's not what I asked."

"I found this great little restaurant across from the courthouse, had their cheese smashburger for lunch, it was incredible, you'd love it."

"O-kay. Are you on your way home?"

"I'm headed back to work. Thanks to the great state of California I'm now way behind on fixing that superbug I was telling you about."

"You're sure you're okay?"

"I'm fine."

"All right. I'll see you later."

"See ya." He ended the call.

A stone dropped through her. She was never sure if he was lying to himself or to her, or if he really operated from such a detached state.

After choir practice, Crystal invited Ester in for a nightcap. Ester would have preferred to continue home, but Crystal clearly needed the company. She stifled an exclamation on entering the messy kitchen, which was even more of a disaster zone than on her last visit after the photo lineup. The scatter of leftovers, clothes, grocery bags, dirty dishes, junk mail, and toys covered every possible surface and bordered on mayhem.

Crystal pulled a full bottle of brandy and two glasses from the cabinet and poured a jigger for Ester, and a double for herself. "Helps me sleep."

Of late, Ester found herself leaning more heavily on wine before bed for the same reason. Problem was, while the alcohol sent her off to sleep right away, she invariably woke up during the night, bleary and dehydrated, and then drifted in and out of an uneasy slumber until the alarm clock cut through the morning.

She again struggled with the brandy's potent fumes. They alone could alter brain chemistry. She'd presumed Crystal had served the alcohol neat previously because they were so shaken after the sheriff's office. "Do you always drink it without a mixer?"

"Why dilute a good thing?" Crystal held her half-drained glass midair. "To us."

"To us." Ester swallowed, and coughed. "We could graduate to fire-eating after this."

Crystal laughed to the point of tears. "Hey, did you ever do anything about that pushy cop?" she said, swiping at the corners of her eyes.

"I emailed and phoned the sheriff's office, but no one has gotten back to me. I'll give it another few days and if I still haven't heard anything, I was thinking I could contact the mayor's office. Although these days a tweet might be more effective. I'm not going to let it go, that's for sure. Obviously Halloran believed they had their man, but nothing justifies his breaking the law himself."

"They do it more than we'll ever know," Crystal said gravely.

"The good news is that the hospital discharged Ms. Wolas, the gunman's elderly victim—"

"I know who she is."

"Yeah, of course, sorry. They transferred her to a rehab facility. Hopefully she'll make a good enough recovery to allow her to return home."

"That's great. How'd you find that out? I didn't see anything online," Crystal said.

"Maria, one of the servers at Blazers, overheard some customers talking. I guess they're Ms. Wolas's neighbors and are in contact with her sister. Maria reckons it's one of the few perks to being overlooked, customers say all kinds of stuff in front of you. I swear in another life she'd make a great CIA agent." Ester dismissed thoughts of how intently Maria had watched her and Allie together, as if their chemistry was a colored vapor she could see. A sapphire blue or dahlia violet. Ester always felt like Bob was surveilling her and Allie too. Not that there was much to observe anymore. She and Allie mostly avoided each other.

Crystal's oldest child entered the kitchen and plucked a mandarin from the fruit bowl. Ester itched to discard the blackened banana crowning the hilly pile of citrus, its carcass baiting fruit flies. "Hi, Brittany."

"It's just Britt now," Crystal said.

"Hey, Britt," Ester said.

"Hey." Britt's large, tender eyes recalled a seal's. She—*they*, Ester corrected herself—had to be twelve or thirteen already. In Ester's head, they were still in third grade and singing "The Little Drummer Boy" a cappella in the school holiday recital, for which they received a standing ovation. That was in the before time, when Ester had yet to meet Crystal through the store and connect mother and child. When none of them had any idea of the trouble that lay ahead.

"You shouldn't be eating this late, sweet pea, and you should be in bed already. It's a school night," Crystal said.

Britt scowled. "I hate school."

"Yeah, well, you don't have a choice, so no point fighting it. And remember the best way to handle the haters is to—"

"Ignore them and carry on," Britt said dully, shuffling toward the door in their pink bunny slippers.

"Night, sweet pea," Crystal said, sad-smiling.

"Night, Britt," Ester said.

"Night." Britt disappeared up the hall and upstairs.

"Is she, sorry, are they all right?" Ester said.

"It's okay, I still slip up sometimes. None of that in our day, my parents would have slapped me silly." Crystal drained her glass.

"You mentioned haters?"

Crystal whacked the table with her palm, making Ester jump. She inspected the flat of her hand and rubbed it on her thigh. "Damn ants."

Ester scanned the table and beyond for the dead ant's army of comrades. There was never just one. She tightened her muscles, making herself smaller. As if that could protect her from ants crawling onto her chair, under her clothes, and over her skin.

"What was I saying? Oh yeah. Some kids at school have been giving Britt a hard time, sneering and taunting, calling them names. The school admin knows, and they've been dealing with it as best they can, but you know how it goes, that stuff never really gets fixed."

"That's terrible. I'm so sorry. You should keep pressure on the teachers and Principal Howe. That torment sticks, and those bullies need to be held accountable." Ester might not fully grasp the gender and sexually fluid revolutions, but people should be allowed to be themselves and no one, least of all a child, should be persecuted.

"Britt said your Jason has defended them more than once." Crystal made to pour Ester a second measure.

Ester held her hand over the mouth of her glass. "Jason?"

Crystal laughed. "You sound surprised?"

"Yeah, well, he's been a lot lately. Withdrawn, acting out, skipping school. I feel like I don't know him anymore, but I'm really glad to hear he's been kind to Britt."

Crystal poured herself a second generous measure. "I'm sure it's just teenage stuff, pushing boundaries and whatnot. He's got a good heart."

"I haven't seen much of it lately but nice to know it's still in there somewhere." Ester relaxed into her final sip of brandy.

Crystal held the bottle high. "You sure?"

"Yes, thanks. I need to get going." Ester's urgency jumped from escaping the ants to spending time with Jason. She couldn't let his growing isolation and the gaping distance between them continue.

"More for me." Crystal lowered the bottle to the table and curved her arm around it possessively.

"You okay?"

"Not really. I'm tired of all the bad news. In this town, this country, this world. I can't keep up with all the crazy and evil. It's choking me."

"I get that, completely, but there are brave, beautiful things happening all over too," Ester said.

"Hmmm. Are there?"

"Is there something else going on?"

Crystal's thumb and finger rubbed her eyes. "Rich hit me with this he's 'decided it's best to not mix business and pleasure' bullshit, making me dumped before we ever dated."

"Don't say dumped. Trash gets dumped, not people, not you."

"Ha! None of my exes got that memo."

"I'd put it on a billboard for you, if I could afford a billboard."

Crystal snort-laughed.

"What about Lily? How's Rich treating her?"

"Fine, as far as I can tell. She and I have been hanging out a bit at shift changes, and she hasn't said anything. I don't see her letting him get away with anything; she's pretty badass."

"We love to hear it. I'll stop by soon to say hi to her and the fish. How are they?"

"Alive."

"Well done."

"I swear Rich coming on to me was to keep me sweet when I was the only one working there; he was afraid I'd up and leave like you, but now he's back to treating me like dirt, and all for an hourly fifty-cent raise."

"Karma needs to hurry up and bite him in the ass, big-time," Ester said.

"Or I will."

Ester was still laughing when she said, "Did you mention the choir to Lily?"

"I forgot to, but I will."

"Great."

"She told me she had the transition surgery a few months back, in Thailand."

"That's commitment."

Crystal looked at Ester hard. "Right? I've been thinking maybe I should take more control of my life too? Move somewhere somewhat affordable, Vallejo, or Portland, and give the kids and me a whole new go at things."

Ester's stomach turned cold. "You can't. I'd miss you too much." It was true, and thoroughly selfish. She didn't think she could stand it if Crystal got to start over when she couldn't.

At home, Ester found Simon watching the sports channel alone in the living room, yet more NBA postgame analysis. He sat sprawled in his armchair, his profile betraying the double chin he'd developed, with that indentation in its belly, like a knife nick. "Where are the boys?"

"The Warriors won. They were down fifteen points after the first half and came back in the third, then down eight in the fourth, came back again, went up three with ninety seconds to go and Green took possession. Game over."

"Great. Meanwhile, what'd you do with our sons?"

His attention remained on the TV. "Kevin's out and Jason's upstairs."

"Kevin's with Mena, I presume? And of course Jason's upstairs. Did you check on him?" He didn't respond. "Did you check on Jason?" she said, louder.

"He's fine."

"So you didn't."

She climbed the stairs and knocked on Jason's door before opening it. The desktop's strobe lighting pitched his face in blues and reds and she pushed down a bad feeling. She also stemmed the lecture gathering in her throat and moved around his chair, to hitch her buttock to the edge of his desk. He tossed her a confused, furious look and returned to his game. She lifted the headset's cup from his ear. He jerked his head clear, his expression an assault weapon.

"Is there something we could play together? A video game we might both like?"

He pulled the ear cup back into place and resumed playing. She lifted the cup again, less gently. "I'm going to research some games, find one we can play together."

He righted the cup and returned to the explosion-riddled battle taking place in a desert dotted with tanks.

She kissed the top of his head. "Night, son." She raised her voice. "Ten more minutes, and then bed."

He dived to the right in his chair, his thumbs frantically working the controller. On the screen, fiery shells detonated, and soldiers' ripped body parts catapulted through the smoky air. She exited the room, disturbed but not deterred. He hadn't seemed to totally hate the idea of them gaming together.

An Artist of Ordinary Things

Ester was dressing for work when the doorbell rang. Moments later Kevin knocked on her bedroom door, his voice tinged with alarm. "Mom?"

"Yeah?" she said, pulling her hair free from the collar of her shirt.

He appeared in the doorway, looking bloodless. "The police are here. They want to talk to you."

"The police?" Her thoughts jumped to Jason, who'd supposedly gone to the shopping mall to buy sneakers. He'd been arrested or was in an accident. She was halfway down the stairs when she thought perhaps it was Simon. Maybe something had happened to him on the basketball court, a heart attack. Or on the drive home, a crash, like his mom. She'd asked for this. She'd brought this on.

She entered the living room, her chest tight. The two officers stood up from the couch. "Mrs. Prynn," they said in solemn unison.

"What is it? Tell me." Her panic was bordering on anger.

The short, lean officer flapped his hand at the couch. "May we?"

Ester nodded sharply. "Please, what's going on?"

The officers sat back down, the cushions buckling beneath them. "Ma'am, we're here about the officer misconduct complaint you wish to file."

"You scared me. I thought something had happened, an accident or—"

The slight officer said, "I'm Corporal Gonzalez, and this is Detective Spencer. We're here to take your statement."

Spencer, thickset and bullnecked, opened his notebook and aimed his pen.

"Thank you. I'm afraid I don't have much time, though. I'm due at work at noon," she said, still flustered.

"We'll get right to it. Shouldn't take long," Spencer said, already writing.

Ester relayed the details of the photo lineup and Sergeant Halloran's subtle but unmistakable coercion.

Gonzalez pressed her. "But how, exactly, did you feel manipulated?"

He and Spencer took turns with her. "I'm afraid we're not following."

"You think that's what he meant, but you can't know for sure, isn't that correct?"

"So he placed his hand on the photo sheet and you thought that meant he was leading you? Wasn't the interview over? Wasn't he simply picking up the photo pack?"

"Have you ever filed similar complaints? Any lawsuits? Harassment claims?"

"Ever lied under oath?"

"Any history of mental illness? Hypersensitivity?" They kept coming at her, still playing at courteous and concerned.

"That's not what I said. You're putting words in my mouth."

They went round and round 'til she was repeating herself. "Yes, he was leading me. I can be sure because it was obvious."

"I haven't done anything wrong. You're making out I'm—"

"Our job is to be impartial, and we're doing just that," Spencer said.

Ester continued as calmly and forcefully as she could. "Sergeant Halloran tried to influence me into making a wrongful ID, and I'm concerned he might be doing the same to other victims. If he is, it's possible people are being wrongly charged and imprisoned. Shouldn't that concern you too?"

Gonzalez and Spencer stood up in unison, their demeanor severe. "Thank you, Mrs. Prynn—"

"It's Ms.—"

"We've got everything we need and commend you on coming forward." Spencer's deadened spiel was a script, and they wanted her to know it.

She doubted she'd accomplished anything besides earning their scorn. "What happens next?"

Gonzalez offered his card. "The matter will be taken up by Internal Affairs, and they'll be in touch if they need anything further from you. I'm afraid that's all we can say for now. You'll be advised when the investigation has been completed."

"How long will that take?" she said.

"Rest assured it's a top priority," Spencer said with a thin smile. She wanted to rip off his overgrown mustache.

Ester parked outside Blazers and remained sitting in the car. Despite the heat, she turned off the AC with its rubbery smell. The sun-grilled landscape surrounding her was largely rural—brown hills, sprawling trees, colorful wildflowers, and long stretches of green. Yet straight ahead stood the huge brick-and-mortar hotel and restaurant, like something dropped from the sky. She wondered about the workers from way back who had built the property smack inside open terrain. Did they think of it only as construction, or did destruction ever cross their minds?

Her brother Rod was a contractor. Ever since he was a boy he was obsessed with building and had even erected his own town,

Rodsville. In his teens he graduated to taking things apart—tossed radios, TVs, engines, microwaves—and putting them back together. His greatest preoccupation proved to be fixing broken things. She wondered when that impulse had left him.

Tim's childhood obsession was bird-watching, and there was a long stretch when he wore binoculars around his neck non-stop. Thanks to the camera Ester's parents gave her for her twelfth birthday, her tween passion was photography. It was her way of collecting things and making them her own. She remembered looking through the camera at the rain shortly after Mom died and thinking the world was crying. Then she wasn't into photography so much.

She needed to exit the minivan and get to work, but it was taking a monumental effort. She was still on edge from the police officers' interrogation. It wasn't so much how intimidating and dismissive they were but that they didn't seem to care about right and wrong, justice and truth. They were never going to side with a civilian over a fellow cop. She felt powerless, and furious. How much more magnified must those feelings be for Black and Indigenous people, all people of color? Time sprinted toward the hour. She forced herself from the van. The slam of the van door startled crows from the power lines, their dark feathered bodies riddling the white sky.

Inside Blazers, Bob's grumpy puss deepened Ester's foul mood. She wanted, needed, to punch something. She tried to not think about what Allie was doing with her day off. Images rushed her, like swiping through videos on her phone—footage of Allie and Marjorie hanging out, and making out. She ached to tell Allie about the police officers in her home. About how it felt like worse things were coming for her.

She escorted her first party of the day to their table, a couple, she suspected, on a first date.

"Something smells good," the man said.

"That'll be our lunch special, a rosemary lamb burger with garlic Parmesan fries and butter-tossed mint peas. I highly recommend it," Ester said, offering menus.

The woman murmured appreciatively, "Sold."

"I'm certainly tempted," the man said.

Ester placed the wine menu on the table. The man, pinching his eyebrow, told his companion he painted everyday things that most people saw without seeing.

"Enjoy," Ester said.

"Like what?" the woman asked as Ester turned away.

"Windows mostly, the regular kind, and their coverings," he said.

"Coverings?" the woman said.

"Curtains and whatnot, whatever blinds them."

That stayed with Ester all night. *Whatever blinds them*. She wondered what she needed to pull back to be able to see clearly.

Line of Duty

Ester continued past Rich's truck and into the store, concerned for Crystal—it wasn't like her to not respond to texts or calls for more than a day. Ester found Lily and not Crystal behind the counter, with Rich nowhere in sight. Her attention jumped to the back corner and the Out of Order sign on the closed restroom door, scrawled in Rich's childish handwriting. She saw him as a boy, hunched over his school desk, his hand cramped around his pencil and his tongue peeking from the corner of his mouth, the child straining to get his letters right but unable to get past stunted and spidery.

Ester introduced herself, trying to be casual, but conscious of the clash of Lily's macho build and square face with her makeup, jewelry, long shaggy hair, and pastel floral blouse.

"So you're Ester Prynn," Lily said theatrically.

"Guilty as charged." Ester's smile dimmed. "I came by to check on Crystal."

"She's home sick, a migraine, Rich said."

"Good to know, thanks. I was worried. Well, I should get going before Rich sees me. You might have heard that he barred me, for life."

"I don't think we'll be seeing him for a while." Lily's long black fingernail pointed to the restroom. Ester pictured Rich standing over the blocked toilet bowl and plunging watery human waste from the repeat offender.

Lily nodded at the goldfish. "I understand we have you to thank for these two."

"Sort of, I guess. I gifted their predecessor, Torpedo, to Crystal and when he prematurely tanked it, excuse the pun, Rich replaced him with this pair. Wonder be."

"I wish they were the only little critters around here," Lily said with an exaggerated shudder.

The store bell tinkled above the double doors, heralding Charlie Neville's arrival, in for his daily supply of whiskey and sundries. Ester greeted him, but he issued only a passing grunt. She'd learned while working at the store that whenever Charlie was friendly, he was buzzed, and when surly, he was in withdrawal.

Lily stage-whispered. "When I opened up this morning, I discovered a huddle of mice in the middle aisle, right below the Triscuits. I jumped so high, I almost broke my stilettos when I landed, and shrieked at such a pitch I'm surprised every dog in the county didn't come running."

Ester was equal parts amused and appalled. She hated vermin. Even a squirrel was too much rat. Had the mice recently arrived, or were they here the whole time she'd worked at the store?

"I tracked their droppings to the storage room, they're getting in through the back wall. Rich better patch over that hole the second he's finished with that mutinous toilet or I'm walking, like you did," Lily finished approvingly.

"If he doesn't do it, call the Health Department," Ester said, breaking out in goose bumps. It didn't bear thinking about how many times she'd been inside the storage room, alone. Or so she'd thought.

Lily's hand swatted the air. "He'll do it. This last while I've been building quite the track record for getting my own way."

"You're giving me goals," Ester said cheerfully. Crystal hadn't exaggerated. Lily was a firecracker.

Charlie shuffled to the counter and paid for his whiskey and beef jerky. The man reeked of himself. Ester's hand twitched, wanting to cover her nose and mouth. Charlie pocketed his change and tucked the brown paper bag beneath his arm. He remained in place, glaring. "What are you?"

"Charlie, meet my replacement, Lily," Ester said evenly.

"Doesn't look like a Lily to me," he said, his vexation growing.

Lily leaned over her elbows on the counter, letting Charlie see down the front of her blouse, to the pink bra cupping her pale breasts. "Believe me, I'm *all* Lily."

Charlie emitted an outraged puff and scuttled from the store.

"I've never seen him move that fast," Ester said.

"I can have that effect," Lily said, her bravado flagging.

"Has Crystal told you about our local choir, Sing, I? It's a lot of fun, and sisterhood."

"Yeah, she mentioned it, but I dunno . . ."

"It's the best thing I've done for myself in an age."

"I did do some gigging to pay my way through college—at bars mostly and a few weddings and farmers' markets."

"Hey, that's great."

"That was a long time, and a different gender, ago."

"Did you like performing?"

"I loved it."

"Well then, there's your answer. That's why I joined, to get back to the things I loved."

"When you put it like that," Lily said.

"Great. The next meeting is tomorrow night. I can pick you up, if you like, right after I get Crystal. Hopefully she'll be feeling better by then."

"Sweet." Lily and Ester texted each other, trading contact information, and issued goodbyes.

Ester was almost out of the store, giving silent thanks that Rich hadn't appeared, when the gunman's sour smell overcame her. She thought she was experiencing a flashback, but the cut of the odor was too vivid. She turned around, seeing Lily dab her elbow with a cotton ball. "What is that?"

Lily froze, perplexed. "I've got psoriasis."

"What are you putting on it?"

"Diluted apple cider vinegar, it really helps."

Ester's pulse raced. That was the gunman's smell. She remembered Rachel talking about apple cider vinegar during their walk a while back. She should have made the connection then. Maybe the gunman had psoriasis or a similar telltale skin condition— another reason why he wears those animal masks. Maybe a local doctor or pharmacist could help identify him, or a supermarket or health store clerk.

"Thanks, Lily. See you tomorrow night for choir," she said, hurrying out.

Ester drove straight to the San Mateo Sheriff's Office, dismissing fearful thoughts of having to face Sergeant Halloran. By the time she entered the station and approached the wiry desk officer, she was almost as keyed up as in the aftermath of the holdup. When she spoke, the rush of adrenaline was also in her voice.

"Can I say what it's about?" Officer Doran said.

"The recent string of local armed robberies."

"Take a seat, please."

Ester waited alone on the bench. She needed to use the restroom but decided it was best to remain in place and wait for Halloran. She was also thirsty but didn't see a water fountain or cooler. Probably also best to not add to her full bladder. Her heart, it was manic.

The minutes stretched, punctuated by officers and civilians coming in and out of the station. An old man showed up at the desk. His dog had bitten a neighbor and was slated to be euthanized.

He pleaded with Officer Doran to stop Animal Control from killing the terrier. Doran offered frail, shrunken Fred herbal tea and words of comfort, but the man was inconsolable. Doran walked out from behind the counter, the lights catching the glints of chestnut in his hair, and wrapped his arm around Fred's slack shoulders. "I can tell that deep down you know what needs to be done."

Ester was so moved by the scene she didn't notice Corporal Gonzalez's approach. "Mrs. Prynn, we meet again."

She rushed to standing, her hand automatically reaching out. Gonzalez ignored it. "How can I help?"

"I'm waiting to speak to Detective Halloran. I have new information on the armed robber."

"You can't enter into any communications with Detective Halloran. You're the claimant against him in an ongoing Internal Affairs investigation. I thought we made that clear."

"Then should I speak with you? I have important information."

"You've got two minutes."

She followed him down the corridor and into the same room with scuffed, cracked walls where she and Halloran had sat together.

"Let's hear it then," Gonzalez said.

Her theory tumbled from her.

"If anything else comes up, do let us know," he said, unimpressed.

She followed him to standing. The frantic feeling had cooled, leaving her legs weak and her head swimming. She'd thought the apple cider vinegar detail was a breakthrough. That it could lead to an arrest. She'd wanted, needed, to set something right in the world.

Her distress must have shown because a glimmer of empathy entered Gonzalez's eyes. "We'll run with it, see what we can uncover."

She thanked him and had almost reached the door when he spoke again. "The majority of uniforms do our damnedest every day in the line of duty, and every one of us puts our life in jeopardy the moment we don our badge, all with the ideal to protect and serve."

She felt mute and immobile with fear, and when she was able to respond it was halting, trembling. "That's not the whole truth though, is it? And if the rot's not faced, then nothing's ever going to be fixed—"

He reached behind her and pulled the door open, his eyes deadened. "I'll let you see yourself out, Mrs. Prynn."

"It's *Ms.* Prynn. I'm Ms. Ester Prynn." She exited, shaken, but with a spine of red oak.

The Burn

Not even the sight of San Francisco's iconic skyline beyond the sparkling bay could shift the sensation of grit in Ester's throat. The gall of that Detective Von from Internal Affairs, phoning her at home earlier and instructing her to provide him with a second statement regarding Halloran. "Slowly. Carefully."

When she finished he said, "I'm not seeing the problem."

"I don't know how I can be any clearer."

"All I'm hearing is that the interview ended and Sergeant Halloran picked up the photo pack."

"That's not what happened," she said.

"So you want to proceed with this complaint?"

"I want to do what's right."

"It was a yes or no question," he said.

"It didn't sound like a question."

"I don't have all day, ma'am."

"Yes, I want to keep going with this."

"So be it." He hung up, leaving her with a taste in her mouth like soil.

She took the Fourth Street exit to downtown San Francisco and followed her phone's directions to the game store. At least this errand, part of Operation Get My Second Son Back, promised to be a small, good thing. She pictured herself and Jason sitting side by side in his bedroom in front of his desktop, both of them wearing headsets and madly working controllers, competing and playing together.

It struck her again how unrecognizable Jason was from his former self. While his mop of reddish hair and those washed-out eyes in a pale freckled face remained much the same, he was staggeringly thinner, *lesser*. An almost overnight reduction that had occurred a few months back and that she'd worried was because of drugs. She'd watched and quizzed him until she was sure mind-altering substances weren't the problem. He insisted that nothing was eating away at him, and that nothing, dire or otherwise, had happened to him—no abuse, bullying, or friend or romance trouble. His teachers corroborated this information, to the best of their knowledge. His doctor believed puberty and social anxiety were the likeliest culprits.

More than Jason's weight loss and vacant, malnourished air, it was the shift in his personality that most alarmed her. The terms "moody" and "insolent" were too tame for him. Beyond his acting out, and those two awful scuffles in his bedroom over his game accessories, what most devastated her was how hard she kept trying to be patient and understanding, forgiving and loving, and how he refused to give her so much as a smidge back.

During Jason's most recent appointment, Dr. Grahame had urged him to exercise, practice self-care and mindfulness, and limit screen time to two hours a day. He also prescribed an antidepressant, which Ester felt conflicted about. The child was only thirteen. It was a moot point anyway, for now. Jason refused to take the medication or to follow any of the doctor's guidelines, no matter how much she and Simon coaxed or goaded. "There's nothing wrong with me!"

She returned to Jason at age five at the San Francisco Zoo, the boy waving at the lone orangutan in his glass enclosure and shriek-laughing when the similarly reddish-haired primate waved back. Inside the zoo's farm, Jason refused to feed the goats with the pellets clutched in his tiny fists, preferring the bleating animals to chase him and the food round and round, and sending Ester and onlookers into fits of laughter.

He also dropped his ice cream cone to the ground to allow the flock of salmon-colored flamingos to feast on it. Next, he dangled upside down on the monkey bars in the playground, demanding to know *Is my face purple yet?* She'd needed to convince him that his face had turned the purplest-purple before he would drop from the bar and take hold of her hand.

On the drive home, he said he wanted to be frozen inside an iceberg so he could stay this happy forever. In the rearview, sunlight caressed his little face, strengthening the yellow in his eyes—that gold-brown of leaves in the fall. Where had that boy gone, and how to get him back? He and Ester gaming together seemed like a good place to start. Her left eyeball twitched, as if laughing at her.

Jason arrived home from school. Ester called him into the kitchen.

"What?" he said, trudging in.

"I went into the city this afternoon and got us this."

"What is it?" he said, unwrapping the folded shopping bag.

"*Labyrinth of Doom*. It came highly recommended." She knew not to admit that she'd tried to buy a game free of explicit and violent content, which it seemed was impossible.

"No thanks." He placed the game on the counter and loped away, his school backpack dragging down his shoulder.

She followed him, the game and new set of accessories she'd bought for herself in hand, and continued her good-humored banter as they climbed the stairs. "I think someone's afraid I'll beat them."

He closed his bedroom door as she reached the landing. She opened it and marched in, still angling for lighthearted. "I'm so going to win."

"I'm so not doing this."

She dragged the second chair from the corner, reserved for whenever a friend came over—which hadn't happened anytime recently—and positioned herself next to him at the desk. She placed her headset around her neck and studied the controller, drawing further cranky looks from her second son.

"You're wasting your time," he said.

She unwrapped the plastic membrane from the game and cracked its case open. "Either you set this up or I will, and we know how badly that could go."

He tugged the disc from her and pushed it into the drive with a huffing sigh. While he typed with frightening speed, she narrated how the sales clerk had raved about the game's tunnels, dungeons, armies, magic, cryptic puzzles, powerful helpers, and formidable enemies. Jason's keen focus encouraged her, his fingers flying through the keystrokes and his eyes darting about the screen.

He threw himself back on his chair, his hands landing on his sprawled lap. "This isn't a multiplayer game."

"What? That can't be right." Her eyes roved the game's home page, seeing little beyond stone graphics and menacing avatars.

"You think I wouldn't know?" he said.

Her disappointment tasted metallic. Jason had seemed to be giving in and she was excited for them to play together. "Dammit. I specifically said I wanted a game for two-plus players. I'll return it and get us something else."

"Too late now." He hunched forward, completing the game set up.

"That game wasn't cheap and isn't what I asked for, which is their mistake, not mine."

His attention was soldered to the screen. "It's already opened and used. They won't take it back."

"Take that disc out now. The game was supposed to be something we could enjoy together."

"I told you I'm not gaming with my mom. That's not a thing."
He selected the advanced game level.

"I miss you."

Something about how she said it made him look at her, his expression shifting from annoyance to someplace softer. But then he was back to the game. She sat working up to more words with the same tone and honesty that had reached him.

Screeching tore the air.

"Shit." She lunged from the chair and rushed downstairs.

She hurried across the kitchen and removed the pot of Bolognese sauce from the stovetop. Then waved a tea towel beneath the smoke alarm in the hallway, her mouth filling with the tang of those pineapple chunks from the day Mom died. She returned to the kitchen and checked the meaty mixture, finding its bottom cremated and the entire dish unsalvageable. All that work for nothing. It summed up her entire day, starting with Detective Von from Internal Affairs. She could cry. Wail. Throw herself down on the floor. She removed her silicone oven gloves and fired them at the wall, sounding two *thunks*.

Simon arrived home and sniffed the air from the entryway. "What's burning?"

The man set her teeth on edge. She reached again for the pot, to toss the ruined food, and screamed on touching its steel handles.

Simon hurried across the kitchen. "What did you do?"

She ripped her hands from the metal, skinning herself and crying out, and dived at the sink as Simon turned on the tap. She placed her flayed palms and fingers below the cold running water, the burns already blistering, stinging.

Simon remained next to her, ordering her to keep her hands under the water. She obeyed, hissing and performing a pain dance in place.

"Can you get me the first aid kit?" she said, her voice also sounding injured.

He opened the far cabinet.

She worked her jaw loose. "Not there. It's in the cabinet to the right of the stove, on the middle shelf, toward the back."

"Found it!" he said, victorious.

When he presented the kit, she couldn't bring herself to pull her hands from the mercy of the falling water. It wasn't only giving up the relief from the cold tap and the return of the worst of the pain that she couldn't bear, but also what she knew would be Simon's clumsy efforts to tend to her.

It

Crystal thumped down onto the front passenger seat, wafting brandy fumes.

"You all right?" Ester said.

Crystal smiled too hard. "I'm fine." She spotted Ester's gauze-wrapped hands. "Yikes. What happened?"

"I burnt them cooking dinner last night. It's the worst kind of pain." As soon as Ester said that, she knew it wasn't true.

"Are you okay to drive?" Crystal said.

"Yeah. I slathered them in this supposedly miracle cream that numbs, sterilizes, *and* heals faster."

"I need to get me some of that," Crystal said, her voice thick.

"Are you sure you're all right?"

"Totally."

Ester reversed out of Crystal's driveway, lyrics coming from the radio about blue-black hair and gold dust eyes.

"Before we get to Lily's, she was saying to me earlier about us being a women's choir, that it's problematic," Crystal said.

"I don't understand? She is a woman," Ester said.

"Yeah, but saying we're a women's choir doesn't make it clear that all genders are welcome, except cis men," Crystal said.

"Cis?" Ester said.

"It's short for cisgender, as in someone who identish . . . identifies with the gender they were asshined at birth."

"There's so much to consider nowadays," Ester said, unnerved by Crystal's slurring.

"Lily and I are going to bring it up at tonight's meeting."

Ester picked her words carefully. "Is that what the brandy's about, Dutch courage?"

"What? No. I had a little one after dinner. It helps with the headaches, until it doesn't."

"Have you talked to a doctor?" Ester said. "You need to get those headaches checked out."

"I'll feel a hell of a lot better when the gunman's caught."

"He will be."

"So you keep saying."

"I want it as much as you do."

"Lily said that before dangerous criminals become offenders, they're almost always victims of violence themselves."

"Makes horrible sense," Ester said.

"If we treated people better from the beginning, gave everyone a fair chance from the get-go, the world would be so much better."

"I agree. It's the same with how we're boxed in from our beginnings and told how to be, women especially. We should be allowed to be whoever we want, as long as we're kind." Ester had started thinking lately that so much of who she was came from who she was expected, instructed, to be—by her parents, schools, society, culture, government. What if she was more of a construction than someone real?

They reached Lily's house, which looked more like a dereliction than a windfall, not that Ester would be complaining if she'd inherited the property from an aunt mortgage-free. Lily was waiting out front, dressed in ruffles and all-black, her hair and smile also big.

"Don't judge my jungle of a garden, or my falling-down house," she said on sliding open the minivan's side door. "I'll work my powers over time."

"You should see my place," Crystal said.

"My mom used to say places can hear us talking about them," Ester said.

"I totally believe that," Lily said, buckling her seat belt. "Our bodies are constantly listening to us too. What isn't?"

"Are you saying I might hurt my rented houshes feelings?" Crystal said. Ester caught Lily's frown in the rearview.

"I'm saying be nicer to it, and yourself," Ester said.

"I feel another headache coming on," Crystal said, sarcastic.

"What happened to your hands?" Lily said.

"My stupidity, that's what," Ester said.

"What did we just say about everything listening?" Lily said, to mirth. She crossed her legs and cupped the peak of her black-nyloned, polka-dot knees, her vivacious energy rolling through the vehicle like a wave. "Let's roll, loves."

Ester entered the high school gym, followed by Crystal and Lily. She located Allie standing with Marjorie and several others and pushed herself straight over. She arrived, clinging to her composure, and introduced Lily. A flurry of greetings followed, as did concern and sympathy for Ester's bandaged hands. She tried making soft eye contact with Allie, hoping to convey a fresh truce, but Allie wouldn't meet her gaze. Around them, several singers sized up Lily's height and angular frame, her large hands and masculine edges. Ester couldn't imagine what it was like to have people inspect and gape at you. If Lily noticed the gawkers, she didn't let on.

Ester fetched Crystal a coffee to sober her up, and then introduced Lily to Monica. "Welcome," Monica said, offering Lily a clipboard with the registration paperwork.

"I hope my baritone won't throw things off," Lily said.

"I can't wait to hear it," Monica said.

"I love your skirt's piebald pony print by the way. Swoon," Lily said.

"Thank you, and you're giving me ruffles envy," Monica said.

"That's an easy fix," Lily said.

"It is," Monica said, amused.

"Speaking of fixes, I had a thought, if you don't mind feedback out the gate from a new member?"

"Of course not."

"I wonder if we can't do better than the limited label 'women's choir'?"

Monica nervous-laughed. "Okay. All right. I admit I haven't given that as much thought as I probably should have. That'll be tonight's first order of business."

"Great, thank you," Lily said, her smile worthy of a dentist's commercial.

Monica called the meeting to order. Ester noted that Crystal had drunk most of the coffee, and the color was coming back into her face. Once everyone was seated, Monica said, "Please join me in giving a warm welcome to our newest member, Lily." Applause and shout-outs followed. "I want to thank Lily for bringing up an important point tonight, and that's our narrow label of a 'women's choir,' which I gave us from the outset. Going forward, we are simply and inclusively the Sing, I choir."

"What does that mean?" Lydia Greeslie said.

"I love that this is a women's choir," someone else said.

"Me too."

Lily raised her hand. "May I suggest Sing, I, a women's and gender-diverse choir."

"A what now?" someone said to laughter.

"Gender diversity," Monica said, reading from her phone. "An umbrella term used to describe identities beyond the gender binary framework."

"We're supposed to be a sisterhood, how's that going to work if we're no longer a women's choir?"

"We're a women's plus choir, that's an expansion of community," Monica said.

"Political correctness is out of control."

Mutters of agreement sounded. "It'll get to the point where we can't say or do anything."

"It's not hard to say and do no harm," Allie said.

The discussion turned loud and heated.

Monica tapped the microphone with the flat of her hand. "Calm down, people. We're trying to figure out how to make our choir as welcoming and inclusive as possible, that's it, that's all. So let's keep this kind and civil, please and thank you."

Lily stood up. "May I?"

Monica nodded.

"The other morning on Moss Beach I saw this little kid running along the shoreline after their grownups. They kept calling out, 'Wait for me.' For most of my life that was me too—calling out to the people I cared about to wait for me, the real me. And whenever I would finally arrive, I longed for them to still be there, accepting me, welcoming me. After I transitioned, some of them were, more of them weren't. And while I may no longer feel like a misfit, I've continued to be treated like one by many, and I'm far from alone in that. It's not only trans people either. There's a ton of us who need to belong and feel safe. This choir could be that necessary, special space."

Lily sat down, visibly quivering. Ester pressed her hand to Lily's back, despite how it smarted her burns. "Well done."

Crystal stood up and managed a few fragmented sentences, her voice mumbly from the alcohol and raw emotion. "I'm trying to say that . . ."

"You've got this," Ester said quietly.

"My oldest child doesn't identify as a girl or a boy. Britt is non-binary and identifies as *they*. I want Britt to grow up in a world that's good and fair and open to them. That's the least they, every-one, deserves." She sank to sitting.

Applause sounded. Lily wrapped her arm around Crystal, and Ester reached across and squeezed Crystal's hand, her burns pro-testing anew.

"Thank you, Lily, Crystal, that was powerful," Monica said.

Lydia took to her feet. "I joined a women's choir, as in the gen-der God gave me, and if it's staying," her arm shot out, pointing at Lily, "then I'm going."

"Oh you're going," Monica said into the microphone. "You're totally out of order." Murmurs of solidarity rippled through the group.

Lydia issued an outraged gasp and descended the tiered rows of bleachers, then tramped across the gym floor to the exit. To Ester's surprise, Gina Simmons, a tattoo artist who owned her own parlor and bore inked sleeves of sunflowers on her arms, seemed like she was readying to leave.

"Can I see a show of hands for Sing, I, a women's and gender-diverse choir?" Monica said. She scanned the rows of raised arms, which included two white-haired seniors. "That's a majority vote, thank you."

Uneven applause followed. Gina hadn't raised her inked arm during the vote and wasn't clapping. Who could figure people out? Ester had presumed Gina would allow others the same rights to self-expression she herself enjoyed. Lily and Crystal sat with their four clasped hands stacked on Crystal's knees, their eyes damp and their expressions shiny.

There Will Be an Answer

Ester chauffeured Crystal, Lily, Allie, and Marjorie to Golden Leaves for the second of the choir's outreach performances. She'd picked up Allie and Marjorie last, from Marjorie's pink apartment building. It was hard to see them standing out front together, showing too many teeth.

This second recital was causing Ester almost as much apprehension as the choir's performance at Kate's cancer treatment center. Most of the spectators this afternoon were too empty to reach, especially Dad, and all were held captive inside Golden Leaves for their own safety, until their last breath. She didn't know how the staff showed up day after day, year after year. She supposed they'd mastered the dubious art of turning numb. For her, the erasure and wasting away got harder to witness with every visit. She would never grow immune.

At least before she left home she and Jason had enjoyed their first civil exchange in a while. "Hey, how's that new game working out?" she said.

"Good," he said. "Thanks," he added. The single word of gratitude reluctant, but he'd said it.

She knew to tread carefully. "Is it difficult to play?"

"Would I be enjoying it otherwise?" he said with just a pinch of snarl.

"What's the objective?"

"The same as it always is. Staying alive and getting the holy grail," he said.

"What's the grail in this game?"

"You don't know until you find it," he said, edging exasperation.

"Huh. Wouldn't you be more motivated if you knew what it was?" She was risking his scorn, and his clearing off, but she was intrigued.

"It's not really about the grail. It's about finding it against all odds, so you can save the day."

"Like going to meet the Wizard of Oz," she said, thinking of the curtain being pulled back.

"You can't compare *Labyrinth of Doom* to a stupid kid's movie," he said, striding from the kitchen.

She loved *The Wizard of Oz* and loved its spinoff maybe even more. *Wicked* managed to uncover additional mind, heart, and courage beyond the original story, and from the unlikeliest and arguably the most interesting of its characters, the Wicked Witch of the West.

"It's so hazy," Lily said, pulling Ester back into the minivan.

"It's from the wildfires up north," Ester said, eyeing the sky like smudged charcoal. "I couldn't believe the amount of ashes on my windshield this morning."

"The world's burning," Crystal said, staring out the front window.

Lily burst into song, startling and then delighting her fellow passengers with a bawdy rendition of June Carter and Johnny Cash's entire duet "Jackson." The way she growled Cash's lyrics, and nailed the falsetto on Carter's, stiffened the hairs on the back of Ester's neck.

"Hot damn," Marjorie said when Lily finished, followed by whooping and cheering from Ester, Crystal, and Allie.

No matter how many times Ester's gaze flicked to the rearview, Allie wouldn't meet her in the mirror.

The choir gathered inside the Golden Leaves parking lot as instructed and entered the nursing home together, Monica in the lead and Ester trailing the group, silently summoning enthusiasm. *If we only help one.*

Inside the main dayroom, the smell of cut grass carried through the open windows, greening its stale air and camouflaging its occupants' musty decay. Ester worried about letting in the poor-quality air, then noticed the four large humidifiers dotted about the space. The choir formed three rows in front of the residents parked around the room in the shape of a huge horseshoe. Ester steeled herself against the wall of shrunken, blank faces, including Dad's.

He was stationed in his wheelchair next to the door, making for an easy exit if he acted up. Despite a steady dose of antipsychotic medication, he was prone to fits of anxiety and could cause quite the scene, thrashing and roaring, and beating off Ester and the staff. During his most recent outburst, he'd reached an especially frenzied, traumatized state and needed to be forcibly shut down with a shot of sedative, like powering him off.

The choir started their performance with their most practiced song, "Let It Be." Dad sat slumped to his right, his head hanging over his collapsed shoulder and saliva leaking from the side of his mouth. At times like this the staff reassured Ester that Dad was comfortable, and it was merely hard for her to watch, but he never looked at ease to her. She sang straight to him, her voice wavering on the lyrics that promised an answer. Dad's only possible answer at this stage was the mercy of a peaceful death. She flinched, feeling Allie touch her fingertips. Their height and vocal types had paired them side by side for the song's performance. Ester opened her hand to Allie's, and they laced fingers. Her skin was still tender from the burns, but the discomfort was nothing next to the balm of holding onto Allie and Allie holding onto her.

The song climbed. Ester willed one of the caregivers to help Dad sit straight and dry his drool. His head twitched, managing to look full forward for a second before it lolled back down. Ester hoped he might have been seeking out her familiar voice, or at least that he was responding to the song.

The choir ended their recital with "Fall." Throughout, Ester hoped Allie would take her hand again. She did not.

As instructed, the choir remained in place at the performance's end. The lights in the dayroom dimmed. Chef Stone appeared in the doorway, pushing a food cart bearing an enormous, white-frosted cake dotted with colorful confetti and a crowd of candles, their flames flickering, struggling. She parked the cart next to Joseph, a former editor of the *Half Moon Bay Record*. He sat gummy and beaming. *Another birthday coming at me*, Ester thought. They were celebrated almost every day at Blazers too. It was as if life were rattling her cage, saying, "What are you waiting for?"

The choir, staff, and several residents sang "Happy Birthday." Throughout, Joseph grinned wide, and his eyes were two bright pebbles. While he attempted to blow out his grove of candles, a chorus of voices encouraged him to make a wish. He closed his eyes and mumbled under his breath. Onlookers clapped and cheered. Chef Stone leaned forward, helping him extinguish the remaining clusters of tiny fires.

Choir members milled about the dayroom among the staff and residents, drinking tea, eating cake, and socializing as best they could. Ester carefully spooned small amounts of mashed cake between Dad's thin, wet lips. Allie and Marjorie stood at the far window, looking out and seeming conjoined.

"Is that nice?" Ester said.

Dad worked the tiny lump of vanilla sponge cake around his mouth. She kept feeding him, kept asking him, and right as she offered him the second-to-last spoonful, she thought he might have nodded.

Glass Instrument

Outside Blazers, the wind rustled the tops of the trees, lending them the gift of motion. Ester ached to be similarly energized. She glanced at the dashboard clock. Twelve minutes until she needed to take her place at the podium and host the night's onslaught of diners. She scanned her surroundings, considering a quick, sneaky power nap, and slipped the dusty Beethoven CD into the player. She reclined her seat, closed her eyes, and counted her breaths. The avalanche of thoughts wouldn't stop.

Where would she go, if she could start over? She had German blood on Mom's side, English on Dad's. Berlin was supposed to be a wonderful city, its art and architecture, its efficiency and cleanliness, its kind, cultured people. She hadn't a word of German, but she could learn. England also pulled. If not an idyllic village like Devon, then maybe Bristol, or Liverpool, the home of the Beatles. *Why was she tormenting herself?* She was broke and tied to Simon and the boys. She wasn't traveling anywhere.

One of those ashrams in India, that's where she could go for an extended stay if she weren't confined by a lack of money and her many commitments—to pray and fast, and sweat out her confusion and angst. In truth, she would much prefer Italy, and sweating out pasta, cheese, and red wine. She had never visited Europe. Never ventured outside America. That dismal travel record needed to change. In Italy, Florence to be exact, she would seek out the small, overlooked churches, and not the vast, famous cathedrals heaving with tourists. She would sit in a pew beneath the colorful stained glass windows, barrels of sunlight pouring through and warming her bowed head and shoulders. She would pray for her living and her ghosts. For forgiveness.

Ester jerked awake. Her eyes cut to the van's clock. 5:10. *Shit.* She scrambled out of the vehicle and dashed across the parking lot. She pushed through Blazers' doors, hurried past the waiting customers, and arrived at the podium. "I'm so sorry."

Bob signed out of the reservation system like he was trying to poke out someone's eyes, likely hers.

"Excuse me, can you check how much longer our table's going to be? I don't understand the delay, the restaurant's empty?" The uptight woman held out her lifeless pager, which Ester dutifully accepted while silently cursing Bob as he strode off. He should have started seating guests already, and not waited for her to show up. What if she'd arrived later than she had or was a no show? Was he going to let diners pile up in the waiting area?

"Wait, is that you, Ester Prynn?" The woman read Ester's confusion. "Dani Kennedy, we worked at LDG together."

"Dani, of course! Hi, how are you?"

"I'm well, thanks. Still at LDG. I'm a partner now."

Ester's smile faltered. She had been a part-time admin assistant at the financial firm until Jason arrived, and thereafter it didn't make parental or financial sense for her to return to work. "Amazing."

"I didn't know you worked here."

"I'm not here all that long."

"Oh, what did you do before this?"

"This and that."

"Easier, I guess, than working downtown, the commute and all," Dani said, like she was offering Ester something.

"Yeah, you know, with the boys, it's nice to be close to home."

"How old are they now?"

"Thirteen and seventeen."

"I thought they had to be about that. You made them sound younger."

"Always our babies, right?"

Dani laughed. "My fourteen-year-old daughter, who refused to join us today, would heartily disagree."

"First time here?"

"No, we've been several times." Dani flapped her wrist, indicating the party of five standing by the door. "This is a good central point for my parents, sister, and me to meet up. We typically walk the beach followed by dinner." She dropped her voice. "I probably shouldn't say this, but I way prefer Capitanis." She hooked her thumb toward her family. "That lot, they're cheapskates."

Next to Dani's family, a boy about seven was sitting on the ground, a glass of water between his open thighs. He licked his index finger and dragged it over the rim of the glass, sending up a haunting hum.

"This is nice, we'll get to see each other again." Dani smiled thinly. "Although the way my mother tells it, our family never gets together."

"Let me just check . . ." Ester scrolled the database and returned the pager to Dani. "I'll get you seated in just a few minutes, in one of the back booths, best seats in the house."

"Excellent, thank you."

"It was nice to see you again." Ester heard her own insincerity.

"So nice to see you too, Ester." Dani leaned closer, her expression serving up pity. "Good luck with everything."

Behind her, the hum of the boy's glass built to a screech.

It bothered Ester that she couldn't remember how *The Catcher in the Rye* ended. She'd read the novel in high school, and again in college, and was gripped by Holden Caulfield's strangeness, so she should recall how everything wrapped up. Did the reader know from the start, or not until the end, that Holden is telling his story from inside a mental hospital? He was confined to a mental institution, right? Or was it jail? She couldn't recollect, and it was sending her into a weird freefall. Sure, it was over two decades since she'd last read the novel, but most everyone knew the coming-of-age story well, and yet here she was, drawing blanks. She needed to start doing focus and memory exercises and whatever else would help keep her mind sharp.

She recalled those wildly popular spit parties from a few years back. Groups would gather to drink, socialize, and send off their saliva for genetic testing, to learn their legacy of disease. She preferred not to know that Alzheimer's, a massive stroke, or whatever else was coming for her. Whatever surprise ending was her fate, she hoped for something sudden and swift. Who didn't? It was perhaps the one upside to dying young like Mom—getting to skip out on dementia and other slow, robbing diseases.

Fancy her meeting Dani Kennedy at Blazers, her former coworker now a high-powered executive. Dani was the type of woman to host a spit party. To demand to know what lay in store for her. Ester burned with mortification, recalling how Dani had felt bad for her in her hostess job and little life.

Ester wouldn't be thinking of troubled, institutionalized Holden Caulfield if it weren't for Jason. That new game she'd bought him, *Maze of* whatever, had only served to steal more of him. Beyond the mandatory reprieve of school, his bedroom was his self-imposed prison, no matter how much she and Simon tried to lure him out.

"Let's shoot some hoops."

"Let's go grab In-N-Out."

"Let's catch a movie."

"Let's try boogie boarding."

"We really think you should see someone. It's not a punishment. We're trying to help you."

Jason's response, like a final, woeful plea, never varied. "Leave me alone."

Kevin also participated in team family intervention, but Jason wouldn't let his big brother as much as finish his sentences.

"Mena and I—" *Go away.*

"Do you want to come to—" *Get out.*

"I'm headed into the city—" *Shut it.*

"You're a little dick—" *You think? You're a way littler dick.*

This from the boy who, when he was a toddler, and wasn't attached to Ester's hip, would continually run to her like an excited puppy, wanting her to scoop him into her arms and swing him round, their laughter gurgling to the ceilings and splashing the walls.

"You all right?" Crystal said from the front passenger seat.

"Yeah, sorry. Just stuff with Jason."

"Jason. I love that name," Lily said from the middle row.

"Me too, but I'm no longer so sure about the boy," Ester quipped.

Ester entered the small, dim restaurant alongside Crystal and Lily, its door emitting a soft squeak. Maxx's was far from the shining star of local establishments, but it offered nightly drink and appetizer specials, the staff was friendly, and the atmosphere bustling. Ester spotted Rachel and Donna seated in a booth off to the side and moved toward them, waving. From the jukebox, Meat Loaf was singing about a man in the shadows with a gun in his eye.

Crystal and Lily piled onto the bench seat after Ester, the three sitting opposite Rachel and Donna. Ester introduced Lily, and Rachel and Donna took turns shaking her hand, their expressions uncertain. Ester had considered telling them Lily was transgender, but decided it wasn't anything she needed to announce in advance, as if in warning. Donna regained her composure, but Rachel's demeanor was stuck on discomfited.

Their drinks arrived at the table, swiftly followed by the appetizers, which drew delighted sounds. Crystal nibbled on a chicken wing with surprising daintiness, a smear of its spicy sauce marking her upper lip. Rachel and Donna swooped down on the calamari. Lily cleaned a rib, turning it this way and that, and sucked on the naked bone. Ester bit into a fat potato skin laden with bacon and cheddar and promptly burned the roof of her mouth. She gulped her Moscow mule, trapping a large ice cube on her tongue and allowing it to sit. When the others realized she couldn't talk, or eat or drink, because of the ice cube turned first aid, they laughed, making her laugh, and choke a little.

"You keep hurting yourself lately," Donna said.

A doused feeling came over Ester.

During the third round of drinks, Crystal tilted her glass, saying, "Aw, shit."

"What's wrong?" Ester said.

"Fruit fly." Crystal worked her finger deep into the drink.

"Order a new one." Rachel waved at their server.

"Got it!" Crystal held up the drowned insect on her fingertip.

The server arrived at their table. In the background, Snow Patrol sang about chasing cars and forgetting the world.

"Can I get another screwdriver, please? There was a fly in this one," Crystal said.

"Sure, but I'll have to charge you, just so you know."

"You can't be serious?" Crystal said.

"The drink's almost finished."

"And I repeat, you're shitting me," Crystal said.

"I'll check with my manager," the server said, sounding less sure.

"Oh, for God's sake just bring her another one, I'll pay for it," Rachel said.

"Hey, I'm handling this," Crystal said forcefully. "We all know you've got money, there's no need to rub our faces in it."

With a guilty start, Ester recalled sometimes complaining to Crystal when she'd worked at the store, saying how Rachel tended to forget that not everyone made the kind of money she did, or could afford to keep up with her expensive tendencies. Back then, she'd never imagined that she, Crystal, and Rachel would ever hang out together.

"Will that be all?" the server said.

"Big spender that I am, I'll take another strawberry margarita, and again no salt, thanks," Rachel said.

"Coming right up," the server said, hurrying off.

The heavy silence that followed was punctuated by the five women stirring the ice in their drinks like they were trying to crush it. The sound of broken, swirling ice built in Ester's head.

Lily laughed, her hand pressed to her red-painted mouth.

"What?" Ester said, grateful for the upswing.

"Tell us," Crystal said, already laughing.

"I'm sorry," Lily said, trying to settle herself.

"Well, share the joke," Ester said.

"Okay, okay, but don't take offense, all right?"

"Now I'm nervous," Ester said lightly.

"No, no, it's not bad," Lily said. "I was thinking that some of you are being a little bitchy, like I said, no offense, and I'm being a model woman, two things I always wanted to be."

She waved her hand, breathy. "It's not as funny when I say it out loud. I blame the killer cocktails, they've gone straight to my head. I'm also buzzed just from being out on the town with you ladies."

"Can't say I've ever been accused of being a lady before," Crystal said. She raised the dregs of her insect-infused drink. "To questionable ladies, and Lily, a model woman."

"I can't," Rachel said, shaking her head and slapping a hundred-dollar bill on the table. She rushed to her feet and collided with the server and tray of drinks. The cocktails splashed Rachel's floral-patterned dress, discoloring its ivory magnolias. "Fuck," she said, wiping her wet front with her hand.

"I'll take those," Crystal said as Rachel hurried off, relieving the server of the remains of the screwdriver and saltless margarita.

"Was it something I said?" Lily sounded impish, feisty.

Ester thought about going after Rachel but decided to leave it until tomorrow, when they'd both cooled off. She and Donna exchanged a wide-eyed look. Rachel was an Olympic gold medalist in riding her high horse, but over the fifteen years of their friendship they'd never seen her make such a rude, dramatic exit. That we never completely know people, never completely know ourselves, added to the icy feeling sinking into Ester.

A Change of Tune

Ester returned to bed midmorning, something she rarely did, but she was running on empty. She attempted to read, hoping it would send her to sleep. The short novel was more of a lengthy poem really, about a freshly minted widower and his two young sons trying to go on as a family of three. In one scene, the youngest son draws his dad, brother, dead mom, and himself. Ester pictured a stick drawing of her family of four, with an empty space where she used to be.

Her phone pinged. She ignored it and ducked beneath the duvet, her sheets the color of gold-yellow lichen on rocks. She lay breathing in the faint smells of her sweat and crotch. She threw off the bedcovers, thinking the text might be from Rachel, and sending the open book to the floor. It planted itself print down, delivering another blow to the novel's dad and two sons. "Oops."

The text was from Lily. *What about getting a service animal for Jason? I had this parrot, Percy, when I was a kid. He saved me. Stop by the store today and I'll tell you all about him, while exaggerating shamelessly.* The text ended with a crying-laughing emoji.

Ester gripped the phone with both hands, her knees a summit beneath the duvet. She liked Lily's suggestion, even as a dart of guilt annoyed her chest—she'd given a goldfish to Crystal as solace and hadn't thought to do something similar for Jason. She reached for the tube of ointment on her nightstand and eased it over the fading burns on her palms and fingers. Then looked out her bedroom window, her thoughts overlaying the tops of the trees and blank sky. She hadn't heard from Rachel since the other night at Maxx's. It wasn't that unusual, it had only been a few days, but the silence felt deliberate on both sides.

Ester had hoped Rachel would apologize or at least reach out. Her finger had hovered over her phone's message icon several times, drafting a text in her head, but she couldn't bring herself to be the one to end the stalemate, whether real or imagined. Rachel was the offender and it was up to her to contact Ester. She wondered if Rachel would show up to the weekly walk tomorrow morning. Angst flooded her. What if Rachel had connected Crystal's jab about her being loaded to Ester's bitching about her?

She stiffened, surprised by the large black feather floating past her window. After the feather disappeared from view, she searched online on her phone. The results claimed a black feather was a sign of protection from your angels. She didn't read further, sure there were also darker theories. She roused herself and responded to Lily. *That's a great idea, thanks. I'll think about it.* She pictured a small aquarium sitting on Jason's bedroom desk, and Jason staring into it rather than his gaming screen.

Except Jason would likely ignore the fish and let it die. He needed a pet that would demand his care and attention, and give him something back. She and Simon were allergic to cats, and she refused to get a puppy. She would wind up being the one to care for it, a commitment almost as big as having a third child. Something she'd wanted at one time, in the hopes it would be a girl, but Simon had ruled that out. Besides, there was no one home most of the time and the dog would be alone too much—she recalled Bob saying the same thing, the man maybe not entirely heartless.

Her phone pinged, another text from Lily. *Seriously. I highly recommend a parrot. But be forewarned! Some of them don't shut up or shit off!*

Ester pressed her phone to her lips, smiling, considering. Before she could change her mind, she placed a call to the pet store where she'd purchased Torpedo and confirmed that they carried a selection of exotic birds, including several parrots. Even Jason would get a kick out of a talking pet. Kevin would also be psyched. It occurred to her to run the plan by Simon, but that was just inviting objection.

Ester herded Jason from the house and into the minivan, her son complaining like a kidnappee the whole way, demanding to know where she was taking him.

When she parked outside the pet store he said, "What the hell?"

"Trust me," she said, her enthusiasm flagging. This already felt like a mistake.

He half rolled off the passenger seat, and duck-walked toward the store, his hands shoved deep inside his jacket pockets and his thin shoulders pulled down.

On this visit, the pet store smelled of botanicals tinged with overripe fruit, from a heavy-handed air freshener or perhaps a vat of potpourri.

Jason shot her a matricidal look. "What are we doing here?"

They wandered the long aisles, Jason's hands still buried in his pockets and his shoulders now pulled toward his ears, as if afraid he might catch something. They followed a volley of chirps and whistles to the back of the store, finding a long row of birdcages. A few of the cages stood empty, while the rest each housed two or three birds in various sizes and colors. Ester gravitated to the two yellow birds in the middle of the row, the pair singing at a marvelous key and volume. Jason continued to the large gray bird a couple of cages over. Its head butted the metal bars, as if trying to get to Jason.

The salesclerk appeared. Ester glanced at his name tag, knowing his name was unusual but unable to recall it. *Thaddeus*. He was thirtyish, squishy, and in possession of dark eyes behind thick glasses. In contrast to his oily hair, his face was scaly and cracked, especially across his cheeks, as though he spent too much time around the store's reptiles and was taking on some of their characteristics. Like how longtime couples start to look alike, and women who live together develop synched menstrual cycles.

Once again, Thaddeus proved helpful and knowledgeable, but he quickly started to drone. Ester didn't need a history, geography, or ornithology lesson. Jason's scowl was turning hazardous. His fidgeting bordered on a seizure.

"Of all the birds here, which one talks, likes to be handled, and is the least amount of work?" Ester said.

"We're getting a bird?" Jason said. She couldn't tell if he was surprised in a good or bad way.

"It's for you," she said, keeping her smile affixed and silently praying.

"The African gray checks those boxes," Thaddeus said, opening one of the first cages in the row. He removed a blue and gold bird about the size of a crow and cupped it between both hands.

"That's an African gray?" Ester said, surprised by its vivid, gorgeous hues.

"No, you'd have to go into the city to find one of those, and I should add that they're really expensive."

"How expensive?" A fist formed in Ester's stomach. How had she not considered the costs involved?

Thaddeus whistled, and several of the birds mimicked him, sending up a shrill chorus. "An African gray would set you back about three grand."

"Jesus." Ester limply gestured to the bird he was holding. "How much is it?"

"Meet Dutch, he's a blue and gold macaw, and is very sweet. He already has an impressive vocabulary, don't you, Dutch?" Thaddeus said, coaxing the bird onto the back of his other hand.

"How much is he?" Ester repeated. Jason appeared next to her, his attention full on the macaw.

"I can give you this little beauty for $800, and believe me that's a steal," Thaddeus said.

"Why's he called Dutch?" Jason said.

Thaddeus's reptilian cheeks flushed bright red. "It's just a name I came up with. You can call him whatever you like."

Not for eight hundred dollars, he can't. Heartburn fanned out across Ester's chest. Jason asked to hold the bird. It wasn't heartburn. Ester was having a panic attack, and quite possibly a heart attack. The bird hopped onto the back of Jason's hand and curled its talons around his index finger.

"Say hello, Dutch," Thaddeus said.

"Hello, Dutch," Dutch said.

Jason's smile split his face. Ester hadn't seen that many of his teeth in a long time.

"What about the cage, accessories, and feed? How much does all that cost?" she said.

Thaddeus whistled, and another piercing chorus burst from the birds. "They're an investment, no doubt about it."

"I'll need specifics," Ester said with a falling feeling. There was no way she could admit to Jason that she hadn't thought this through, especially after the whole fiasco with St. Francis High School. She sneezed, her allergies, her every fiber, acting up.

Thaddeus counted on his fingers. "The bird, cage, accessories, feed, vaccinations . . . you're looking at a couple of grand, give or take."

"Vaccinations?" Ester said. It came out like a squeak.

"Watch this." Thaddeus pulled his phone from his sweatshirt pocket and instructed Jason to hold his arm straight out. A country music song floated from the phone, about boots lying under the wrong bed. Ester tuned out thoughts of betrayal. Dutch started to dance on the back of Jason's hand, small, rhythmic hops and kicks that delighted the boy.

By the time the song reached its energetic finale, Dutch was dancing back and forth along Jason's arm in a nimble sidestep while bobbing his green, tufted head and flapping his gold wings—the length of their blue-trimmed span impressive. The bird opened his large, hooked beak, accompanying the singer and delivering the last line of the song in perfect harmony. Jason looked so ecstatic, Ester didn't recognize him.

"Have you anything like him, only cheaper?" she said, seeing a shower of black feathers puddle around her feet. The universe cackled. *You thought that was a good omen falling past your window earlier.*

She felt a silent outpouring of sympathy from Thaddeus, as if he could also see the growing pile of feathers about her ankles.

"A budgie might be a good compromise. They're like twenty-five bucks," he said, moving down the row. "Or this gray cockatiel your son was looking at earlier, I could give him to you for, like, eighty bucks. That's with my staff discount."

"What about the gray cockatiel, Jason? You seemed to like him?" Ester said, following Thaddeus.

"It's a good choice. Although they're more whistlers than talkers, and can be noisy," Thaddeus said.

"Are they as friendly as the macaw?" Ester said.

"They're social and like to be handled, all right, but they can get a little intolerant and have been known to bite on occasion, so they're not a good fit for kids. Do you have younger children at home?" Thaddeus said. Ester shook her head. "Great. Shouldn't be a problem then."

"Why don't you take the cockatiel out and we'll have a closer look." She'd aimed for upbeat, but her tongue sounded like it had developed a limp.

Jason's attention remained on Dutch. He and the bird kept saying hello to each other. Ester didn't know if her credit card would
cover the cost of the macaw and all its paraphernalia. She did
know that if it did, Simon would demand they return the lot.

"Here's Johnny!" Dutch said in a flawless impersonation of Jack
Nicholson's character in *The Shining*, making Jason laugh so hard
he shot snot.

Ester's head snapped back to Thaddeus. She mouthed, *Help*.

"Birds are a big investment and commitment. You shouldn't
rush into it. Best to go home and think about it," Thaddeus said.

"You're right. There's a lot to consider. We can always come back
if we decide to take the plunge," Ester said.

"I knew it," Jason muttered. Ester felt sick. The boy expected to
be disappointed. His finger continued to stroke Dutch's small green
head. It was an age since Ester had seen him show such tenderness.

"You should also consider bird sanctuaries, there are several in
the Bay Area," Thaddeus said. "I've heard really good things about
the one in San Jose. They care for all kinds of rescued birds and are
always looking for good foster and adoption homes."

"That could work," Ester said heartening. "We'll head there
tomorrow, the whole family. Thank you. Thank you so much."
They would go after her morning walk. She wondered again with a
fluttery feeling if Rachel would show up.

"You're welcome to come back and visit anytime," Thaddeus
said, taking Dutch from Jason and returning the bird to his cage.
Jason looked to be in need of a blood transfusion.

"What's his name?" Jason said of Dutch's almost identical companion inside the cage.

Thaddeus colored with fresh embarrassment. "Holland. It's
hard to keep coming up with different names."

"I bet," Ester said.

"He'll be going to his forever home tomorrow, won't you, Holland?" Thaddeus said.

"Hasta la vista, baby." Holland sounded exactly like the Terminator.

Thaddeus chuckled. "I may or may not be their acting coach."

"Dutch will be alone," Jason said miserably.

Ester coughed, a sensation like black feathers plugging her throat.

Ester and Jason arrived home and she parked in the driveway. They hadn't spoken since leaving the pet store. She knew not to try.

He opened the front passenger door and said without malice, "Thanks anyway."

She swallowed what felt like a peach pit. "I've a really good feeling about this bird sanctuary tomorrow in San Jose. You'll find the perfect pet there, wait 'til you see."

He slid from the van and slouched to the house, leaving her alone in the vehicle, her words hanging over her like foreboding. *Wait 'til you see.*

This Better Work

Shortly after Ester and Dad moved to Half Moon Bay, she started the tenth grade. Her first day, Dad failed to pick her up. She waited outside the school gates while her fellow students filed out around her, until she was alone and left behind. A similar panic hit her as she pulled into the coastal trail's parking lot and spotted Rachel's SUV. She considered stalling in the driver's seat until Donna arrived.

At the mouth of the dirt path, a twig snapped beneath Ester's sneaker. Rachel turned around, looking pained. A tender wave came over Ester and she quickened her pace, her arms open. She and Rachel hugged.

"Are we okay?" Rachel said.

Ester eased from the embrace. "I hope so."

"I really wish you'd told Donna and me about Lily."

"I didn't think I needed to."

"It was so awkward."

"I don't see why?"

"Oh, come on," Rachel said sharply.

"I didn't expect this from you."

"I think we should stop this conversation."

"I can't leave it here," Ester said.

"I just wanted to go for a nice walk this morning."

"So did I."

"I don't see what you're so upset about. I was the one blind-sided, and your friend Crystal practically attacked me. My favorite dress is ruined too."

"Hardly blindsided or attacked. But you know who that does apply to? Crystal. She's a really good person who recently survived a terrifying assault and also has a ton of other stuff going on. She's having a terrible time of it."

"And I feel bad for her, but she didn't need to take it out on me. Why would she say that anyway, about me having money? She doesn't know me."

Ester's panic resurfaced. "It's kind of obvious you're doing well for yourself."

"You said something about me, didn't you?"

Ester was going to throw up. "No, I didn't."

"You did. You bitched about me. Unbelievable." Rachel scanned the parking lot, her gaze furious. "I think I'm going to head home."

"You can bitch about someone and still love them," Ester said, her voice thin.

Rachel seemed about to say something belligerent, and stopped herself. After a sullen pause, she spoke carefully. "I didn't think I had a biased bone in my body but I'm not going to lie, the other night was hard for me. Crystal was rude, and Lily's so obviously masculine it was uncomfortable. I wasn't sure if she was a cross-dresser or whatever else, and I didn't know what to say or how to act. Besides all that, I'm not sure I like her or Crystal. That's just the truth, and I'm sorry if that makes me a bad person."

Ester tamped down her anger. "If I'm being completely honest, I had some of my own bias and sense of . . . I don't know what to overcome with Lily—embarrassment, discomfort, ignorance, the whole mix—but I knew that was on me and not on her."

"Okay, fair point," Rachel said.

"And you don't have to like Lily, or Crystal, I agree she was rude, but you don't get to judge them, or to be unkind," Ester said.

"Also fair . . . so we both behaved badly."

"I behaved—"

"You bitched about me, one of your longest, closest friends, or so I thought, and to Crystal, whom you've known for like a second."

"You are one of my dearest friends, and I wasn't bitching-bitching . . . Not really," Ester added with a small smile.

"Oh, good, because I never really bitch about you either," Rachel said, amusement tugging her lips.

Donna arrived, catching Ester and Rachel in a second hug. "Thank God," she said, laughing and wrapping her arms around them both.

On the passenger seat of Simon's car, Ester turned her attention from the oncoming traffic, like a metal army speeding toward them. In the rearview, Mena sat sandwiched between Kevin and Jason. Ester wasn't keen on her tagging along to the bird sanctuary. She and Kevin saw each other constantly now, both in and out of school, and the lovestruck couple had started to fray Ester's last nerve. Every second word they said was "literally" and "rad," and they'd also taken to dressing alike, with a high dependency on floral and paisley shirts paired with skinny jeans and white tennis shoes. They were way too young to be this infatuated and inseparable, and Ester refused to continue to encourage them. It was inevitable the relationship would lead to a brutal breakup. Or they could wind up getting pregnant and staying together because of it. She wouldn't want that for either of them.

She tried to get back to the ease in her mood since making up with Rachel. It was a weight lifted, and while everything wasn't entirely smoothed over—she couldn't unsee Rachel's bigotry and sense of superiority—she was hopeful that Rachel would do better going forward. In the mirror, Kevin reached for a strand of Mena's dark hair and curled it around his finger. Mena eased her head free, grinning. Ester glanced at Jason next to the window, wearing headphones and fixated on his phone.

"A penny?" she said to Simon. He'd hardly spoken during the drive.

"Just focusing on the road," he said.

She worried that was true, his mind emptier than she ever wanted to admit. She tapped the Maps icon on her phone. "Do you need directions?"

"Not until after the freeway."

"Heads up, you'll be taking an immediate right once you exit."

"This better work," he said, dropping his voice.

"It will. You should have seen him in the pet store."

"A service bird? What next?" Simon muttered.

"I'd get him a service anything if I thought it would help."

"Have you looked into how much work and expense this bird is going to be, and how noisy? Plus, what's its lifespan? Because you know it's going to be you and me who'll end up taking care of it, including cleaning out its shitty cage every day."

He was sinking her mood and her hopes. She had the same concerns, and she hadn't considered the bird's lifespan. Which, everything crossed, was a lot shorter than a cat's.

Inside the bird sanctuary, Ester, Simon, and the kids were greeted by a haze of dander and a fury of birds.

The director, Claire, spoke over the avian ruckus, her height, reedy build, and blunt bangs enviable. "We can go bird by bird if you like, but our current population stands at sixty-plus, so you might want to take a look around at your own pace and let me know which birds strike your fancy."

The prospect of touring so many vocal, abandoned birds unnerved Ester almost as much as their insistent noise, like cries for help.

She realized Claire was waiting for a response. "It's Jason, our youngest, who's interested—" She coughed, fighting back the blitzkrieg of motes.

"Jason, do you see any birds you like?" she continued, sounding like she had laryngitis.

"Do you have any African grays?" he asked Claire.

"The guy in the pet store told us they're the king of parrots," Ester said. Jason threw her an exasperated look, flattening her smile.

"We don't see too many African grays here. They're expensive, highly desirable birds, so people tend to sell them rather than turn them over to shelters. For the most part, birds wind up here because their humans can no longer care for them for various reasons and can't find anyone to take the bird off their hands. As a result, our population is primarily made up of your more affordable household pets, like the many cockatiels you see here," Claire said, gesturing vaguely.

"What about this one, Jason?" Simon moved in front of a cage housing a multicolored bird splashing about inside a bowl of water.

"That's Frannie, a lorikeet, and quite the character," Claire said.

Simon sneezed. Frannie sneezed. "She's an utter mimic," Claire said. Simon sneezed a second time, as did Frannie. The duet of sneezes persisted.

"Oh dear," Claire said.

"A cold," Simon said, rubbing his dripping nose.

"This one's so cute," Mena said of a small bird with a green body, yellow-orange head, and bright-red beak. "Hello, there. Can you say hello?"

"Hi, sugar." The bird pushed its beak through the cage's front mesh, directly above a bulky padlock.

"That's Houdini, a Fischer's lovebird. We have to double lock his cage because he's so good at getting out of it," Claire said.

"What's wrong with this one?" Kevin pointed at a large white bird with several bald spots dotting its body.

"That's Patches, a cockatoo. We're eager to find him a family ASAP. Unfortunately, he gets bored without full-time attention and bites off his feathers. Don't you, Patches?" Claire said.

"I'm a naughty boy," Patches said, winning Jason's attention. But not for long.

"Do you have any macaws?" Jason said.

"What's the typical lifespan of these birds?" Simon said, the edges of his eyes pink.

"A lot longer than most people realize. That's the main reason so many are abandoned, they outtire or outlive their owners," Claire said.

"For example?" Ester said.

"Let's see. The budgies last about five to ten years. The canaries and cockatiels, we're talking ten to twenty years. The cockatoos and macaws, it's anywhere between forty and sixty," Claire said.

"Sixty years?" Ester said. She and Simon exchanged a panicked look.

"I found one!" Jason sang out. "Mom, he looks just like Dutch." The group moved to the cage in question.

Claire removed the macaw. "Meet Masie."

"Does she dance?" Jason said, offering his hand for Masie to perch on.

"Does she ever," Claire said. Mena played a rap song about checks and money from her phone. The irony of the lyrics wasn't lost on Ester, or on Simon no doubt. While the sanctuary only asked for a donation in exchange for a bird, the long list of other expenses remained. Masie delivered a stage-worthy performance, dancing and strutting up and down Jason's arm.

"Does she talk?" Jason said, looking drunk with delight.

"Say hello, Masie," Claire said.

"Hello, zucchini. Hi, zucchini. Howdy, zucchini," Masie said.

"You'll never guess what her favorite food is," Claire said.

"Hello. Hello. Hello," Masie said.

"Once she gets going, she sometimes doesn't know when to stop," Claire said, scratching Masie's chest with her fingernail.

"Great, Mouthy Masie," Simon said below his breath.

"Help!" Masie said.

"She's also a terrible attention seeker," Claire said.

"I love you," Masie said.

"And a master manipulator," Claire said.

"The black markings around her eyes, they're like a white tiger's coat," Jason said.

"Oh yes, now that you say it," Claire said.

"She's beautiful." Jason sounded like he was having a religious experience.

The group turned to gape at Simon, who was leaning forward, wheezing and clutching his chest. Ester was thrown back to the store and Crystal's asthma attack. Claire rushed Masie back inside her cage and flapped around Simon, babbling concern. Ester's head filled with the sound of suffocating. Simon's. Dad's. Crystal's. Marcus's.

"Do you need an ambulance?" Claire said.

Simon shook his head, gasping. He struggled to the exit, accompanied by the others.

Outside, the group remained in front of the sanctuary, Claire still asking if she should phone for an ambulance. "I just need a minute," Simon said.

"I think he's going to be fine, thank you," Ester said.

"I'm sorry, it's clear you're chronically allergic," Claire told Simon. "There's no way I can allow you to take a bird."

"He could take antihistamines," Ester said, unable to bear the look of growing devastation on Jason's face. She sneezed. "We both could."

"For the next forty to sixty years?" Simon said breathlessly.

Jason charged toward the parking lot.

Ester hurried after him, promising they would make it up to him, and hating how hollow and panicked she sounded.

The silence on the drive home was only somewhat masked by the radio, and punctuated by Simon's coughing and sneezing. Ester had offered to drive, but he insisted. "I need the distraction."

Ester repeatedly checked on Jason in the rearview, half expecting him to throw himself from the moving car. He remained intent on whatever was piping through his headphones and on gnawing his thumb knuckle. Ester recalled how much it had hurt, and bled, when she'd accidentally bitten her thumb. She turned in her seat, trying for tender. "Hey, stop that."

Jason looked livid, but he obliged.

She kept checking the rearview. His teeth didn't return to his knuckle.

They were nearly home when she received the text from Crystal. *gunman did it again   another home invasion & serious assault old man this time*

Ester stifled her noises. *Please tell me they caught him?*

nope but got him on CCTV he wore gorilla mask

Ester's scalp remained tight. Her phone pinged a second time. *cant shake feeling hes going to hit here again*

He won't. It's like each robbery is a trophy and he wants a different, bigger prize every time. Ester knew no such thing, but if there was ever a time to fabricate.

r u around??????

Im driving back from San Jose. Long story. I'll check in with you later, ok?

ok

Ester's teeth slyly closed around her thumb knuckle, inflicting pain that took over her thoughts.

Intertwined

Ester awoke the next morning thinking about Pryor Mountain. She hadn't dreamt about the mountain range during the night, at least not that she could remember, yet there it loomed large in her mind first thing, presiding over fields of dancing wheat. She could almost taste Billings's sweet breeze coated in the height of summer. Most distinct, the wild horses pounding through the valley, their muscular bodies glistening.

Maybe it was fantasy and not memory, but she swore that as a girl she'd seen a full eclipse hang over the mountain. In her recollections, she was the only one to have witnessed the phenomenon. A secret, an omen, studding the sky. But that couldn't be possible. And yet, the more she thought about it, the more it seemed as if that blackened coupling of the sun and moon had continued to hang over her ever since. She broke out in a cold sweat, remembering the black feather falling past her bedroom window.

She wished there was a power button for our thoughts. There was, she realized. Disease, and it had permanently shut down Dad's mind. From the bathroom, the shower dial squeaked open and water pummeled the tub. She glanced at the alarm clock on her nightstand, surprised that Simon was up before her. She was almost always the first one up in the mornings, even now that she was working regular night shifts and often didn't get to bed until well past midnight.

She reached for her phone next to the clock and her tower of books impatiently waiting to be read. There were no further texts from Crystal. She checked the local news for more on the gunman's latest victim, Stuart Jordan. As previously reported, Mr. Jordan was stable, despite suffering multiple lacerations and broken bones, including several ribs. Ester read the update at the bottom of the article, her screen seeming to turn gray. Doctors were unable to save the sight in Mr. Jordan's left eye.

Kevin's bedroom door opened, and he shuffled along the landing and into the main bathroom. Ester strained to hear sounds from Jason's room. There were none. She saw his crushed, furious face as they'd driven away from the bird sanctuary. The quiet, the stillness from his bedroom drilled her. She moved from her bed and into her bathrobe, fighting a bad feeling. She hurried into the hall, cinching the belt of her bathrobe at her waist. *Waste*, she thought with a start.

She rapped on Jason's bedroom door and pushed it open. Her legs almost went out from under her. He was lying lengthwise across the middle of his mattress on his stomach, his eyes closed and his mouth slack. She rushed to him, about to shout to Kevin to call 911 but up close it was clear his breath was flowing and his eyes were moving behind their lids. Much of his back was uncovered, the groove of his spine like a long dent. She remembered holding him skin-to-skin as a baby and singing him to sleep.

She considered letting him lie in and stay home from school. But he'd missed enough classes lately, and she was working a private event at Blazers that afternoon in addition to the night shift. If she left him home alone for that length, he would play video games until he'd stupefied himself.

She shook his shoulder. "Time for school, sweetheart."

He groaned and pulled the comforter over his head.

In the kitchen, Ester fixed herself coffee and buttered toast and set about preparing the boys' lunches. She reached for her phone, about to text her brothers to ask them if she was remembering or imagining a full eclipse in the Billings sky but stopped herself. It wasn't like either of them ever contacted her on a whim, or for much of anything else beyond the obligatory holiday greetings.

Simon appeared, humming to himself. Kevin soon followed. The two sat on their barstools at the island, reading their phones and spooning cereal. Jason also surfaced, his scowl scorching. He settled on his barstool and surfed his phone, like father, like brother. She braced herself for them to read about Stuart Jordan's sight loss. Meanwhile, the silence stretched, a resistance band about to snap.

Ester arrived at work in the early afternoon, her agitation growing. She'd spent the entire morning at home doing laundry and various other chores and felt exhausted yet restless. Her legs wanted to walk out from under her and break into a sprint.

She found Allie in the kitchen, pouring coffee. "Hey."

"Hey." Allie flashed a tentative smile.

Ester also helped herself to coffee, her hand tingling with the memory of her fingers braided with Allie's inside Golden Leaves.

"I can't believe the gunman did it again. Are you doing okay?" Allie asked.

"It's like a bad day that you have to keep reliving."

"I'm sorry," Allie said.

"Another elderly victim, it's sickening."

"I know, but try not to think about it. That's only spreading the gunman's damage."

"I'm trying, thanks."

Allie exited, a steaming mug in hand. Ester fixed on the carafe in the coffee maker and considered pouring its dark contents over her feet. Anything to not feel this other pain that she couldn't so much as put into words.

Ester entered Blazers' private room and studied her bookings list. A biotech company had reserved the space for a lengthy meeting, followed by a social mixer. Over the next hour, she supervised and assisted with the setup and reconfirmed with housekeeping the timing and menus for the coffee break, luncheon, and evening reception.

The company's management team arrived. Ester double-checked with the CEO's assistant that everything was to their liking and addressed the last-minute technical and dietary needs. A remarkably attractive woman entered the room, parading long raven hair and a brilliant white skirt suit. "Let's bring on another assistant to support IT's beta team," she said to the two men in skinny suits.

Ester's heart jumped, as if struck by a baby's foot. She knew what she could do for Jason.

During her free hour before the start of her evening shift, she drove back to the pet store and discovered Thaddeus inside the rear storeroom, smoking. He dropped the cigarette and stubbed it out beneath his steel-toed boot. "You never saw that."

"Saw what?"

He glowered at the red bulb protruding from the opposite wall. "That light's supposed to come on whenever someone enters the store." He flashed his toothsome smile. "Had a change of heart, did we?"

She filled him in on the disastrous trip to the bird sanctuary. "So I had a thought, and a favor to ask. I was wondering if there was any way Jason could work the odd shift here, with a focus on the care of the birds?" She sneezed, and sneezed some more.

"You okay?"

"Sorry. It's a cumulative effect between here and the storm of dander at the bird sanctuary. What about it? Any chance you could use Jason's help, even for a couple of hours a week? You saw how he was with the birds, and Dutch in particular. I haven't seen him that engaged, or content, in a long time."

"That's wild. Just yesterday I was telling the owner we needed to hire a part-timer to help me reorganize and better maintain this place."

Ester's mood soared. "Is that a yes?"

"Does he have any experience?"

"He's a fast learner."

"How about this? He can work Saturday mornings to start, from nine to noon, and we'll see how it goes."

Ester hugged him. "Thank you."

"Oh," he said with fresh surprise.

She didn't remember driving back to Blazers and seemed to arrive by sorcery. She could barely wait until she got home after her shift to tell Jason the happy news and see his reaction. In an ideal world he would be sound asleep by then and she would tell him first thing in the morning.

She was stationed behind the hostess podium, working on the desktop and configuring the night's seating chart, when a pair of worn, familiar Keds approached. She looked up, surprised to see Simon. She almost broke into a smile and was poised to tell him about the pet store, but his grave expression stopped her. "Dad?"

He nodded, his eyes damp and cracks spreading over his face.

Secret Find

Simon drove Ester to Golden Leaves. En route, she regretted leaving the minivan at Blazers. She or Simon would need to return for it later, and she would have been fine driving, although her insides had yet to stop pulsating. She hadn't anticipated this strange cocktail of shock and heart-pumping panic. Not when she'd expected, wanted, Dad's death for years. The all-too-familiar slice of his dying alone, that was what she couldn't bear.

"Can we stop by the house first? I won't be a minute," she said.

"Sure," Simon said.

She sat gripping her phone in her lap, as if it could take off on its own. She needed to call her brothers and let them know. Would it be wrong to text them? It would be so much easier to text them.

"You better let your brothers know," Simon said. He and Ester used to do so much more of that. Reading each other's minds. Being in tune.

They entered the empty house. Kevin was at soccer practice, and Jason was finally seeing the school counselor. "The boys. They need to be told."

"I'll go get them after I drop you off," Simon said.

Kevin and Jason didn't really know their granddad. Even before the onset of Alzheimer's, he hadn't bonded or bothered much with either of them, but they would at least grieve the idea of him.

"Do you want me to phone your brothers?" Simon said.

"Yes, please." She no longer cared that she was shirking her familial duty. Tim and Rob did it all the time.

In the bedroom, she pulled open the top left drawer in the tall dresser and rifled through the clutter of pens, creams, makeup, and costume jewelry, finding the needed black jewelry box, its velvet coated in lint and dust. She removed the pale blue locket inside, its metal back cool against her fingertips. Her thumb caressed the embossed white flowers on the locket's ceramic front. She opened the chainless locket, its interior painted cerulean blue speckled with gold. Just as when she was a girl, she raised the open locket to her right eye, as if about to take a photo, and peered through the fissure between its gold hinges, spying on a tiny sliver of the world.

The afternoon she found Mom dead at the bottom of the garage stairs, the locket lay on Mom's open palm, as if waiting to be plucked. Ester had never seen the locket before that day. She took it from Mom, and never told anyone about it. After the paramedics carried Mom from the house and disappeared with her, Ester sneaked a trembling look inside the locket, and cried on finding it empty.

Throughout the following days of mourning and forced mingling, Ester told herself stories about the locket. It was a secret heirloom from Mom's side of the family. It was a gift from Mom's first love. Mom discovered it at an estate sale and its speckled, cerulean interior, its open-mouthed emptiness, whispered to her. Mom bought it in a fancy jewelry store as a gift for Ester. Mom was going to write down her burning wish, fold the paper into a miniature square, and store it inside the locket. Mom liked tiny things. Mom liked pretty things. Mom liked giving gifts. Mom liked secrets.

Similarly, throughout Marcus's funeral and burial, Ester had invented better stories about his death. Anything but his dying because of something as simple and stupid as an asthma attack. Anything but his not being able to get to his inhaler in time. Anything but his not wanting to live.

She squirreled the locket into her coat pocket.

Simon was waiting for her at the bottom of the stairs. "All set?"

"Did you get ahold of Tim and Rod?"

"Yeah. They'll be here tomorrow afternoon."

"Are they all right?"

"They seemed fine."

A bitter taste flooded her mouth. "Of course they did."

"Hey," he said gently. "Family's family."

Was it worse, she wondered, to be like him, an only child growing up with a dead mother and lone dad. Or to be like her, growing up feeling like an only child with a dead mother and lone dad.

Back in the car, she counted up her in-laws in her head. "Do you know if they're all coming?"

"Tim or Rod didn't say." Simon clapped his hand to her thigh and shook her leg a little. He let his hand rest above her knee in that steadying way she liked.

"Let them know I can get them a discount at the hotel, will you? And find out who's coming and how long they plan to stay."

"Will do," he said.

She wondered how many others would come to the funeral, and if Dad had enough savings to cover the various costs. She, Tim, and Rod might have to chip in some. That would be fun. There wasn't a life insurance payout coming either. Dad had signed his policy over to Golden Leaves to cover their outrageous costs until death did them part.

There was also the expense of a reception. She texted Allie, inquiring about the costs to book Blazers' private room for a buffet lunch, nothing fancy but nice enough, and with a cash bar. She could still feel Allie's arms tight around her inside Blazers earlier, and her warm breath at her ear, murmuring condolences. Despite Simon looking on, they'd clasped each other for several beats too long, Allie's ponytail smelling of grapefruit.

"You never talk about your mom," Ester said.

"It was a long time ago," Simon said.

"You were nine."

"Like I said, a long time ago."

"Or your dad," she said.

He pressed his palm to hers and kissed the back of her hand. "This is about you and your dad."

She glimpsed the red brick wall he'd built between himself and his parents' shocking deaths, their torn, broken bodies.

They arrived at Golden Leaves, his hand back on her thigh. They kissed, a brush of lips. "You okay?"

"Yes, thanks," she said.

He made to get out of the car.

"Don't. I'll be fine on my own. Please, go get the boys."

"You sure?"

"Yeah."

"Okay. We'll see you soon."

Simon waited until she'd reached Golden Leaves' entrance before starting the car. He waved, his dropped head pushed close to the windshield and his expression a mash of encouragement and grief. She recognized that he'd scaled his wall for her and dared to look out at the wasteland. She raised her hand in thanks, in a salute.

Alone, she pressed the nursing home's intercom and announced herself. The buzzer sounded and she stepped inside, smelling lemons, the synthetic kind. She didn't greet, didn't really register, the staff or residents around her, but continued down the long corridor toward the back bedrooms, a dull path worn into the middle of the linoleum like a green, supersized snake.

She arrived at Dad's room, finding a laminated sheet displaying a large red admiral butterfly affixed to the closed door. To indicate the occupant had died, she presumed. The admiral, its name shortened from admirable, was the only species of butterfly she knew by name. A white butterfly seemed a more fitting symbol for the occasion, but she was sure there was apt meaning to the choice. She entered the room and the reek of disinfectant.

She stood over Dad's pale form, sensing before ever touching him how cold and stiff he was turning. Someone had placed two dull quarters on his eyelids and wedged a white, rolled face cloth below his chin, to keep his mouth closed. She hadn't known about the face cloth trick and had thought the coins were a myth, or at least a custom no longer practiced. She batted away thoughts of the holdup and the quarter she'd flipped but hadn't turned over. Someone had combed Dad's hair to the front again. She would need to fix that, for the final time.

Tears and violent body shakes ambushed her. She reminded herself that Dad's death was a blessing. He was at peace at last. But her sorrow demanded its way, grieving not so much Dad's passing but the second half of his life, when he lost his wife and for the most part his two sons, and later his mind, his entire self. Throughout that harrowing regression, his saving graces were Ester, to some degree, or so she hoped, and riding the highest sea waves he could hijack.

She remembered the surfboard decorated with a dolphin that Dad bought for her soon after they moved to Half Moon Bay. He tried his hardest to teach her to surf, but she couldn't manage it. Even with a wetsuit, the icy waters chilled her to her skeleton. As did terror. Nothing Dad said or did could convince her that she wouldn't be swallowed by the waves or ripped apart by sharks. She persisted with the lessons for his sake but couldn't as much as fail better and eventually gave up.

"Please, let me at least give you this much," Dad pleaded. It was the closest he'd ever come to saying he was sorry for taking her away from her home, with its traces and memories of Mom, and from her brothers and school and friends, her entire world. But his need for her to put surfing over her fears, so that he would feel better, only made her feel worse. To soothe herself, she cut the soles of her feet on the shoreline's seashells.

She reached inside her coat pocket and closed her fingers around Mom's locket. She tightened her grip, squeezing until the keepsake turned damp and warm in her fist. Until its edges marked her skin.

When she was able, she released the locket and placed that final piece of Mom in Dad's hand, reuniting them.

Shark

The following evening, a small group of mourners gathered inside the funeral home for what the undertaker insisted on calling the "visitation." Ester kissed Dad's marble brow, and its cadaver chill set her lips tingling. The dim, airless room pressed. There weren't enough windows in the dismal space. It needed more bulbs. Voltage.

A hush fell. Rod and Michelle filled the doorway. They crossed the threshold and approached the coffin. The group watched a son see his deceased father for the first time.

Ester floated toward her brother and sister-in-law and hugged them in turn. Rod looked well. Tall and slim, his curly, graying hair nudged his shirt collar, adding to the rugged look of his bushy brows and acne-scarred cheeks. His tailored suit brought out that blue shade of mountain in his eyes.

Simon appeared next to her and solemnly greeted Rod and Michelle.

"You didn't bring the girls?" Ester said.

"We thought it best not to, at their age," Rod said. Ester guessed the girls were now five and seven. She'd only met them a handful of times and had lost track.

"My parents are taking care of them," Michelle said, looking oddly orange-tinged while her teeth and platinum hair were too white.

Rod reached into the coffin, his slender hand covering Dad's laced fingers with their knuckles like frost-capped hills. Michelle placed her hand over Rod's. Ester moved away and stopped next to Kevin, Mena, and Jason, wishing her own hands had something to do. Her kids were doing okay with it all. That was something. Although it was a little upsetting that they didn't seem to care more. It was also honest.

A group arrived from Blazers, Allie among them. They each hugged Ester, murmuring condolences, and commiserated with Simon and the boys. Bob didn't hug her, thankfully, but his handshake was firm and his expression earnest. Allie was the last of the group to greet Ester. In Allie's arms, the sensation that had annoyed Ester all day eased, allowing her muscles, her entire body, to stop their constant gripping.

Lily appeared next to Ester, sad-smiling. Ester reluctantly released Allie.

"Do you want to join me for a smoke?" Lily said.

"I don't smoke," Ester said.

"Neither do I," Lily said.

Outside, Lily broke a cannabis brownie in two and offered Ester a piece. Ester hesitated, tempted. Weed was on her bucket list. "I better not."

"Your loss." Lily closed her teeth around the larger of the brownie pieces. "I just heard myself. Sorry, that came out wrong."

"Don't worry about it."

"I'm also a member of the adult orphan club, but by disownment."

"I'm sorry," Ester said.

"Me too."

A white rideshare pulled up. Tim and his family emerged. Ester moved to the group and reached to hug Tim. He offered his hand, which she shook, her lips clamped. She hugged the others, start-ing with Sara and ending with the youngest child. For a horrible second she couldn't remember her niece's name. Tara, she recalled with relief. The child was three, maybe four years old.

Tara's liquid blue eyes latched onto the last of the brownie in Lily's hand. "Me want some!"

Ronnie and Tommie echoed her pleas.

"Tara, boys, show some respect." Sara grimaced at Ester. "Sorry."

"It's fine, really," Ester said. It was several years since she'd last seen her sister-in-law, and Sara wasn't wearing the time well. Ester wondered what lay behind her premature wrinkles and the gray bags under her eyes, her brittle body.

"We'll get you some treats very soon, I promise," Ester told the children.

She introduced Lily to Tim and Sara.

"I'm sorry for your loss," Lily said.

Tim nodded stiffly. "Thank you."

"Hello," Sara said, ushering the children past Lily and inside. Tim followed, throwing Lily a disturbed look. His disdain hurtled Ester back to her freshman year in college.

"Dad said you're dating an African American," Tim had said through the phone.

"What if I am?"

"You're embarrassing Dad and yourself."

"You don't know what you're talking about." If Dad had an issue, he hadn't voiced it. As with much else, Ester doubted he was paying attention.

"End it, Ester," Tim said.

"End you." She slammed down the phone receiver so hard, she worried she'd broken the cradle.

"Earth calling Ester," Lily said, giggling.

"You're high already," Ester said.

"Thank bleep for that." Lily held up the remaining brownie, her eyebrow arched.

"Oh bleep it." Ester rushed the cannabis-laced chunk into her mouth.

Tim stood leaning over Dad's coffin, Sara and their three children stationed next to him. His broad shoulders started to shake, and he emitted loud, alarming sobs. Sara placed her blue-veined hand on the center of his back. The children gathered around his legs, their faces pressed to his trousers.

Tim quieted, and he and his family joined Rod and Michelle on the other side of the room. Ester stepped into a quiet corner opposite them to field a string of texts about the logistics for the funeral wreaths and mourning cars. She also responded to Crystal, who was working at the store and kept checking in. Her housekeeping finished, she scanned the room, finding Allie, and started to make her way over.

Tim intercepted her. "What happened to Dad's beard?"

"They shaved it off in the nursing home." The cannabis high hit and her mouth and mind turned woolly. "His beard's been gone a long time." Her words sounded like slow motion, meanwhile her brain was spinning and her pulse was on fast-forward.

"He's not Dad without his beard," Tim said.

"He looks like Dad to me," she said with another squirt of vindictiveness. More than two years had passed since he and Rod had visited Dad.

She stepped around him and reached Allie. "I could do with some air."

"Lead the way," Allie said.

Ester and Allie walked out of the funeral home and around the back of the gray stone building, taking shelter beneath the boughs of a giant cypress tree. The leaves above them murmured, as if adding to the refrain of condolences. Ester tried to push down her anger and steady her whirling insides.

Allie wrapped her arms around the tree's broad trunk. Ester moved to its other side and pressed herself against its peeling bark.

When she touched her brow to the trunk's splintered crust, the top of her head lifted off. Her brain had halved, and its upper portion was flying away. Escaping. She laughed, in awe of that little lump of brownie. It was no slacker. She stretched her arms around the tree, straining to the point of pain in her shoulder sockets. Her and Allie's wriggling fingers struggled to make contact.

Reaching, grunting, laughing, they managed to defy the tree's circumference and touch fingertips, setting off sparks that shot through Ester's hands and up her arms. She wished she could see Allie's face right then, to know if she was similarly lit up. It was the electricity that she had craved inside the funeral home. A savage thirst cut through her euphoria. Her entire mouth felt sucked of saliva, making her tongue a desert. All memory of liquid was lost to her. She was the world without water.

She hurried around the tree and reached for Allie. "Hold me, please."

Allie returned the hug. "Hey, hey, it's okay. I've got you."

Outside the crematorium the next afternoon, the mourners praised the moving funeral service.

Rachel wrapped her arms tight around Ester. "You gave him a great send-off."

Donna also hugged her. "His surfboard on top of his coffin, his getting to take it with him, that did me in."

During the service, Ester had sat between Tim and Rod in the front pew. They both draped an arm around her. Her brother bandages. Where had they been the many other times she'd needed them?

With Monica at the helm, the Sing, I choir sang "Amazing Grace." Lily delivered a divine falsetto solo on the first chorus, and Allie performed a chest-twinging solo on the final chorus. All of that was seared in Ester's mind. As was the image of the red velvet curtains closing on Dad's coffin and surfboard, before being engulfed by flames.

Everything else about the service was a blur, including her eulogy. She'd written a lengthy tribute but couldn't bring herself to read it. It wasn't only that she was a nervous wreck having to speak in front of so many people. The speech seemed too prepared. Performative. She opened her mouth and trusted that she would speak from her heart. On an evening a few weeks into the future, while surrounded by violet twilight, she would tell Allie that she couldn't remember a word she'd said about her dad from the pulpit. Allie would tell her that she'd said she felt like she'd lost Dad three times—when Mom died, when Alzheimer's took him, and when his heart stopped. He had looked to nature for lessons on how to live, Allie continued, and his favorite season was spring. He liked to brag that surfing—riding the highest waves he could snag for a few sensational seconds—was how he bested Jesus Christ Himself, who had only managed to walk on water.

Allie said that when the laughter quieted, Ester told mourners that *shark* was the last word Dad had retained before he forgot language entirely and stopped speaking. He said shark often and vigorously. "I used to sit with him and silently play out the possible reasons why a man-eating sea predator above all else would have such sticking power over Dad in the end. Maybe he was saying just that, a shark. Maybe shark was shorthand for the entire watery world that, really, he grew to prefer to the one on land. Maybe shark captured how Alzheimer's was circling him. Maybe he was saying 'Watch out!' to the rest of us. Watch out for whatever the shark is in our lives. That thing or things we need to escape. That's it, I like to think. To the very end, he was warning us. To the very end, he was trying to be the best, however imperfect, citizen he could be. The best, however imperfect, dad."

"It was beautiful," Allie said.

"You took in all that?" Ester said, stunned.

When they kissed, soft, sultry, Ester broke open.

Telltale Scar

After the crematorium, Simon drove Ester and the boys to Blazers for the reception, his hand on her thigh. In the aftermath of the heartfelt funeral service—its song and speeches and sacredness—the car seemed lifeless.

Inside Blazers, Ester tried to not track Allie throughout the private, jabbering room, but it was futile. She was tipsy, and her focus singular. Allie had taken the day off work to attend the funeral and reception, but that didn't stop her from monitoring the food, organizing the wreaths transferred from the crematorium, and ensuring the dirty dishes and napkins disappeared in a timely, discreet fashion.

"Your boss is going above and beyond," Rod said.

"Yeah, she's great," Tim said.

"She is," Ester said, not caring that a thick tenderness bled through her voice.

"Should we settle up with her now?" Tim said.

"Do we know the final number?" Rod said.

She moved off before she said something her brothers would regret and stopped next to the large arrangement of white lilies by the room's entrance, their smell a punch. She scanned the mostly jovial gathering of mourners, silently talking down her fury. There were more people present who didn't know Dad than those who did. His few surviving, weather-beaten surfing friends stood in a cluster next to the bar. A handful of his former coworkers from the medical warehouse remained next to the buffet table. The trio of staff from Golden Leaves hovered next to the door, as if readying to slip out.

The largest group in the room was the Sing, I choir. Ester's skin broke out in bumps recalling their performance of "Amazing Grace" as they'd surrounded Dad's coffin. Their collective voice had floated over the mourners and brushed the chapel's walls and ceiling like a soothing vapor. Lily's and Allie's solos further graced the holy haze and swaddled everyone present, including Dad. There was something of the angels in the choir, and Ester wished everyone everywhere could be visited by such voices and inspired by such power. What the choir did to her during Dad's service, that's what thoughts of Allie did to her too.

Simon appeared next to her. "How are you holding up?"

"I need a coffee."

"I'll get it."

Alone again, she watched Mena and her sons talk with their cousins and Crystal's three children. Close by, Sara held Tara on her sharp hip. Tim and Rod were nowhere to be seen.

An older man joined Ester. His blue eyes flecked with gold recalled the interior of Mom's locket. "Your father got a sad ending."

"It was certainly drawn out." Ester recalled the temptation to take a pillow to Dad's bony, sunken face.

"I'm sorry."

"Thank you." She'd lost count of the number of times she'd engaged in this same exchange in recent days. He turned to go and she spotted the long, thick scar running alongside his ear and down the curve of his jaw, as if someone had attempted to remove his face.

Crystal and Simon reached Ester at the same time. She ignored the cup of coffee Simon offered. "What if the gunman doesn't have a skin condition? What if he's hiding a telltale scar on his face, or tattoos, or a birthmark?"

"I'm sure the police have considered that," Simon said.

"You don't have to worry about any of that right now," Crystal said.

"He needs to be found." Ester's thoughts leaped to the little English girl from years back. The one who disappeared from a vacation resort somewhere in Europe, Portugal perhaps, and was never found. She had a telltale eye, its misshapen iris like a keyhole.

Simon touched the top of Ester's arm. "Are you all right? Do you want to take a walk?"

"I should check on dessert. It's time for dessert."

"Drink this coffee first."

She drifted away, needing to find Allie. She pictured the gunman's scar positioned below his left eye, where it glared out jagged and knotty.

Tim blocked her path. "There you are. Rod and I both leave tomorrow on afternoon flights. We were thinking the three of us should meet in the morning, to discuss Dad's affairs."

"His affairs?"

Tim's flinty eyes narrowed. "His finances and whatnot."

"There's nothing to discuss. Everything Dad owned was liquidated and used to pay the nursing home. The little money that's left will go toward his funeral expenses, and even that isn't quite enough to cover everything. We'll all need to chip in, but it won't be much, you'll be glad to hear. I got us good deals on everything."

"You're upset. We can talk about this another time," he said.

"Like I said, there's nothing to talk about. Now if you'll excuse me, I promised your kids dessert."

"You're acting like this is only happening to you. He was our dad too."

"Nice of you to remember," she said, spotting Allie.

She reached Allie, wishing she wasn't drunk. Glad she was drunk. "Let's go outside."

"Marj and I are about to leave, she's gotta be someplace."

Ester's head reeled. "Marj."

"Are you okay?"

"You can't leave, you haven't had dessert."

"We're good, thank you."

"Please don't go. Not yet."

"I can ask Marj—"

"I should drink some coffee."

"I'll get you a cup."

"No." Ester hadn't intended to sound abrupt. But Simon had gotten her coffee. She couldn't have Allie getting her coffee too. She would get her own coffee. She turned away and almost tripped over Tara.

"Look!" Tara held out a half-eaten cookie that resembled a pink crescent moon. She stood waiting, mashed shortbread caking her baby teeth.

"I see!" Ester scooped Tara up and spun her round, the child's small black shoes digging into her thighs.

Breathless, dizzy, Ester stopped still. As woozy as she was, as much as Tara's shoes continued to stab her, she held the little girl airborne in her arms, not wanting the lifting to stop.

Road Spill

At brunch at Blazers, Rod told the party of eleven that Dad used to place two socks over his hands and act out a play he called *The Last Dinosaurs of Montana*. Ester didn't remember the play or Dad ever goofing around with sock puppets and wasn't sure if any of it was true, or if Rod was simply entertaining the kids.

Rod placed his white napkin over his fist, cinched it at his wrist, and charged the cloth phantom toward the children's scrunched, retreating faces. "Boo!"

Everyone laughed.

While gap-toothed Maria and two busboys delivered the food and refilled coffees and juices, Michelle passed around her phone, showing photos of her and Rod's two girls—snapshots of big eyes, missing teeth, and long, honeyed curls. Even Rod and Michelle's Labradoodle could win contests.

"I'm sorry now that we didn't bring the girls with us," Michelle said.

"I still think it was the right call," Rod said, his fork cutting into his poached eggs, spilling yellow. "The girls are sensitive."

Ester stopped herself from asking him what he knew on the subject.

Simon asked Tommie if he had a girlfriend. The six-year-old giggled and squirmed on the vinyl seat.

"How about Kevin and Jason?" Tim said pleasantly.

"We met Kevin's girlfriend yesterday, remember?" Sara said

"So we did," Tim said, his color rising almost as high as Tommie's. He had never liked to be corrected.

"Jason's a gamer. He won't ever leave his room long enough to find a girlfriend," Kevin said.

"Shut it." Jason bit into his French toast like it was the wrongdoer.

"I've always liked my own company too," Rod said. Jason's furious expression softened.

Tim and Simon traded work updates. Tim was hoping to be promoted from personnel manager to head of human resources. "It would mean travel, and more stress, but better benefits, obviously."

Ester would have wished Tim good luck, but Sara wouldn't stop talking about her gastric problems. "Everything runs through me. I've had tons of tests, but they found nothing. Which is great, of course, but you want answers."

As Sara prattled on, Ester regretted ordering the breakfast burrito with its oozing ingredients. She pushed her plate aside, wondering if she should have invited the group to her house for brunch. Blazers made the most sense, on a number of levels. Breakfast was included with the hotel stay, for one, and it was convenient and more practical to eat here rather than trying to entertain this large number at hers, but it didn't seem intimate enough, especially under the circumstances. She suspected the arrangement suited Tim and Rod just fine, and that they were as eager as she was to make this brunch and their farewells go as smoothly and quickly as possible.

Tommie and Ronnie rolled toy cars over the white tablecloth, their small mouths issuing loud engine sounds, and their spittle and tiny vehicles flying. Ronnie's car wheels caught in the tablecloth and the bunched fabric dragged his water glass.

"Careful!" Sara said, catching the glass before it spilled.

The cars crashed in a premeditated head-on collision, the boys making furious ramming, revving, and crunching sounds. Tara sat next to her brothers, serenely ripping off and reattaching Barbie's blond head. Kevin and Jason watched their cousins, looking a mix of amused and horrified. The five children, flesh and blood, hardly knew each other. Ester eyed Simon, concerned the crashing cars and mutilated doll were affecting him. He appeared oblivious.

Michelle mentioned coaching her oldest daughter's school basketball team. "Good for you," Ester said. The conversation morphed to Kevin's soccer successes. No one asked Ester anything about herself.

"Are you into sports?" Rod asked Jason.

"Not really. That's Kevin's thing."

"What's your thing? Kevin mentioned gaming," Rod said.

"Yeah, I'm big into it. I'm also about to start working Saturdays at the local pet store." Jason told Rod about the birds, and Dutch.

"Nice. My first Saturday job was mowing the neighbors' lawns, and not with any fancy motorized machine," Rod said. "I had to use Dad's manual lawnmower, a clunker of a metal beast that I pushed and dragged over and over again until I hated every blade of grass ever. That summer, my biceps turned thicker than my thighs."

The laughter quieted, and the conversation lulled.

Maria reappeared and started clearing the table.

Tim wiped his mouth with his napkin. "I guess it's about that time."

"It's a pity your flights are so soon, you could have come over to ours for a bit," Ester said, meaning and not meaning it.

Her brothers and their wives issued reassurances. "You've got enough going on. Next time."

Tim, Rod, and Simon removed money from their wallets for the tip. Ester excused herself.

Inside the restroom, she touched her brow to the cool wall tiles, consoling herself that Dad was released from his particular prison, and she was free from ever having to visit Golden Leaves again. Her relief evaporated as quickly as breath on glass.

"Why did you both stay behind in Billings? Why didn't you move with Dad and me?" The bathroom's acoustics made her voice sound deeper, almost serrated. She'd never said as much out straight to her brothers but had sometimes skirted the issue.

Rod once said, "Dad never asked us right."

Tim said, "Our whole lives were in Billings."

So was hers.

Moments after Ester returned to the table, Allie appeared at its head and addressed the group. "How was everything?"

"Everything was great, thank you," Simon said. The adults issued a chorus of thanks and praise. Ester remained mute.

Allie wished Tim, Rod, and their families safe travels. "I hope we meet again under happier circumstances."

"I hope so too," Ester said. The pointed admission made her feel faint with fright, but it was also liberating. Allie's smile faltered. Tim threw Ester a perplexed look, like yet again she wasn't playing her part right.

Maria materialized and set about refilling the water glasses. "That's okay, thanks. We're good," Simon said.

"Are we?" Ester rasped.

The adults' keen attention returned to her. Simon stood up and touched her elbow. "Come on, hon. It's time to go."

Outside, Ester hugged her nephews and Tara goodbye. She also hugged Rod, Michelle, and Sara. She and Tim shared a handshake. She, Simon, and the boys stood waving both families off as their cars cruised forward. Later, with a fresh wave of regret, Ester would find out that Tim had slipped Kevin and Jason twenty dollars each. Every visit with her brothers and their families, she was left wishing that it had gone better. That they'd each tried harder.

Simon wrapped his arm around her shoulders. "Let's get you home."

"Yes, let's get me home," she said, slipping out of his hold.

Inside the car he said, "I know that was hard for you." She looked through the passenger window.

"Why don't we ever go to Montana?" Kevin said from the back seat.

"Your uncles never asked us right," she said, echoing Rod.

"Why do you need to be asked? Isn't that where you're from?" Kevin said.

"She doesn't want to talk about it," Jason said, surprising her.

"Shut it," Kevin said in a high-pitched mimic of his brother from earlier.

"I'll make you shut it," Jason said.

"Cut it out," Simon said.

"I'd like to go see your hometown sometime," Kevin said.

"Maybe," Ester said.

"Gaming's my home," Jason said.

"You're such an idiot," Kevin said.

Ester spotted a black garbage bag dumped on the shoulder, its contents spilling over the asphalt. "Stop!"

"What is it?" Simon said, hitting the brakes.

He and the boys followed her out of the car. The four stood over the fat bag and its spread of litter. "Who does this?" Ester said.

"This is why we stopped? You could have gotten us into an accident," Simon said, turning back for the car.

"Let's clean it up," she said.

"It's not our problem," Simon said.

"Yeah," Jason said.

"Just leave it, Mom," Kevin said.

Ester doubled at the waist, gingerly gathering the loose garbage with her bare hands and returning it to the refuse bag—damp crumpled paper, sticky food wrappers, dirty coffee cups, and sachets of tomato ketchup.

"What are you at?" Simon said, wound up.

She tied the refilled bag and hauled it into her arms, struggling to bear its weight. Simon rushed to her aid. "What do you think you're doing?"

"We're taking it home," Ester said.

After a short protest, Simon and the boys surrendered and the four performed a clumsy dance together, carrying the bag of garbage to the car, and placing it inside the trunk.

At home, the four carried the garbage bag from the car and around the side of the house. On the count of three, they tossed it into the black garbage bin. Ester and Simon could have managed without the boys, but by then Kevin and Jason seemed to want to be a part of the cleanup.

"What were you thinking?" Simon said, wiping his hands on his chest. "Braking like that, you could have gotten us rear-ended if not worse."

"I'm sorry." Ester got why that would be upsetting for him, even if maybe he didn't connect it for himself.

She told Jason that she'd heard him in the car saying gaming was his home. "I get it, I do, but there are better ways to find that feeling."

"Like what?"

She took so long to answer, he'd already entered the house. "Like in people. In yourself," she said to no one.

Who's There?

Jason arrived home from his third Saturday working at the pet store and deposited a brown paper bag on the kitchen counter. "Check it out."

"What's this?" Ester dried her hands on a tea towel and reached for the bag, pleased it was paper and not plastic, and half afraid he'd brought home an animal. She saw a flash of a coiled, hissing snake. She removed the plastic case, titled *NBA Jam*.

"Thaddeus had it lying around his house. It's for two players."

She pressed the video game to her chest, beaming.

"Don't make it weird."

"Last one to your room gets the crappy chair." She dashed for the door.

"I didn't mean right now."

"Ester Prynn for the prime chair and the win," she said, taking the stairs two steps at a time. He charged after her.

In his bedroom, she claimed his swivel chair. He pulled the second chair from the corner, grumbling. It took him only moments to set up the basketball game on his desktop. She had to pin her butt to the seat to stop herself from getting up and closing his closet and the dresser drawers. Had to clamp her mouth shut to stop herself from ordering him to gather up his dirty laundry and bus the herd of dusty glasses dotted about. So his room was a mess. It wasn't worth getting upset about and ruining this chance with him.

He flipped a quarter to determine who would get their first choice of the teams. Ester relived her flipping the quarter inside the store right as the gunman burst in.

Her call, tails, showed up on the back of Jason's hand. She recovered and selected the Warriors, playing as Steph Curry. Jason selected the Lakers, playing as LeBron James.

"This game can't be that old, and yet the graphics look so dated," she said.

"Game software ages fast. Why do you think Thaddeus gave it away?"

"You can't tell your dad about this. He'd hog it."

Jason chuckled. "He's such a wannabe."

It hit Ester that she was the wannabe, and one at a major crossroads. Following the brunch with her brothers and in-laws, Allie had checked in with her, concerned. Embarrassed, and her thoughts full of Simon and Marjorie, Ester had assured Allie that she was fine. Ever since, Allie had kept her distance, and she and Marjorie, "Marj," appeared to be inseparable. Meanwhile, Ester was growing more restless and confused and discontent.

"Is this seriously the best you can do?" Jason raced up the court and dunked yet another basket. She threw herself into the game.

The first quarter ended 26-10 for the Lakers, with Jason scoring the final basket on the rebound. Ester, her competitive streak in full swing, wasn't sure she'd ever felt this much tension and enjoyment simultaneously. The front doorbell rang. It was likely a delivery. The driver would drop and go. She chased LeBron up and down the court uselessly. The doorbell rang a second time.

"Are you expecting anybody?" she asked.

Jason shrugged, his avatar dribbling the ball down the court.

Peeved by the interruption, she reluctantly moved to the top of the stairs and peered at the front door. The two women's lumpy silhouettes in the door's glass looked familiar. The woman on the left, her pillbox hat, gave them away. A hat the color of eggplant, Ester recalled, with a gold angel pin.

It was the Jehovah's Witnesses on her doorstep. Simon liked to talk to them, asking how, if there was a God, He could keep letting catastrophic things happen the world over? Ester heard the question he was really asking. How could God let his mom die like that, and later his dad? Or maybe she was hearing herself in those questions. These same two matronly women reappeared sporadically, asking for Simon and armed with parables they hoped would satisfy and convert him and the entire family. The mailslot creaked open, a booklet dropped to the floor, and the metal flap clanged closed. The women about-turned.

Ester returned to Jason's bedroom, relieved to find him willing to resume their game.

"We sold Dutch today," he said, scoring a three-point hoop.

She hesitated, wary of saying the wrong thing. "How was that?"

"It's the goal, getting them a good home. Hildy Hampton bought him. I think it was mostly because of the wild way he dances."

Ester pictured Hildy freeing Dutch from his cage, and her reveling in the bird dancing on her arm, like an extension of herself. "You should see if you can join her whenever she lets Dutch out for a free flight."

"A free flight?"

"Yeah, like over the woods or wherever. She'll want him to fly far and wide."

"Won't he fly away?"

"Hildy will train him to come back. That's what those birds do."

He nodded, seeming impressed.

Almost halftime, the score was 48-14 for the Lakers. The whistle blew as Jason's ball sailed through the air and scored a two-point basket. She wished it was the police who'd appeared on her front step, with news of the gunman's capture and disciplinary action against Sergeant Halloran. She worried she should have gone down and answered the door. Maybe the two faith-filled women would have said something timely, enlightening. She imagined it was the gunman on her doorstep, back to finish what he'd started, in a wolf's mask. He would pick up where he'd left off, first planting a rough, plastic kiss on her mashed mouth and then—

"Are you playing or not?" Jason said.

"Sorry."

Jason continued to outmatch her throughout the third and fourth quarters, winning the game for the Lakers 82-23.

"That was fun," she said, overheated and breathless. It was a workout—shouting, bucking in her chair, and working the controller hard and fast. She almost thought to tell Dad about this happy development on her next visit to Golden Leaves.

"Try winning, that's really fun," Jason said.

"Okay, that's it. You're going to eat those words." She straightened in her chair and gripped her controller like it had magical powers.

"Haven't you got something else to do? Or somewhere to be?"

She sniffed the air. "I smell weakness."

"You know I'm unbeatable," he said, setting up a new game.

He proceeded to also annihilate her in the first, second, third, and fourth quarters of the second game. Throughout, she was a continent of content. It was far from ideal, her drawing Jason further into gaming when the ultimate goal was to wean him off it, but the game was benign and this was the most fun they'd enjoyed together in a long time. It was the most wholesome fun she'd had in a long time, period. Aside from the choir. She looked forward to every second Tuesday more and more now, and she wasn't the only one. Most choir members had taken to arriving at the school gym early and staying late, talking and laughing together, encouraging and inspiring one another and, if need be, consoling one another.

"We're raising the vibration for ourselves and for everyone else out there," Monica said, gesturing toward the gym doors. "We all benefit."

At the last choir meeting, Lucy Neville admitted to the group that she didn't think she could bear another day of watching her husband drown himself in whiskey. A raw, moving discussion followed, with several others also sharing their pain and struggles, and many more members offering advice and resources and support. It would never cease to amaze Ester the deep, dark things we can tell acquaintances, strangers even, but can't say to our loved ones. Throughout, Crystal picked at the scar on her forehead.

"Boom!" Jason said, throwing himself back on his chair in triumph. The cartoon Lakers fans inside the desktop clapped and roared, their loudness drowned out by the whoosh of tinnitus in Ester's ears as the cartoon Superman on the front of the gunman's tote bag flew at her. On-screen, the Lakers hugged and smacked each other's backs. The Warriors congratulated the winners and walked off the court, hanging their heads. The game credits scrolled, and the screen turned black. Ester's reflection stared out from the desktop's dark rectangle. She blinked, dispelling the image of herself back inside the giraffe mask.

She knew not to push her luck and ask Jason to play another game. Her thoughts returned to the Jehovah's Witnesses at her front door and morphed into the scene from that British romantic comedy. The one where the guy shows up at the front door of his best friend's newlywedded wife with a boombox and handwritten signs, declaring his love, a love he knows will never be requited. Ester imagined Allie at her front door, also with signs.

"Seriously, you need help," Jason said.

It took her a second to realize he was talking about her terrible game skills. She forced a big smile. "It was my first time. Wait until I've got more practice in."

"It would take a miracle."

"You and Kevin, you're my miracles."

"And just like that, you had to go and ruin it."

She laughed. "How about spaghetti and meatballs for dinner?" Simon wouldn't be happy, meatballs gave him indigestion. The pickings in the kitchen were slim though, and she hadn't the energy to go grocery shopping.

"I thought you said you weren't up for cooking tonight?"

"I did," she said, also falling back into her chair. She was so tired it felt like her spine had folded in on itself.

"So order takeout," he said, suddenly the logician.

She supposed he felt sorry for her, over Dad. Although she thought she was bearing her grief well. For the most part. Maybe his burst of thoughtfulness—the NBA game, the takeout suggestion—was a thank-you for her getting him the job at the pet store. Or maybe his efforts were because of the other day, when he threw a textbook at Kevin's head and Simon told him to have a long, hard think about the man he was shaping up to be. It hardly mattered what had brought on his turnaround. It only mattered that this was the first time in she couldn't remember how long when they'd sat together for this length of time, ribbing each other and laughing.

It was that evening that she texted Allie and asked to meet with her at the wine bar where she'd seen the catalog couple who seemed wholly put together. But when she arrived she couldn't bring herself to go in—what if they were spotted?—and Allie had joined her in the minivan. Again. It was then that Allie recited Ester's eulogy for her dad almost word for word. It was during the height of Ester craving that feeling she'd experienced earlier with Jason—the ecstatic headiness of connection after many misses—that she and Allie kissed for the second time. It was like getting to taste one of those stars twinkling above them.

Wrecking Ball

From her earliest memories, Ester had told herself stories. They mostly worked to soothe her, like how the dark is fun and not frightening, the place where dreams happen. Her brothers also told her stories, back when the three siblings lived together in Billings. The worst of their stories was the one about the bogeyman. How he has a tail that he wraps around his child victim's neck. Once he traps his prey in his tail noose, he whispers into their young ears, his tongue flicking their fleshy lobes. He tells each child in long, great detail how his tail is going to cinch their neck—tight, tighter, tightest—cutting off the air in their windpipe and forcing their lungs to empty. They will die slowly, silently. Utterly.

As Ester grew older, some of the stories she told herself also punished. Like how Mom's death, and later Marcus's, were her fault. Over coffee, inside her kitchen, she narrated a new story to herself. One about Simon and her, four years into the future, when Jason had also left for college and they were back to living alone together and nearing fifty years of age—a couple for almost a quarter of a century. In this narrative, she has no exit strategy or unsettling desires. Instead, she and Simon recommit to each other and rediscover the love that brought them together in the first place. Their marriage not only survives but thrives, their best years lying in wait. Of all the stories, that one felt most like fiction.

Her phone pinged. A text from Lily. *My shift ended 15 mins ago & Crystal is still a no show. I texted & phoned her. Got zip.*

Ester texted Crystal and likewise didn't receive a reply. She tried phoning, similarly getting nothing. She responded to Lily. *I cant get ahold of her either. Its my day off. Ill swing by her place. See whats up.* She grabbed her purse and jacket and hurried from the house. Crystal had spiraled since the gunman's last attack, despite the small solace in Mr. Jordan's return home after the hospital. Meanwhile Ms. Wolas remained in the rehab facility.

On the drive over, Ester continued to phone Crystal, but the calls kept going to voicemail. She told herself everything was fine. Crystal had probably taken a nap before work and slept through her alarm. Or she'd forgotten to set an alarm. Or she'd gotten delayed at one of her sporadic cleaning or childcare jobs. Ester dismissed thoughts of another asthma attack. Of Crystal not getting to her inhaler.

Crystal didn't answer her front door. Ester tried phoning her again, and again Crystal didn't pick up. She rang the doorbell repeatedly, then rapped the front door with her knuckles and banged it with the side of her fist. She called out to Crystal, and peered through the large front window veiled in a once-white curtain. She scanned the two upstairs windows, also draped in discolored white and also revealing nothing.

Ester walked along the side of the house, which was flanked by a tall row of weeds crowned with yellow flowers. The rusty latch on the side entrance squeaked when she lifted it, and the wooden gate stuck when she tried to enter. She pushed her shoulder to the gate until it gave way and continued around the back of the house, sending crows shooting from the roof.

She tried the back door, finding it locked. She moved to the dirty, naked window next to the door, beyond which Crystal sat slumped over her kitchen table next to an empty brandy bottle. Ester's relief was overtaken by anger, and then alarm. Maybe Crystal was more than passed out drunk. Ester returned to the back door, retrying the handle, hoping it might miraculously open this time around. Unsuccessful, she rushed back to the window and banged on the glass, calling to Crystal, who remained unresponsive.

Ester should call 911, but there was no way Crystal could afford an ambulance and ER visit on her own dime. She was already buried in workman's comp paperwork and bureaucracy, trying to get them to pay her unconscionable medical expenses following the gunman's assault. Plus there were so many bizarre and terrifying stories in the news lately about people getting arrested for the craziest things. Ester didn't dare risk getting Crystal, a single mom, into trouble for drinking herself unconscious and missing her work shift. Most likely that's all this was. Crystal was passed out drunk, not having a medical emergency.

Ester tried shouldering the back door open and kicked it as hard as she could several times, but it wouldn't budge. She did succeed in hurting herself, her right ankle and collarbone smarting with pain. She phoned Simon.

"You can't take that kind of chance, you've got to call an ambulance," he said.

It was the right advice, but she couldn't bring herself to follow it. Not just yet. She banged on the window with both hands, rattling the glass and shouting Crystal's name. Crystal remained as still as death. Ester raced to the small back garden, looking for a rock, anything, to break the window. She found baked earth, burnt grass, and more weeds flowered in yellow. She was turning back to the house when she spotted the football in the far corner. She jogged to the ball and scooped it up, considering whether she could kick it hard enough to smash the windowpane. Hitting on a better idea, she removed her jacket, wrapped its body around the oval ball, and gathered its sleeves and tail in both hands. She stood to the side of the window and swung the makeshift wrecking ball with all her might. To her shock, the window didn't give. She was aiming for the glass a second time when the kitchen door opened and Britt entered the room, trailed by Crystal's two younger children. Ester's arms fell, and the padded ball slapped the front of her legs. The three children, fresh from school, stared at their unconscious mother.

Britt opened the back door. Ester rushed to Crystal. Britt ordered Jim and Julie to go watch TV in the other room. The two remained rooted in place.

"Go on, get, Mom's fine," Britt said, their voice raised. Jim and Julie scurried out.

Ester placed her hand on Crystal's back, relieved to feel its warm rise and fall. "Crystal? Can you hear me? You need to wake up."

Britt shook Crystal's shoulder hard. "Wake up, Mom! Come on, you need to go to bed."

Crystal groaned, and her right shoulder rolled backward, revealing her damp, swollen face in profile. Britt pulled on Crystal's arm, trying to get her on her feet, but Crystal was a dead weight. Ester grabbed Crystal's other arm, hoping to heave her to standing, but she and Britt weren't strong enough, and Crystal dropped back onto the chair. Britt moved to the sink, filled a mug with water, and poured its contents over Crystal's head. Crystal reared upright, gasping and spluttering.

"That worked," Ester said. She and Britt went at Crystal again, hooking her arms around their necks and hauling her out of the chair, across the kitchen, and up the stairs. Ester's injured ankle and collarbone screamed. Jim and Julie watched big-eyed from the living room doorway as the messy, loud procession made its way to the top of the house.

"Your mom's fine. She just needs a good sleep," Ester told them, struggling to half carry, half drag Crystal up the final steps to the landing.

She and Britt put Crystal to bed fully dressed, aside from her sneakers. Ester rolled her friend onto her side at the edge of the bed, both to lessen the cleanup if she was sick and for fear she would choke on her own vomit. Crystal's wet hair was plastered to her head, revealing her gray roots and receding hairline, her pink scar from the whack of the gun. She looked so much older, and achingly fragile.

Downstairs, Britt promised Jim and Julie a snack, and in a short while dinner. Ester followed Britt into the kitchen. Britt washed and sliced two red apples, refusing to let Ester help, and served Jim and Julie the fruit with a dollop of peanut butter. "If you behave, you can have ice cream after dinner."

Back in the kitchen, Ester asked Britt how often something like this happened. "That's the first time," Britt said, refusing to look at Ester.

"You can tell me the truth. I want to help."

"I better bring Mom up some water." Britt moved to the sink and filled a glass.

Ester cleared the dirty glass and empty bottle of brandy from the table. The alcohol fumes alone, they were tiny bites.

"You don't have to stay. I've got this," Britt said, water dripping from the full glass in their hand.

"You don't have to go it alone," Ester said. Britt carried the water to the door. "What are you going to do for dinner?"

"Probably pasta or frozen pizza. I'll let the kids decide." Britt, at all of twelve, didn't seem to think they were also a child.

"Would you like me to make something?"

"No, thanks. You should go."

"Wait," Ester said, stopping Britt short. "I'm leaving my phone number on the table, you can call me anytime, day or night. I mean that. Your mom's going to be okay, you know that, don't you? You all are." She hoped Britt might turn around, but they kept their back to her and continued out.

Ester hesitated in the kitchen, voices carrying from the TV in the living room and Britt's footsteps sounding on the stairs. She decided there wasn't much more she could do, not until Crystal sobered up, and not when Britt wanted her gone. She entered the living room and said goodbye to Jim and Julie. They responded half-heartedly, engrossed in the TV. From the bottom of the stairs, she called up to Britt, asking them to please phone her later. "Let me know how you're getting on."

Outside, she texted Lily, saying Crystal was home sick. She and Lily exchanged a flurry of texts, which ended in Ester reluctantly agreeing to work at the store for an hour to allow Lily to go home, take a shower, and eat dinner before returning to finish the unexpected double shift.

For the entire hour at the store, Ester worried Rich would spot her through the security cameras or arrive in person and catch her behind the counter. She could picture his furious response to finding her in her old post, and it didn't bear contemplation. She watched Es and Gish float and flit inside the yellow-lighted aquarium, their flickering choreography slowing her heart rate some. The odd time the bell above the entrance rang out, she looked over with a fresh rush of dread, half expecting to see Rich coming for her, or the masked gunman, or the bogeyman with his forked tail curled in a noose.

Déjà Vu

The night out was Ester's idea, an attempt to do over the happenings at Maxx's. For this go-around she decided on Kehoe's, a dive Irish bar on the outskirts of town with an energetic jukebox and spirited atmosphere. Beyond summoning the original group—Rachel, Donna, Lily, and Crystal—Ester also invited Allie and Marjorie, confident their vibrant presence would loosen the group's mood. Anything to diffuse tensions between Rachel and Crystal and Lily. Ester told herself she had no ulterior motive, even as she couldn't stop reliving her and Allie's last kiss. Now here they all were, sitting around the same table, where Allie was a magnet and Ester metal.

Ester scanned the appetizer menu, the artichoke croquettes and tempura green beans tugging. Her composure belied how the fraught scene at Maxx's insisted on replaying in her head, right up to the moment Rachel stormed off, the front of her dress stained with the spilled cocktails. She couldn't shake the sight of Crystal passed out at her kitchen table either, after which she'd pleaded with her to join AA, but Crystal refused to acknowledge she had a problem. "I overdid it, that's all. It won't happen again."

"I didn't get the impression that was your first blackout," Ester said.

"What did Britt say? They'd no business saying anything."

"They didn't say anything. They didn't have to," Ester said.

"I'm handling it, okay?"

Ester hadn't broached the subject again until she decided on this replay of Maxx's, and Crystal had insisted it wouldn't be too much too soon. "I won't even drink."

The mental reel jumped to the last choir meeting, when Ester had invited Allie and Marjorie to Kehoe's, her face burning so badly it felt like she'd left a chemical peel on for too long. Allie had hesitated, clearly uncomfortable, but Marjorie readily agreed. Ester didn't blame Allie. She knew she kept turning hot and cold.

Their server appeared, asking in a lilting brogue what they'd like to drink. Lily worked her charms on the young brunette, uncovering that Roisín was a recent arrival from the west coast of Ireland.

"How'd you get all the way from Galway to Half Moon Bay?" Ester said.

"An airplane, I hope," Lily said, drawing laughter. Ester noted with relief that Rachel was part of the chorus.

It came to Crystal's turn to order, and she asked for a brandy soda. "Easy on the soda."

Ester's jaw pulsed. While the conversation swirled around the table, she oscillated between chastising herself—she shouldn't have picked a bar for the occasion—and leaning into optimism. Maybe Crystal could control her drinking and her manners. So far it didn't seem like she and Rachel had spoken to each other. At least that meant they hadn't antagonized each other. Not yet anyway.

Crystal chirped to Lily about the impending demise of the US Postal Service. "Who mails anything anymore?"

"It'll get to the point where our entire lives are online," Lily said.

"Seriously," Rachel said, with feeling. She and Lily ruminated on a not-too-distant future where we'd never need to leave our homes and robots would be more visible out in the world than humans. Their chattiness softened Ester's misgivings about the night out being a mistake.

Allie was deep in conversation with Marjorie and Donna. Ester caught snippets of Allie saying she loved to fly and used to be an avid hang glider. Marjorie spoke of her fear of heights. Donna lamented how we lose our equilibrium as we get older. In her youth she'd craved roller coaster rides, the bigger and more death-defying the better, but now she couldn't tolerate as much as a spin in a revolving door. Allie and Marjorie laughed hard. Ester wanted to join the lively conversation but was stuck in her seat down the other end of the table.

"What's up?" Lily said next to her.

"Nothing. It's all good," Ester said.

Roisín returned with their drinks. "Keep coming back to check on us, you hear?" Lily said, winking.

Roisín laughed. "I will for sure."

She moved off, and Crystal leaned toward Lily. "Okay, I have to ask."

"This is going to be good," Lily said.

"I'm curious, so you're a lesbian—"

"Honey, I'm a little bit of everything."

The group laughed loudly. Ester glanced at Rachel, who still appeared to be in a high mood.

"I was wondering if, before you transitioned, you liked women then too?" Crystal said.

Lily turned thoughtful. "I did like women, but I liked men more, and I thought once I transitioned I would finally get to be with men, fully I mean, but it turns out now I'm totally interested in women."

"Well mostly," she added, drawing more laughter. "Really though," she continued. "Don't you think most of us are on a spectrum, and we could go any which way depending on attraction and connection. If it weren't for centuries of persecution, that is." Her gaze landed on Rachel.

Rachel visibly tensed, making Ester's insides also tighten. "I've never thought about things like that before. Growing up, we weren't allowed to."

"And now?" Lily said.

Rachel nodded, a concession. "I'm learning."

"Maybe I should turn to women. I keep striking out with men," Crystal said.

Lily shrugged. "Honey, if you're feeling the call . . ."

Allie raised her glass. "Here's to being and loving whomever we want."

Ester looked straight at her. "I'll drink to that."

"Me too," Marjorie said, with maybe an edge.

"Cheers," the group chorused, Rachel's enthusiasm almost matching everyone else's. They drank in unison.

"This song is tragic. Belt up, everyone, I'm going to go fix the music." Lily slung the strap of her gold glittered purse onto her shoulder and struggled up from the table. The group cheered and applauded.

"I'll help." Crystal hurried after Lily, the last of her drink in hand.

Marjorie signaled to Ester to move into the chair Crystal had vacated. "Come on over."

Ester rushed to oblige, landing next to Allie.

"Did you hear Bob's news?" Allie said.

"No, what?" Ester said, painfully aware of how attractive Allie was. Her eyes, her mouth, were mazes that Ester didn't ever want to find her way out of.

"I don't think it's confidential, but maybe I shouldn't say anything just yet," Allie said.

"You can't stop now," Marjorie said.

"I guess it's no big deal. Bob's going after the manager position at Horizons, and if he gets it . . ."

"His assistant manager position will be up for grabs." Ester's mood soared. If she got the promotion it would mean a raise and an advancement to add to her résumé.

"You should totally apply," Rachel said.

"Absolutely, and maybe I'll go after your hostess job," Donna said.

Ester rolled her eyes playfully. How many times had Donna threatened to quit social work, and when was she ever going to do it? Never, that's when.

A song with "twerk" in the chorus blasted from the jukebox. On the small dance floor, Lily and Crystal started shrieking and shaking their asses, the first drink already casting its spell. Several customers erupted in guffaws and applause. Marjorie placed her thumb and first finger in her mouth and whistled with impressive force.

Ester asked Allie, "If I did get promoted, could we consider Crystal for my hostess job?" It would be the break Crystal needed, financially and beyond.

"I don't see why not," Allie said.

"There is one thing. She has a police record, for shoplifting, but it's from a lifetime ago."

"Hmmm, not ideal, but I'm pretty sure we can get past that, especially on your recommendation."

"Thanks so much. I'm going to let her know, she'll be thrilled."

"I'm not guaranteeing anything—"

"No, of course not. I'll make sure she understands that."

"And tell her to keep it to herself for now."

"Will do. I'll be right back." Ester sprang from her chair.

She filled Crystal in, negotiating the need to raise her voice above the music against the need to be discreet. "It's a lot of ifs, but hopefully."

"That's awesome, thank you. Let's celebrate!" Crystal grabbed Ester's wrist and started for the bar.

Ester pulled her arm free. "I'm still on my first drink."

"Slowpoke." Crystal doubled back and grabbed Lily's hand. "Come on, at least you can keep up."

"My queen commands," Lily said, following Crystal to the bar. Beyond them, Ester spotted Allie cutting through the crowded space. Ester dallied in place, torn.

She found Allie standing last in line outside the restroom. "Hey."

"This is a fun spot. Thanks for getting us all together," Allie said with only a hint of stiffness.

"Of course. Although I can't guarantee what the food's going to be like."

Allie moved up the shortening line. "Right. I don't think the Irish are known for their cuisine."

Ester laughed. "We can hope."

The line progressed and they moved into the restroom. "I'll keep you posted on the Bob business," Allie said, before entering the vacant stall.

"That'd be great, thanks."

A woman emerged unsteadily from the second stall, and Ester entered. Next to Ester, Allie flushed, and exited. When Ester reappeared from the stall, Allie and another woman stood washing their hands. Ester joined them, willing the woman to hurry up and leave.

She did.

Ester and Allie alone together in the restroom, it was the night in the Late Bar all over again, the scene of their first kiss. She stopped herself from saying "déjà vu."

Allie finished drying her hands and tossed the paper towel into the basket on the floor. "See you out there."

Ester watched Allie in the mirror, her heart a jackhammer. "Wait."

Allie faced her. Ester turned around and leaned back against the sink for support. "Do you think we could meet up? Just the two of us." She sad-smiled. "Someplace besides a restroom and my van."

"Why now? You've said nothing, given me nothing, since the last time we were alone together."

Ester wanted to admit that their second kiss had tasted of stars. That Allie reciting Ester's eulogy for her dad back to her, and with such exactness, was the kind of being heard and seen that Ester hadn't known she'd waited her whole life for. She said none of those things. She couldn't express either the tangle of her insides since that night, not only because of the oppositional feelings sweeping through her, but also her fear that she wouldn't ever have the courage to claim the exhilaration Allie caused her. And even if she did, it wouldn't matter. She had a lifelong pattern. She lost people.

The little she did manage to say, even that ripped through her chest. "Tonight's talk of being true to ourselves, that's why."

"You're seriously confusing, you know that?" Allie said.

"I know, I'm sorry, but this, us, it's undoing who I always thought I was, and everything I believed was my entire life."

The pain in Allie's face mirrored Ester's, but when she spoke, she sounded resolute. "You've been through a lot lately. I'm not sure exploring what may or may not be going on between us is really what you want right now, and I don't think you are either."

"I have been through a lot, and it's given me a sense of urgency. Life's too short, at least when you're doing it right. Meet me, please. Let's see where this leads."

Allie's teeth released the inside of her cheek. "Okay."

"Okay?" Ester was trembling.

"Text me."

Ester swore her smile touched her ears. "I will."

"Until then, then," Allie said, and slipped out.

Ester delayed in the restroom, to cool her telltale elation. When she recovered, she returned to her original seat at the table, catching up on an animated discussion of the best and worst makers of swimwear.

"This is the intel I need," Lily said.

Ester and Allie sneaked risky glances, Ester's insides doing gymnastics. She felt as trippy as she had after eating that piece of pot brownie outside the funeral home, and the desire she'd kept pushing down ever since meeting Allie surged to the surface, its hunger wonderfully, wickedly ferocious.

The Yellow Cottage

Simon entered the bedroom right as Ester was circling sleep. He sat on her edge of the mattress and handed her a sealed card, his expression mischievous. "Careful of your eyes," he said, turning on the bedside lamp.

She rolled onto her back, squinting against the yellowed glare and annoyed that he'd roused her. Her day shift at Blazers was chaotic, hordes drawn to Sunday brunch and its bottomless mimosas. At its height, the wait for tables was up to ninety minutes long, and she'd needed to placate the press of impatient customers, an absolute drain of her energy and goodwill. Meanwhile, Bob was nowhere to be found. She would do such a better job if, when, she was hired to replace him. At one point, a buzzing pager had brought her back to Golden Leaves and the sound of its secured front door unlocking. She saw the door opening and letting her in, showing her Dad's goneness.

"What's the occasion?" she said, yawning.

"You'll see," Simon said.

With a groan, she maneuvered herself to sitting and opened the envelope. The front of the *Especially For You* card was decorated with a bouquet of lilacs. When she opened the card, a folded sheet of paper dropped onto her middle.

"Read the card first," he said.

I'm whisking you away. You're overdue for a much-deserved break. All my love, Simon. She opened the quartered page. It was a typed, homemade gift certificate granting Simon and her a night together in a rental cottage in Sebastopol.

"Surprise. The boys are in on it too. They're going to take care of themselves for the next two days. We leave in the morning."

"What? I can't. I'm working tomorrow night."

"No, you're not. I texted Allie, and she gave you the night off. Your next shift isn't until Tuesday at five."

"Why would you do that? You can't just text my boss and ask to change my work schedule. That's so juvenile." She was meeting Allie on Tuesday night, at Allie's apartment. Her annoyance turned to confusion. Was she now down on the schedule for Tuesday for real, or had Allie lied to Simon to cover up their getting together?

"Hey, relax. Allie was totally cool about it."

"You had no right to contact her." She rushed the card and gift certificate back inside the envelope.

He reached for her bare shoulder. "Hey, come on, this is a good thing. I thought you'd be pleased."

Maybe months earlier she'd have appreciated his taking the initiative and doing something this thoughtful and necessary for her, but right now it felt ruinous. "I wish you'd talked to me first."

She slipped into the bathroom and texted Allie. *Sorry about Simon asking if I could take tomorrow night off. I had no idea what he was up to. I wanted to check. Am I really working Tuesday, or are we still meeting?* She hit Send, her breath held.

Those reply typing bubbles appeared on her phone screen and remained for several long moments. Allie's response finally came through. *Ur working Tuesday. It was the only night this week Bob could swap with u.*

Ester responded before she lost her nerve. *Ok. What other night suits you to meet?*

Allie also responded quickly. *Let's wait. See how ur getaway goes.*

Ester typed several rapid responses but deleted each of them. She would talk to Allie in person at work during their shift overlap on Tuesday and explain that her feelings hadn't, wouldn't, change. Their chemistry, Ester's infatuation, were undeniable.

She returned to bed. Simon was sitting on his side of the mattress, making it list to the right. He pulled off his shoes and stood up to remove his trousers. She willed him not to try for sex.

He climbed into bed in his underwear, still defending his decision to surprise her. "You need this."

"I need you to go about things right." Even through the haze of temper and disappointment she could hear the depths of her hypocrisy.

"You don't take my job, anything about me, seriously," she went on.

"Of course I do."

"That time I was let go from Solsavers, I saw the look on your face, like you expected as much, and you were the same when I quit the store."

He sat up on his elbow and peered down at her. "What are you talking about?"

"I can see right through you, you know."

"Clearly, you can't."

"Tell me that you don't expect me to screw up."

"What you maybe see is that I expect things to go wrong, that's nothing to do with you, that's life. And I see things too, just so you know."

She waited for him to say more, her body rigid. He did not.

The next morning Simon's car cruised toward Sebastopol, encountering little traffic. He serenaded Ester with a playlist he'd compiled especially for the occasion, songs ranging from Neil Diamond's "Sweet Caroline" to Sara Bareilles's "Armor."

"I'm impressed," Ester said, thawing.

"Kevin helped with the song choices. I think he might have also recruited Mena to assist."

"They have it bad for each other."

"So did we, remember?" He rested his hand on her thigh, something he'd done while driving since they first dated.

She remembered how popular he'd been back then. How he readily chatted and joked with his friends and acquaintances, everyone in his orbit. That's what she'd first found so attractive about him, beyond his good looks and solidness and causing her grievous belly laughs on the regular. Soon into dating him, she was most impressed by how he kept his word, right down to his punctuality, and opened up to her about his dead mom that one time, allowing her to do the same.

As mad as she was about him back then, she'd go so far as to say it was love at first sight, once she became pregnant and they got engaged she was never one hundred percent convinced they were meant for each other for life. Right up to the present day, she couldn't shake the feeling that they'd held out on each other this whole time. Hiding, distrusting maybe, she wasn't sure. She only knew that they had never offered each other their complete hearts, their full selves.

The rental cottage was more remote than the property listing had led Simon to believe, but they hit on it eventually. "All praise GPS," he said.

They cleared the property's long driveway, Ester silently admiring the fir trees and bumpy hills, the acres of green stretching out as far as the horizon. The yellow cottage was located at the back of the owner's matching yellow house, the distance between the two properties a mere couple of hundred feet. The cottage itself was almost as small as the area between the buildings and was in fact a one-room converted garage.

Ester tried to camouflage her disappointment. She'd already voiced enough criticism of this getaway, but the space was chilly, despite the sunshine beyond, and its leaf-themed decor was dated and kitschy.

A woman appeared in the open doorway, startling Ester. "Sorry, I didn't mean to sneak up on you. I'm your host, Sage."

Sage shook Simon's hand, and next Ester's, flashing yellowed teeth. She whipped her long silver hair off her shoulder and ran her hands down the front of the green caftan that fell to her ankles, like she was checking herself. "Do we have a special occasion?"

"Just getting some R & R," Simon said cheerfully.

"Excellent. There's an information sheet on the kitchen counter, some housekeeping notes about the heating, garbage, and the like, and recommendations for local hiking and dining. Do let me know if you need anything else." She ducked out and pulled the door closed.

Ester surveyed the cramped space, trying to make peace with the profusion of leaf patterns on every possible surface. "More foliage than Golden Gate Park."

Simon opened the fridge. "Hello. Things are looking up." He removed the chilled bottle of white wine and thick wedge of Gouda cheese.

Ester located the wine glasses and discovered more snacks in the cabinet over the short counter. She arranged the crackers on a plate and poured the roasted almonds into a bowl, wishing she'd thought to bring chocolate.

"Now we're talking," Simon said, pulling the cork from the wine bottle with a splendid popping sound.

They moved outside with the modest feast, into the small, colorful garden, and settled at the white plastic table. Aside from birdsong and the rustle of trees, the quiet was remarkable.

"It's so peaceful," she said.

"Just what the doctor ordered."

"Makes me realize how much our boys fight." She hoped Jason was at school and not gaming at home.

"I don't want you thinking about them. I don't want you thinking about anything but here and now. I carried you off for a reason, remember?"

"Sounds very medieval."

"I was thinking less knight and more dashing superhero."

She looked into her glass of golden wine, suppressing thoughts of the Superman tote bag.

"I don't like to see you sad." His hand rubbed her thigh up and down.

She forced out the question, her skin prickly. "Is that what you meant last night, about you seeing stuff?"

"I'm not blind. You've been working really hard lately, on top of everything else that's happened—the holdups, your dad, seeing your brothers again. It's taken its toll."

"I'm fine, really." She drank deep from her glass, almost disappointed that he hadn't mentioned Allie. There was so much he never saw.

She was guilty of not seeing too. "What you said last night, about expecting things to go wrong, I didn't know you felt that way too, and I'm sorry. Life's not supposed to be like this."

"I think most people think that way."

"I'm not so sure."

He checked his phone. "I've no service. Unplugged, just how you like it," he said, slicing off a hunk of Gouda. He handed her the cheese on top of a cracker.

She accepted the offering, hoping for more real talk.

"Before we know it, both boys will be in college and we'll be able to do so much more of this," he said.

She pushed away thoughts of obstacles like money, and discontent, and Allie.

They finished the food and wine. She felt full and overheated from the sun. She was also a little buzzed. Her thoughts drifted to Crystal. She'd gotten drunk that night at Kehoe's, and Ester had needed to take her home and hold her hair back while she vomited and wailed into the toilet bowl—all within earshot of her three children.

"I wouldn't mind taking a nap before dinner," Simon said.

"Sounds good," she said.

They cleared the table and moved inside.

They stripped down to their skin and cuddled together in bed.

"We need to escape like this more often," he said.

"We can't afford to." She considered mentioning her possible promotion to assistant manager but decided to wait until, hopefully, it was official.

"Thankfully the best things in life are free," he said, rolling on top of her.

She felt numb while he worked on her, until she imagined it was Allie kissing her mouth, sucking her nipple, licking her navel.

"You're so wet," he said, ejaculating with a long groan.

Ester and Simon awoke in the thick dark. Neither could remember when they'd last slept so deeply. He switched on the bedside lamp and reached for his phone on the nightstand.

"What time is it?" she said.

"Ten after nine. We better hurry if we're going to get dinner."

"I'm still full from earlier."

"We can eat something light. It would be a shame to not go out. We've come all this way," he said.

"I know, but I'm so tired, and I'm really not hungry."

He threw off the blankets and stood up on the bed. "Get up here."

"What are you doing?" she said, bemused.

He grabbed her hands and pulled her to her feet. "Come on, this'll wake you up." He started jumping on the mattress, his head almost colliding with the ceiling.

She tried to pull free. "You're ridiculous."

"Simon says, Jump! Jump!"

She performed small, reluctant bounces.

"See! It's fun!" He looked delighted, and years younger, and handsome. It sparked in her again, that persistent hope that they were salvageable.

"I haven't done this since I was a kid," he said.

"I've never done this," she said.

"Never?"

"Never." She jumped harder, higher.

The next day, on the drive home, he would say with amused wonder, "I can't believe you never jumped on a bed before. What kind of a childhood did you have?"

She would laugh softly and look through the passenger window, past her watery reflection. For the ninety miles of road that followed, it would seem as if she and Simon had stopped still and everything outside was flying past them.

The Split

Ester and Simon arrived home to an empty house. In the kitchen, he gathered her into his arms and kissed her full on the mouth. "I love you."

She eased from his grip and moved to the sink. They didn't tell each other they loved each other very often. Not even in the beginning, when they were young and more full of feeling.

He moved behind her as she was filling a glass of water and wrapped his arms around her waist. "I want you to be happy."

"I want that for both of us," she said before drinking from the damp glass, her swallows loud.

"I am happy."

She faced him. "Are you?"

"As I'll ever be."

She moved to the island and lowered the glass of water.

"I could be happier. Who couldn't?" he said.

She was still formulating a reply when he spoke again. "I'll go get us some groceries. I fancy more Gouda. Do you want anything besides the usual?"

The usual. She wanted anything besides. He left while she was gripping the edge of the island, and in his wake she screamed. Her entire life, she'd never screamed. Not even during childbirth. She'd imagined that was virtuous. *Stupid. Stupid. Stupid.* She leaned over the countertop, screaming. She tipped back her head, screaming. She screamed until she couldn't. She dropped to the floor and pressed her back to the island's base, crying, laughing, her throat raw. She lifted her chin and dispatched another, lesser scream. It still felt like power. Like medicine.

Upstairs, she filled the bathtub and submerged herself in bubbly water, determined that this soak would be more relaxing and restorative than her last. She lathered herself in buttery French soap, rehearsing what she would say to Allie when she got to work. She would apologize again for Simon reaching out. She would say that she still wanted to meet. She would admit to the swell of feelings gathering inside her like a symphony building to crescendo.

She climbed out of the bathtub and took the rare time to cover her body in moisturizer, the fancy one with argan oil and orange blossom. The lotion was part of the gift set Simon had given her for her last birthday, and she was wearing it for Allie. The twinge of guilt didn't stop her from also putting on sexy lingerie—a matching purple lacy bra and boyfriend panties—and the black skirt suit with her ivory blouse that people always complimented. She teased and sprayed her hair into a high, sleek bun, and took so much care with her makeup it was like painting a self-portrait.

She stopped at the bottom of the stairs, taking in the silence, the stillness. She imagined this was her real life, living here alone in the calm. She was free and single, and on the verge of a new, thrilling relationship. It occurred to her that her jumping on the bed inside the yellow cottage had rearranged something inside her. She was different, more confident and clear-eyed. Or maybe it was her screams that had loosened the hinges on her former self and let out this new person.

Neither, she decided. Change was coming long before her screams, or that mattress turned trampoline and her pretending that she was a girl again, when Mom and Dad were still alive and

Marcus was a laughing boy. She said *asunder* and *a rendering* out loud, like she was testing their meaning, trying to get to the bottom of them. The holdup she realized with a shiver, and the crack to Crystal's head, that was what had first split Ester into someone else.

Inside Blazers, Ester scanned the bar and dining areas, searching for Allie. Sal waved from behind the bar, and Ester sang out hello. Bob, finished for the day, ignored her while beelining for the exit. "You have a fabulous night, Bob!" she said.

Inside the bathroom mirror, she thought she looked thinner and wasn't sure if it was a trick of the glass, or if the fractured, lighter incarnation of herself was actually visible. She'd never looked at her reflection this kindly, serenely. She kissed herself in the mirror, her eyes open, and stared a little longer before exiting. She turned back in the doorway and erased her lipstick from the glass.

On her way to the office, still in search of Allie, Alejandro appeared at her side. When he spoke, it was with a slight nervous stutter. "Can I ask f-f-favor, please?"

"Sure."

"I want to surprise propose to Jacinta and would like for choir to please do flash mob but with no dance, just sing. No need the whole choir, but as many as possible would be very nice."

"That's a beautiful idea, and congratulations. I'm so happy for you both."

"I only hope she say yes," he said laughing, but with a note of fear.

"Of course she will. When and where are you thinking?"

"Two weeks. Saturday, May 12 at six o'clock please. It's Jacinta's birthday and we're going to dinner, but first I propose at the harbor. I have perfect song, 'Hero' by the Enrique Iglesias!" His voice had climbed in tandem with his excitement.

Ester laughed, his high mood contagious. "Two weeks to pull off a new song, that's a tall order, but if anyone can do it, our choir can."

"Thank you, thank you." His face was a sphere of joy.

"It'll be a pleasure, and an honor," she said, mentally running through her calendar. Her schedule was about to get hectic with Jason's upcoming graduation and the many ceremonies and parties planned around the milestone for the entire eighth grade, but she would ensure it was all doable.

"Remember, please, top secret," Alejandro said.

"You have my word."

"Okay, I get back to work," he said, moving off.

She continued to the office, the knot in her stomach tightening. Like Alejandro, she was nervous-excited. She knocked on the closed office door and waited. She checked the time on her phone. Three minutes to five. She needed to take her place at the front of house. She knocked once more and opened the door to an empty office.

"Looking for someone?" Allie said from behind her.

Ester swung around, the sting of disappointment replaced by delight. "Hi there. I was hoping to catch you."

"Consider me caught," Allie said.

Ester dropped her voice. "I'm really sorry Simon asked you to change my work schedule, that was totally inappropriate."

"He wanted to surprise you. Clearly, he cares about you, a lot."

"I care about him too, a great deal, but not in that way."

"Which means what exactly?"

"I really want to see you, alone."

Allie's expression darkened. "This is messy and will only get messier, and we have to work together."

"It doesn't have to get messier. We can figure this out."

"There's also the power imbalance. I am your boss."

Ester's fingertips brushed Allie's. "I'd like to think I have some power over you too."

Allie rolled her eyes, fighting a small smile. "This is serious."

"You don't have to tell me that," Ester said, tears heating the back of her eyes.

"You're sure this time?"

"Yes, completely."

"How about Friday night, at seven? I'll cook dinner at my place," Allie said.

"Sounds great, if you're sure you're comfortable meeting at yours?"

"Of course. Why not?"

"You're not worried Marjorie might show up?"

"Ah, gotcha. Marj and I broke up. She had stronger feelings than I did, and I thought it best to end things sooner rather than later."

"Oh. Okay."

"What's that look?"

"No, no look."

"Definitely a look."

"I'd like to be honest with Simon too."

"The stakes are much higher for you, and we don't know where, or what, we are yet."

"That's true. Thank you for understanding that."

"We don't have to do this, you know."

"We do. I do, at least."

Allie's smile returned. "I was hoping you'd say that."

"I'll see you Friday, and I'll bring wine, and dessert."

"I look forward to it."

"Me too."

Ester headed for the hostess podium, her cloudlike insides seeming to defy gravity.

Lockdown

Thursday afternoon, Ester visited the hair salon for a color touchup. She and her stylist prattled about the heat wave, the climate crisis, and San Francisco one day winding up under the sea. Despite the apocalyptic conversation, Ester was thoroughly enjoying her second day off work in a row, nothing in her head but tomorrow night's dinner with Allie. She imagined Allie's apartment—neat, artsy, tasteful—and pictured Allie and her dancing together in the living room, slow and up close. Like in a movie. Like in a parallel universe.

Ester was working the day shift tomorrow until five and would pick up the wine and dessert on her way home. She would get dressed up and painted up and tell Simon and the boys she was going to a potluck at Allie's along with several others. These were the actions she could plan and contemplate with bearable spurts of fear and guilt. Fully stepping into her new self, however, and confessing that seismic shift to her family, and everyone else, was something she couldn't face. Not yet. She would, after Jason's graduation, or maybe she should wait until after he settled into high school.

Her thoughts returned to Allie and getting to kiss her again and do and say what had previously felt forbidden, impossible. She sat quivering, never having felt this kind of date delirium. An arrow shot straight for her, gold and scarlet-tipped, like the colors of the letter *A* that adulteress Hester Prynne was forced to wear on her chest at all times. She moved her goose-bumped arms beneath her salon cape, fending off thoughts of the consequences of her having been unfaithful to Marcus. The person she needed to be most faithful to now was herself. She would come clean with Simon, and the boys, soon enough.

An old Joni Mitchell song piped through the salon's surround sound, the one about a seagull. It brought back Chekhov's play, *The Seagull*, which Ester and Marcus had attended together on a college field trip. Students were supposed to sit with their respective classes inside the theater, but she'd sneaked into a seat next to Marcus, a giddy junior among seniors. She still had the theater ticket. Still remembered that the play was about characters loving the wrong person.

The stylist powered off the hairdryer, her eyelids smoky and her blue bob streaked in hot pink. "Do you want me to run the flatiron over it, or do you want to keep the volume?"

Ester appraised herself in the mirror and decided on the straight and sleek effects from the iron, an elevated look she could never quite pull off herself at home. She only hoped the style would hold until tomorrow evening. With each careful, steamy pull of the iron through her hair, Ester's eyelids turned heavier. Her bones melted. At the washbasin earlier, while her toner was developing, she'd drifted a little and taken a road trip to Billings, where her car cruised alongside the wild horses in the fields. Almost asleep, her driving had turned to cantering, to galloping, to her becoming the muscled, gray-dappled horse itself, thundering across the green plains below Pryor Mountain, everything before her vast and open.

Ester's phone pinged. She almost ignored the text, but the Pavlovian impulse won out. She read the message, horror falling over her like a second salon cape, and rushed to standing with a wounded sound.

"I have to go," she said, struggling out of the salon's scratchy black wrappings.

The stylist was talking, alarmed, concerned. Ester could only hear whooshing. She hurried to the coat closet, her eyes filling and everything blurring. She grabbed her jacket, returned the strap of her purse to her shoulder, and stabbed Simon's speed dial. She raced past the receptionist, mumbling about a family emergency and promising to pay later. She exited the salon, frantically trying to remember where she'd parked. Simon's phone went to voicemail. She dialed his number again, swearing, crying. Her phone's screen lit up with an incoming call from him.

"You got Principal Howe's text?" she said, breaking down.

"Yes. Where are you?" he said.

"I'm leaving the hair salon, I'm headed to the school."

"They said to stay away and wait for updates, so we don't add to the chaos."

"I'm going to the school," she said, thrumming with panic and sudden anger.

"I'll meet you there," he said. "Ester," he said right as she was hanging up.

She returned the phone to her ear. "Yeah?"

"Drive safe."

She climbed into the minivan and half blindly sped toward Jason's school, Principal Howe's text overlaid on the windshield. The school was on lockdown, an active shooter in the area. This would be the perfect day for Jason to have played truant. She hoped, her heart thumping, that he had, but knew in her gut that he hadn't. She phoned him via the car's speaker, even as she knew students' phones were confiscated every morning and not returned until after the final bell. Maybe on account of the lockdown . . .

Jason's phone went to voicemail. Ester, drawing a ragged breath, ordered her nerves and voice to steady. "Jason, it's me. I'm on my way to the school. So is Dad. We'll be there soon, you just hold tight until then. Everything's going to be okay. We love you. We'll see you in a few. Bye. Bye. Love you."

She hung up, already unsure of what she'd blathered. If she'd said the right things? If she should have said more? Less? If it might be the last message she ever left him.

"No!" she said aloud, her hands gripping the steering wheel tighter and her teeth locking so hard she thought of powdered enamel. Jason was going to be fine. Everyone at the school was.

Her chest contracted. Crystal had to be freaking out. All three of her children attended Centro. She phoned, and listened to the line bleat. She thought she was going to get voicemail, but Crystal picked up, sounding groggy. "Hey."

"You haven't heard?" Ester said.

"What?" Crystal said.

"Centro is on lockdown, there's an active shooter in the area. They're saying it's just a precaution but they're not letting students out until it's definitely safe to do so. I'm on my way there."

"I'm reading Howe's text now. It says to shtay way and let the police do their job."

"Where are you?" Ester said sharply.

"I'm at home. Where are you?"

"I told you, I'm driving to the school. I'm not going to just sit around."

"I'm going to follow the school's inshushions and wait here," Crystal said.

Ester pictured Crystal's shaky fingers worrying the scar at her hairline, the woman too drunk to show up for her kids in an emergency.

"Keep me posted, won't you?" Crystal said, asking for much more.

"Yeah, I will," Ester said as evenly as she could, and hung up.

Moments later, her phone rang again and the minivan filled with the caller ID saying Kevin's name. "Oh God," she said to the empty vehicle, her voice cracking. She swiped her tears with the side of her hand and tried to breathe normally. "Kevin, hey," she said, hearing the watery mix of tender, grim, fear, and falsity.

"You heard about the lockdown?" he said.

"Yeah, it's just a precaution. Jason, everyone at the school, they're all okay." She glanced at the dashboard clock. "Shouldn't you be in class?"

"I'm supposed to head in there now, it's business as usual here, but it doesn't feel right. They're saying the shooter is still active."

"I don't want you worrying, okay? The police will catch the shooter, if they haven't already. Every cop in the Bay Area will be after him."

"Are they saying anything about who he shot?"

Ester's head was a balloon adrift and floating upward. "They've said nothing yet. Go to class, sweetheart, and I'll text you as soon as I know more."

"Okay. Be sure to text me."

"I promise. Everything's going to be okay, all right? You and your brother will be back to tormenting each other by dinnertime."

He laughed tightly. "Love you."

"I love you too." She ended the call, her tears falling unchecked.

Blocks from the school, she was confronted by motorcycle officers standing guard in front of orange barriers and redirecting traffic. She circled the streets, trying to outsmart the police and their roadblocks, but she couldn't find an open route into the school. Her phone pinged incessantly, panicked texts from other school parents.

At the bottom of Dolores Street, she coasted up to the beefy officer winding his arm like a twirling baton, urging her to keep moving. She thrust her head out the driver's side window. "My son's a student in the school and he's . . . he's vulnerable. Can you please let me through?"

"I'm sorry, ma'am, I can't let anyone through," he said, one arm still stretched out and the other still going round.

"Please, I need to know he's all right." Behind her, an irate man shouted, and drivers honked their horns.

"I really am sorry, ma'am, there's nothing I can do, and you're not helping your son or anybody else by blocking up the area. We need to keep this traffic moving."

"Can you at least tell me if the shooter's been caught?"

"We've got every possible officer trying to do just that and this should all be over soon. Now, please, you've really got to move along."

"What about who he shot? Any update on them?" If she knew any of the victims, she didn't think she could take it.

"Ma'am I can't speak to that either, and don't make me have to ask you again to keep moving."

She peeled the car to the left, and turned the corner, a tsunami of panic and frustration engulfing her.

Simon phoned. He was also stonewalled by the road diversions. "What do you want to do?"

She spotted a small white church on her right, its doors open. "Meet me at the church on Reina and Castellan."

She parked and hurried back down the block, reading her phone. The latest message was from Crystal. *Any new?* Ester texted back, livid. Crystal couldn't even type that much coherently. *Nothing yet.*

Ester entered the empty church and walked up the red-carpeted center aisle, thinking with a sick feeling of her having wanted to escape to hideaway churches in Florence. She sank onto a front pew, taking in the altar, the stained glass windows, and the scatter of bibles over the bench seats. The church was maybe Methodist, or Lutheran. She dropped to her knees and prayed with a fervor she hadn't felt since Mom died, and later Marcus. She rested her forehead on her clasped hands, her knuckles hurting her brow. Within minutes, her kneecaps on the kneeler's thin padding also ached. As in her youth, she apologized to God for her sins, and asked them to show her, her loved ones, and every living being mercy. *Hurt me, punish me, if you must, but not Jason, not Kevin. Not now. Not ever. Please, God. Please. I'll stop whatever this is with Allie. I'll stay faithful to Simon and keep my family together if that's what it takes. Please.*

As if in response, Simon appeared. She pushed herself to standing, her knees and lower back protesting. She and Simon clung together.

"You heard the shooting victim died?" he said.

"No."

"She was pronounced dead at the scene."

"There's just that one casualty?"

He nodded. She heard herself. *Just one.* In the era of regular mass shootings, anything less than multiple victims brought relief, if not something close to apathy, especially when there were no children involved. Most Americans kept saying this is not who we are. Yet it is who we are. And worse.

She searched her phone, scanning the local news headlines. "That's all it says here too. One shot dead outside the bank on Purissima, and the shooter is still at large."

Simon dropped onto the pew.

"Do you think . . ."

"What?" he said, anguished.

"It has to be the same gunman, right? There can't suddenly be two in the area. Stuff like that doesn't happen here."

"Stuff like that happens all over now."

"Kevin is going to freak out when he hears. He checked in with me a short while ago and was trying to be strong, but he's scared."

"Yeah, he called me too."

Their phones pinged. Another text from Principal Howe reconfirming that everyone at the school was accounted for and safe. The school remained on lockdown while the police continued to search the area. Howe promised further updates as they became available and the release of their children as soon as possible. Ester felt another fleeting sense of relief followed by loathing and a return to panic. It was the masked gunman. She could feel it in her bones, her blood.

She and Simon alternated praying, checking their phones, fielding messages, and trying not to say or think the excruciating. Almost forty minutes passed. Ester had lived entire days that seemed shorter. Her heart marked every second with a too-loud tick.

Her phone rang. She answered, almost jumping out of her skin. "Jason!"

"We got let out. Can you come get me?" His voice held only a trace of a tremor.

"Yeah, of course. Dad and I are on our way. Are you okay?" she said, tilting the phone so Simon could hear.

"Yeah, fine," Jason said.

"They captured the shooter then?" Ester said.

"I guess not, but the police said the area is clear and we're free to leave."

"Okay, we'll see you in a few. You're in the back parking lot, yeah?" she said, racing after Simon up the aisle and out of the church.

Surrounded by fog, the long line of vehicles snaked over the final four blocks leading up to the school gates. Parents and guardians exited their cars and moved up and down the stalled traffic, checking in with each other, giving thanks, complaining about this latest maddening delay, and swapping whatever scant information they had on the escaped shooter and his murder victim. Ester checked her phone compulsively, but breaking news and social media failed to tell her anything more than what she already knew. Crystal phoned, crying and slurring, asking Ester to pick up her kids.

"Get yourself sober," Ester said as gently as she could. "Don't let them come home to you like this."

It took over twenty minutes for her and Simon to finally cross the school property line. Their car then crawled at a sloth's pace behind the procession of vehicles inching along the main driveway and toward the rear parking lot. Impatience licked like flames. They reminded each other that everyone here was safe and conceded that what could easily have devolved into crowd and traffic mayhem was being well controlled by faculty and volunteers. To that end, Principal Howe, teachers, and several elderly community members directed parents to their relative section of the yard, the space divided into nine designated areas for grades kindergarten through eighth. Everywhere, clusters of adults and students in barrels of hugs, the air trilling with the sounds of relief and rejoicing.

Ester spotted Jason and rushed from the car while it was still rolling. He allowed her to hug him, and she held onto him, jabbering and giving thanks, declaring love. Simon parked the car alongside them and hopped out. He and Jason hugged. Ester wiped her wet face with her hands, overcome by Simon and Jason holding each other up, and by the rapidly multiplying emotional reunions happening throughout the schoolyard. Her thoughts tumbled and throat thickened, mindful of the school families and beyond who didn't get this ending with their loved ones and precious children.

She panned to the sixth-grade meeting spot, finding Britt standing off to the side, holding Jim and Julie by the hand. Britt's anxious gaze searched the yard, like they were looking through a coin-operated viewfinder with the time running out and no money left.

Ester hurried over and hugged the three siblings. "Your mom sent me. I'm taking you home."

Once upon a Time

Ester arrived at Kehoe's before Allie, her heartbeat tripping over itself. She sat at a high-top table for two, close enough to the entrance to be visible without being too obvious and a healthy distance from the jukebox's blare.

"Hiya, welcome back," the Irish server said in her cheerful brogue.

"Hey," Ester said, trying to remember the server's name. "Can I get a Maker's neat, please?" She didn't drink bourbon, if Maker's was bourbon. Maybe it was scotch, or whiskey. She only knew that it was strong, and its name seemed appropriate. She was here to make good on her oath.

Allie arrived before the Maker's, looking radiant in a red silk shirt and skinny jeans. Ester, wearing putty-colored khakis, a pilled blue sweater, and a messy bun, had chosen to not make an effort. She did regret her minimal makeup, which did little to hide her puffy eyes and the red splotches on her cheeks—ongoing fallout from crying so hard, at first out of terror for Jason, and next relief, and then this sundering ache.

Allie arrived at the high-top, her perfume bringing the forest into the bar. Ester stood up, her smile wobbly. "Hi."

"Hi," Allie said, full of concern. They hugged clumsily and sat down. "How are you doing?"

"I'm okay, all things considered," Ester said.

"How's Jason?"

"He's fine. Surprisingly so, to be honest."

"He might be masking."

Mask squeezed Ester's head. "We're keeping a close eye on him."

The server reappeared with the Maker's and greeted Allie. "Hiya."

"Hi, Roisín," Allie said with that powerhouse smile. "I'll have the same, please."

It softened Ester, Allie remembering Roisín's name. She pressed on, light-headed, struggling to stay strong. "I'm sorry about canceling dinner."

"Don't worry about it, what a nightmare. That poor young woman," Allie said.

"She was just going to the ATM, thinking it was another day, probably worrying about money and who knows what else."

"It's horrific."

"Those farm workers help feed us and most of us never so much as consider them."

"I was thinking the same thing."

"For him to rob and shoot her like that, leave her bleeding to death on the sidewalk. That he was likely the last thing she saw on this earth, taking aim and firing at her, wearing another of his stupid masks—"

Allie gripped Ester's hand on the high-top. "It's heartbreaking. She should be getting married, not buried."

"Makes me sick. Jesus. Her poor fiancé and family and friends, everyone who knew her."

Allie's other hand covered Ester's. "Softly, softly."

It was an instruction Monica often issued at choir. Ester blinked back tears and tried to store up Allie's touch before she detonated whatever might have been between them. "If I'd done more that day in Rich's store, hit the alarm or—"

"Don't do that to yourself."

"It's one thing I excel at, scathing guilt," Ester said.

Roisín arrived with the second Maker's. "Anything else?" she said above the music and the rising chatter from the growing number of patrons.

"I'll take another," Ester said, lifting her glass.

"Me too, thanks," Allie said.

"Someone's on a tear," Roisín said with a laugh.

"What?" Ester felt herself pale. She was about to tear down Allie and her.

"What is it you say over here? Painting the town red?" Roisín said.

"Painting the . . ." Ester said faintly, her free hand rubbing her brow. Allie shook her head, and Roisín slunk away. Ester's legs, her whole body, was shaking.

"Talk to me," Allie said gently.

"I'm trying."

"You were saying, about your guilt, do you want to go back to that?"

"It's mostly stuff from long ago, stories I tell myself that won't go away. I could contain them well enough until the holdup, but ever since . . ."

"We've all got those stories."

"Not like mine, you don't."

"In one form or another, everyone's got demons and blistering regrets."

Ester's annoyance climbed along with her despair. She didn't need her feelings minimized. From the jukebox, Queen bellowed the final chorus of "We Are the Champions," with its pledge to keep fighting 'til the end. That's what Ester was trying to do for her family, only right then it felt like she was defending the wrong cause. The next song, Carly Simon's "You're So Vain," also swiped at her. *Fair*, she conceded. It was self-absorbed to imagine she had any kind of an exclusive on suffering.

"It helps me to consider that if anyone else was telling the stories that I punish myself with, they would likely cast me much more favorably," Allie said.

"Hmm. I'm not so sure."

"You need to be kinder to yourself."

Ester nodded absently. She'd taken Crystal to her first AA meeting earlier, and while Crystal couldn't bring herself to tell the group she was an alcoholic, she did promise to keep going to the meetings. The group applauded her, and the chairwoman said, "It's essential we keep showing up for ourselves." Crystal didn't seem convinced.

Ester, tingly from just sitting across from Allie, wasn't feeling much assurance either. They sat looking into their empty glasses like something was going to appear within their fragile walls.

Roisín arrived with the second round of Maker's.

Ester swallowed another gulp of fire. "I was beside myself yesterday, thinking about what could happen to Jason, to everyone at the school. While we were waiting for them to be let out, I visited this little church in town, to pray, beg. I made a promise, an oath, to stop this and hold our family together."

Allie pulled her tongue from the bulge of her cheek. "I didn't know you were religious."

Ester sniffle-laughed. "Only in times of tragedy it seems."

Allie drank.

Ester looked away from the matching flecks of amber in Allie's eyes. "The second I saw Jason, all those children, at the school, it solidified what I need to do. I can't destroy our family, I just can't, especially not . . ."

"With me."

"No . . . yes." Leaving Simon for another man would send enough shock waves, never mind betraying him for a pansexual woman. "I was going to cancel tonight entirely, but that was taking the easy way out."

"How noble," Allie said.

"I'm making a total mess of this. I'm sorry, I really am."

"Don't be, I get it. I wish you and your family nothing but the best." Allie finished her drink in a single swallow and coughed a little.

"I know it sounds cliché, but I really do hope we can stay friends, and that this won't affect us at work."

"Don't worry, I'm nothing if not professional. This won't jeopardize your bid for assistant manager."

"That's not what I meant. I know you better than that."

"Funny. Right now I don't feel I know anything about people."

Ester forced herself to watch Allie walk away, and it was like she was the one leaving.

Ester returned home from Kehoe's minutes before the Chinese takeout arrived. She was shaken, and drained, but mostly relieved. She had done the right thing, and she and Allie would be okay, one way or another.

Ester, Simon, Kevin, Jason, and Mena plated up in the kitchen and moved into the living room, bearing iced drinks and mounds of steaming noodles. Simon, Kevin, and Mena commandeered the couch, leaving the armchair to Ester and relegating Jason to the beanbag on the floor.

"You sure you're okay?" Ester said, referring to more than the beanbag.

"I'm good," Jason said, almost agreeably.

Simon worked the TV remote, scrolling the long list of available movies, and fielding the varying opinions from the group on what they should and shouldn't watch. Ester sent up silent thanks for how well this part of the night was working out. She'd taken a gamble, it might have been the wrong call, for Jason and for her. But the mood was relaxed, homey. She even welcomed Mena's presence, the girl's dark head soldered to Kevin's collarbone and his arm affixed to her slight shoulders. Let them be happy together for as long as it lasts. Better to have loved, and all that.

It took awhile, but the five finally agreed on *Green Book*, a film based on the life of jazz virtuoso Dr. Don Shirley. Partway through the movie, Ester's attention strayed. There was something off about a story depicting segregation and Black brilliance having a white hero in the lead. She eyed Jason fondly, giving fresh thanks, and scanned the others "softly, softly." The tender moment fizzled, dissipated by how Simon sat squinting at the TV, his mouth partly open, his absorption childlike.

Jason, groaning, twisted his torso left and right on the beanbag.

"You okay?" Ester heard how often she asked him that, especially since yesterday, and half expected him to snap at her.

"My back's tight."

She stopped herself from scolding him for sitting over his desktop for hours on end day after day. "You need help?"

He pulled a face. "How exactly?"

She smiled, shaking her head.

Her interest in the film continued to flag, and she circled back to Jason, still fidgeting on the beanbag. "Where are you with that game I got you? Have you found the grail yet?"

"I did, but I didn't claim it."

"That doesn't make sense?"

"Once I do, it's game over."

"You don't want it to end," Ester said, her scalp crawling.

"Stop talking over the movie," Simon said, his attention locked on the TV and the revelation that Dr. Shirley is gay.

Ester moved into the kitchen, pushing away the return of the wrenching sensations. She imagined this is how she would feel if she opened her mouth to sing, discovered she'd no voice, and learned it was never coming back.

She reappeared with five servings of lemon sorbet on a tray. While the others scraped their bowls, her spoon steered her remaining lump of dessert round and round. Its cold, citrus sharpness had done little to cut through the aftertaste from the spiced noodles and vegetables, and the coating in her mouth remained, of garlic and ginger and demolition.

"I've a confession," Jason said, looking up at her.

"You do?"

"*Labyrinth of Doom*, it is a multiplayer game." He somehow looked both contrite and pleased with himself.

The barb of hurt passed, and she nodded. "Thank you for being honest with me."

"What are you thanking him for?" Kevin said. "He just told you he lied to you."

"He's telling me the truth now," she said, holding back tears.

"Are we watching the movie or not?" Simon said.

The movie ended. Simon yawned and stretched his arms overhead. Jason returned to his room. Kevin walked Mena out. She stopped in the living room doorway. "Thanks for a great night. I keep telling my family we need to be more like you guys."

No, Ester wanted to warn her. *You don't want to be like us, like me.*

In bed, impassioned, Simon again told Ester he loved her.

"I love you too," she said, testing, trying, but her words emerged as colorless as air.

Fetch

Ester scrolled her phone in bed while Simon slept, checking in vain for news of the gunman-turned-murderer's capture. At least he hadn't struck again. Not yet. She willed herself to get up, but she was a mangled rag doll, her limbs hanging on by scant threads. One who hadn't yet recovered from working alongside Allie the previous night. While their interactions were polite, the strain that hung over them had creaked and buckled like a metal roof about to cave in. Afterward, she'd come home and lain awake for hours, twitchy and turning, telling herself her attraction to Allie would fade, eventually. But the robbed, hollowed-out feelings had only worsened in the depths of the silent dark.

As night fought back the dawn, she'd considered looking for another job, but the challenges of her hireability for a decent job remained, and she couldn't pass up the chance to get promoted to Bob's position if he moved over to the hotel's management team. Simon stirred next to her and released a faint moan in his sleep, almost as if he were in pain. He resumed snoring, softly, forgivably. Throughout the restless night, his snores at their height had sounded like a car engine running without its catalytic converter, and she'd recalled how Rachel had said that for those first few minutes each morning she hated Robbie. She checked the time on her phone, tempted to cancel the weekly walk. She didn't think she could face Rachel and Donna. Didn't think she could hide the metastasis of her unraveling.

She moved downstairs, glad to have the kitchen, the quiet, to herself. Bleary-eyed, she fixed a pot of extra-potent coffee, desperate to shake off the brain fog and the loom of her becoming entirely undone. She groaned aloud, recalling how yesterday was ruined before she'd ever set foot inside Blazers and suffered through the tense shift with Allie. The morning mail had brought a letter from the police department's Internal Affairs division, informing her they'd concluded their investigation and ruled that Sergeant Halloran had followed policies and procedures in full, clearing him of any suggested wrongdoing. She'd ripped the letter to shreds, which had maybe felt satisfying for half a nanosecond.

Fueled by possibly toxic levels of caffeine, she pushed herself out the front door, resigned to the weekly walk. Better than moping around the house and gorging on chocolate before noon. Inside the minivan, she gripped the steering wheel with both hands, but it was futile. No matter how hard she held on, she couldn't temper the sense of being unmoored. She moved her hands to the base of the rim, where her left thumbnail picked the stubborn potting soil from her right. Before she'd gone to bed last night, in an inspired, arguably demented, burst of determination, she'd reattempted her resurrection of the dead money tree. What started out as pruning ended in her amputating the skeletal, brown-leaved branches until all that remained of the plant was its braided trunk. Her fingers traced that resilient weave with reverence, her thoughts thick with how much she would have loved a daughter. But Simon's limit was two children, as was their finances'.

She'd dropped to her knees and sliced and hacked the plant's soil with the trowel while also removing with surgical exactness thoughts of being daughterless, of all absences. She exposed the dirt-clumped roots right down to their webbed capillaries and with excessive care removed the plant from the pot. She disappeared the caked soil into the compost bin and returned to the living room and onto her knees. She refilled the large blue pot with fresh earth, sending up the smell of spring, of creation.

She spoke over the rehoused stick plant. "Come on, baby. You can do it, grow. Come back to us."

Ester arrived at the coastal trail's parking lot, surprised to not see Rachel's or Donna's vehicles. Whatever about Donna, it wasn't like Rachel to run late. She used the wait time to text a reminder to the flash mob's group chat, confirming the details for their first practice. Monica and twenty-two choir members, in addition to Ester, had signed up to participate in the surprise performance on the pier, everyone excited to rally for love.

Rachel's white SUV lumbered into the parking lot, followed moments later by Donna's red jalopy. Ester hauled herself out of the minivan, her stomach flipping. They would see right through her rickety smile.

Rachel and Donna hugged her hard, repeating condolences for the school lockdown and its surrounding ordeal. Ester closed her eyes, soaking up their care. Already she felt better. Buoyed.

"I can't sleep knowing he's on the loose. I can't imagine what it's like for you," Rachel said as the group hug ended.

They walked, Ester telling them about the letter from Internal Affairs. "It's not right."

"No, it's not," Rachel said.

"So much for transparency and accountability," Donna said.

They entered the trail, Donna admiring the shimmery weather. Ester murmured agreement. No matter how wretched she might feel, she didn't think she could ever not appreciate their astonishing surroundings, and on such a glorious morning—the bright sun already filtering through boughs so verdant their leaves seemed lacquered.

"Perfect day to barbecue," Rachel said, also trying to cheer Ester.

"Isn't it?" Donna said.

The outdoor grill was the only cooking appliance Simon ever courted. Ester already knew he would make burgers with the works for dinner that evening and, in a rare nod to variety, insist that they eat outside on the peeling deck. Ester would agree, glad of one less thing to do and welcoming the break from routine.

Rachel and Donna steered the conversation to summer vacation plans. Rachel had arranged a family camping trip to Sedona in June. Donna wished her family could afford the time and money needed to travel across America in an RV or even a camper van. Ester said she wasn't sure where she and her family were going.

While Rachel and Donna chattered on, Ester worried she couldn't feel her heartbeat. Typically, by the time they reached this incline on the path, the vital organ would be taxed. She sneaked her hand to her chest, checking, feeling foolish. Up ahead, the air crackled with the sound of breaking twigs and skittering gravel. That hardened dog owner appeared around the bend, followed by the husky off leash and trotting downhill toward the women. As if by telepathy, Ester, Rachel, and Donna swerved to the opposite edge of the trail and continued forward in single file, giving the animal a wide berth. Despite the beauty of the breed's glacier eyes, regal hulk, and luxurious coat, this dog's heightened wolfishness and bounding energy were its most striking, and intimidating, features. Before Ester had fully formed the thought that the dog might sense the women's fear and be triggered, the animal charged.

The husky brushed against Rachel's leg as it galloped past the three petrified women. Rachel hopped upward with a whimper, as if trying to clear the swing of a lethal jump rope. Ester and Donna flanked her, murmuring concern. Rachel bent her leg back at the knee and swatted the side of her calf, as if trying to remove the dog's traces. Ester kept an eye on the husky, ensuring it wasn't doubling back.

Rachel gingerly sniffed her hand. "Ew. It smells like vinegar. Stupid dog's gotten it all over me."

Ester stiffened, her distress growing as the dog's owner reached them. Rachel, her expression thunderous, said, "You need to keep that dog on a leash."

"They should keep you on a muzzle," he said, barreling past.

Ester grabbed Donna's forearm. "Oh my God."

"What is it? What's wrong?" Donna said.

"Are you all right?" Rachel said, rubbing her hand on her thigh.

"It's him, it's the gunman," Ester said in a harsh whisper.

"Are you sure?" Rachel said.

"Yes. I'd know his shredded voice anywhere." Ester, peppery with adrenaline, pulled her phone from her jacket pocket and dialed 911, her attention trained on the gunman's retreat. When the operator answered, Ester spoke in a frantic jumble.

"Ma'am, I need you to slow down."

Ester tried again, Rachel and Donna standing close, looking terrified.

"You're sure, ma'am?"

"I'm positive," Ester said, flighty, swaying slightly.

"Our patrol units are on the way. Where is the suspect right now?"

"He's headed back toward the start of the trail with his dog, it's a large husky. He doesn't seem to have any idea that I recognized him." It hit Ester with a wallop that he had no clue who she was. To him, she was faceless, matterless.

"The suspect is considered armed and dangerous, ma'am. Under no circumstances are you to approach him. Officers will be there shortly."

Ester backtracked on the trail. "I'm following him at a safe distance. There's no way I'm letting him escape again."

Rachel and Donna fell into step beside her, urging her to follow the operator's instructions, but she was beyond caution or good sense. She remained on the phone while pursuing the gunman, struggling to keep a casual air and pace. He continued to appear oblivious. She was a mass of quivering fear.

A woman jogger appeared on the trail, her athletic pace quickly clearing the distance between her and the gunman. Ester wondered with a sick feeling if she should shout a warning. The jogger passed the gunman without incident and continued toward the three women.

"Should we say something to her?" Rachel said, low. Ester shook her head sharply.

The woman pounded past them, clueless to what was happening.

In the distance, sirens wailed. Ester's pulse accelerated, convinced the gunman would take off running. He continued walking for several paces, then stopped and doubled over at the waist. Ester continued her commentary to the 911 operator, her voice low, guarded. The gunman lifted a stick from the ground and fired it through the air, sending the husky on a chase. He resumed walking but stopped short as the sirens drew unmistakably close.

"He knows," Ester said into the phone. He looked left and right, as if about to hurtle into the woods. The three women also stopped, Ester no longer in any doubt that she was still in possession of her heart. The gunman looked back at them. Ester readied for flight—whether to take after him or run from him, she wasn't sure. The husky returned and dropped the retrieved stick at his human's feet. The gunman seemed to assess the stick. Maybe he was weighing it as a weapon. Or maybe he was looking at his hiking boots, calculating how fast and far they could take him. He started to move again, keeping on the trail. His pace remained languid, as if he'd convinced himself the sirens weren't coming for him.

He disappeared around the longest curve on the trail. Ester hurried after him, followed by Rachel and Donna. She could hear her panicked breath coming back to her through the phone.

"Stay back. Do not approach him," the emergency operator said.

The parking lot came into view. Ester froze. Rachel and Donna stopped next to her. The gunman was on his knees on the tarmac next to the women's parked vehicles, his hands laced behind his head and a barricade of squad cars and clamorous police surrounding him, the officers shouting orders, the eye of their pistols aimed.

Breaking News

For days reporters and news vans descended on Ester's home. Various media outlets also repeatedly called her on the landline, her cell phone, and at Blazers. She declined to speak with any of them, still scarred from seeing her face multiplied on super-sized TVs after the holdup. She was also uncomfortable with how the media increasingly sensationalized crime and criminals for clickbait.

Others, including Crystal, the gas station clerk, and Sylvia Velda's distraught fiancé, seized the opportunity to speak up for justice and gun control. Unable to resist, Ester consumed every mention of the gunman (she refused to use his name) in print, online, and on the radio and TV. She found familiar details—about his grating voice and the zoo of plastic masks—and gleaned new information—his sour smell stemmed from the apple cider vinegar he rubbed into his dog's coat to repel fleas and ticks.

Ester shared people's surprise that the gunman, single and without children, was a college economics professor. A cast of coworkers, students, neighbors, acquaintances, and a nephew in Miami claimed they had no idea he was capable of such a heinous crime spree. They described him as a loner, aside from his dog, and brusque, antisocial even, but nothing in his behavior had raised alarm bells. Police found his gun and mask collection beneath his bed, a reporter noting that it was the place where monsters lurk.

Ester returned to the day of the holdup and how the gunman had reduced her to faceless, meaningless. Is that how he also saw himself? Is that why, beyond disguise, he wore the masks? Or maybe it was that he had fully given himself over to his bestial side.

"Why not take your fifteen seconds of fame?" Jason said, yanking Ester back to the kitchen.

"That's a hard pass," she said.

"You could get a book or movie deal out of this, possibly both," Simon said, only half joking. "Wouldn't that be something? You a heroine of the page and screen, just like Hester Prynne."

Those taunts from Ester's high school classmates resurfaced. *Here comes A, and not for apple, if you know what I mean. Hahaha. If it isn't Scarlet the slut. Hahaha. Ester is a cheater. Hahaha.* Ester wanted to reach back and urge her younger self to not give her tormentors the power to mortify and reduce her. Her stomach lurched. Is that why she'd cheated on Marcus in college, to self-fulfill her former classmates' ridicule?

"You should be lapping up the accolades, Mom, you helped catch the killer," Kevin said.

She harbored zero desire for such attention. Best to have never encountered the gunman. For him to have never entered Rich's store. Never committed any of his indefensible crimes. Yet underneath that yearning there also flickered in her an almost awful gratitude. The holdup had pitched her out of her deadening existence.

"A college professor, it makes no sense. Why did he do it?" Simon said.

Ester wanted him, and her sons, to stop talking.

"A robber a professor of economics," Bob had said inside Blazers with a chuckle. He was especially insufferable these days, having landed his promotion to manager of Horizons Hotel.

"He can't have needed the money," Simon continued.

"Can you not?" Ester said. He was amplifying the noise in her head and asking the impossible. They weren't likely to learn much more about the gunman and his depraved urges until the trial.

She returned to the afternoon she'd stood in front of the closet mirror in her bedroom, wearing the giraffe mask and trying to see herself and Crystal through the gunman's eyes. It came at her just how far removed he must be from his soul, and his victims' humanity, to allow himself to terrorize, maim, and kill. Her phantom breath brushed her face inside the giraffe mask. The gunman must have felt the same damp circular current of his breath behind his animal masks. But that sacred flow wasn't enough to give him pause and invite him to consider that we are all living beings trying to make our way in this world while hoping, deserving, to go unharmed.

Ester closed the news app on her phone, shutting down another article heralding her courage. This reporter went so far as to call her a vigilante. She exited the minivan, shaking off the cold, bleak feeling that such supposed praise draped her in.

She reached Crystal's front door and, composing herself, pressed the bell.

Lily opened the door wide. "Welcome to the tea bar!"

Ester followed her into the kitchen and a waft of peppermint. The mess of items heaped and scattered about the room remained, as did the ant traps. Crystal sat at the table, presiding over a platter of triangular sandwiches and a plate of scones with a side of yellow-orange jam.

"Rich is really covering the store for you two?" Ester said.

"It's a miracle," Crystal said with jazz hands.

"I told him we were having a 'life happening,' and I think he was too afraid to ask what that meant, so he just said yes to us taking the time off," Lily said, to growing mirth.

"He'd be seriously pissed if he knew it's afternoon tea," Ester said.

"Not any afternoon tea," Crystal said, pouring a third cup of brew. Ester suspected Lily had provided the fancy yellow rose–patterned china for the occasion.

Crystal proposed a toast. "To Ester—criminal catcher, local hero, and an incredible friend."

"Hear, hear," Lily said.

Ester waved off the tribute. "Please."

Crystal lowered her teacup to its matching saucer. "It's such a pity there's no reward money."

"I know," Ester said. "Simon and the boys said the same, more than once."

"Imagine," Lily said with feeling.

"Oh, I have," Ester said.

"Me too," Crystal said mournfully.

"I'm going to get promoted, and you're going to get my hostess job, I know it," Ester said.

"Does this mean I get custody of the fish?" Lily said.

"So long as we get visiting rights," Crystal said.

"Cosigned," Ester said.

"D'accord. Visits are mandatory," Lily said.

Crystal pulled her inhaler from her cardigan pocket and puffed.

"You okay?" Ester said.

"I'm not going to lie, I really, really want a drink right now," Crystal said.

"You're doing great," Lily said.

"Yes, you are," Ester said.

"Thanks to both of you," Crystal said.

"You're the one doing the hard work," Ester said.

"Tell me about it. It's not one day at a time for me, I'm clawing my way minute by minute," Crystal said.

"Clawing one minute, powering through the next," Lily said.

"She's right, it'll get easier," Ester said.

Crystal pushed the sandwiches and scones toward them. "Eat up, please."

"I should have gotten a cake," she added, almost to herself.

"This is perfect, thank you, and totally unnecessary," Ester said.

Lily tackled a jam-slathered scone and emitted stage-worthy moans. "What is this divinity posing as jellied fruit?"

"Apricot, it's local, from the farmers' market," Crystal said.

Ester's mouth tingled with the memory of Mom's juicy apricot pies. Ester had never attempted to bake one. Her next day off, she was going to set that right. She flashed forward to herself placing the flaky, golden pie on the dining room table, her mouth pooling, her heart full. Only it wasn't Simon and the boys smiling back at her, hungry, glistening. Her throat hardened, like a stone lodged.

Crystal's hand pressed her forehead, her pink scar visible above her thumb. "It's wild that you walked past him on that trail way back."

"Stop. Imagine if I'd figured it out then? There would be at least three fewer victims in the world, and Sylvia Velda would still be alive," Ester said, forlorn.

"You couldn't know before you knew," Crystal said.

"I wonder what's going to happen to his dog?" Lily said.

"Don't even think about it," Crystal said.

"It's not the dog's fault. Poor animal deserves a happily ever after," Lily said.

"It's amazing you ever figured out it was him," Crystal said.

"I could never forget that scrappy voice and his sharp smell. The way he spoke to Rachel too, hateful, vicious," Ester said.

Lily paused the lift of her teacup midair, her baby finger standing straight up. "That's exactly what you need to do, forget."

Crystal topped up their tea, scenting the air with fresh bursts of mint. "I never thought I'd be throwing a tea party, and for adults!"

"Don't get me started on what we never thought we'd become." Lily turned serious. "No wait, that's not true. I always knew."

"You never second-guessed yourself?" Ester said.

"All. The. Time. Until I realized that voice wasn't mine. It was my parents and the haters, and white-hot fear."

Lily's words landed on Ester like sparks from a fire. When Ester spoke, she sounded faint. "How'd you get past that?"

"I drowned it out with the truth. Below all that toxic noise, I knew who I was, and I gave myself to her fully."

"Brava," Crystal said.

"You're a force," Ester said.

"Let's not get carried away," Lily said. "Who am I kidding? You should totally get carried away."

Their laughter quieted. Crystal gestured at the last of the fruit scones and cucumber sandwiches. "Finish them, please. I don't want any leftovers."

The three women disappeared the food and drained the teapot. The blueberry stains on the crumbs dotting the plate, Ester thought they looked like ink.

Rise Up

On the drive home from Crystal's, Ester pulled the minivan onto the shoulder, killed the engine, and silenced the radio. The traffic ripped past, as if its occupants were being sucked into a super-velocity vacuum. She closed her eyes. She felt a little ridiculous, sitting there in plain sight with her eyes shut, trying to tune out the rushing vehicles and concentrate on her breathing.

It took a while, but she succeeded in getting her insides, her entire body, to relax and settle. Her thoughts continued to swirl. When she reached a state that seemed as calm as she would ever arrive at, she silently asked the voices that weren't hers to quiet down and allow her to hear herself and know the truth of her wants and needs and next steps. She didn't expect anything to happen, not really. She imagined she would sit there until she satisfied herself that she'd given the experiment her best effort and then continue home. Instead, a voice sounded from deep within her, as clear and measured as the virtual assistant on her phone. Only the voice didn't belong to her.

Mom said, "Ester, sweetheart. Ester Prynn. Rise up to meet yourself."

Yet again, Jason crushed Ester at *NBA Jam*. She demanded a rematch.

Simon appeared in Jason's bedroom doorway. "I want in on this."

"Another lamb to the slaughter," Jason said.

"Whoa, big talk," Simon said, dropping into the chair Ester had vacated.

"I'll be back," she said in a deep-throated impersonation of the Terminator.

The sound of Simon and Jason's jovial ribbing followed her downstairs. She passed the living room, where Mena and Kevin were sitting on the couch, reading their phones. A dart of irritation needled her. No one had acknowledged the money tree's budding reincarnation.

In the kitchen, she set about fixing a dinner of roast chicken, oven fries, and a goat cheese salad. She'd met Lydia Greeslie when she was getting the groceries, in the supermarket's meat section, the pair surrounded by the slaughtered. Ester knew her face looked similarly reddened and raw. Inside the minivan, she'd cried at length, like she was wringing herself out. That was after she'd committed Mom's honeyed words to memory exactly as she'd heard them, like a voicemail she could replay on repeat.

"Well done on catching the gunman," Lydia said, near admiration tossed in with begrudgment.

"You should come back to the choir, if you've seen the light, that is," Ester said.

"As if," Lydia said, scoffing, but with an undercurrent of something like longing.

"Tell me you don't miss it," Ester said kindly.

Lydia pushed her cart and its sparse contents away, but not before her pinched face betrayed the truth.

Ester pulled her thoughts from the exchange and removed the wheel of goat cheese from the gurgling fridge. If Simon and the boys had noticed her swollen eyes and blotchy face following her crying jag, they, like Lydia, hadn't acknowledged it. She peeled off the cheese wrapper, and it was like stripping herself. Uncovered, revealed, she pictured Simon and Jason upstairs, and Kevin and Mena in the living room. So near, and yet she felt far away, inside another house altogether, another life.

Simon complimented the goat cheese salad, his mouth a white-coated mash of arugula and beets. Ester looked away from the crushed ingredients between his teeth, feeling a similar, obliterated upheaval.

"Lots of dressing, that's the trick," Simon went on. "Time was, farm foods smacked of flavor. Nowadays most of it tastes like next to nothing."

Jason pulled a face and removed a piece of candied pecan from his mouth. "I'm pretty sure lettuce always tasted like nothing."

"Your dad has a point," Ester said.

"See," Simon said, winking at Kevin and Mena.

"Did you put lemon on the fries?" Kevin said, appreciatively.

"Mmm, I'm getting that too," Mena said.

"We shouldn't accept bland, tasteless," Ester said, her fork spearing a mandarin segment.

"What are you going to do?" Simon said.

"We can be more discerning. We can demand better," Ester said.

"How?" Simon said.

"So you'll take whatever you get, no matter how underwhelming," Ester said.

He shrugged. "I'm easygoing."

"You're never going to change, are you?"

In another show of ambivalence, he held out his knife and fork. "What's to change?" He shook his head good-humoredly, his utensils zeroing in on the chicken. "Forget I said that. You probably have a list."

Everyone but Ester continued eating, as if nothing had happened, as if she wasn't fighting for air.

The Proposal

Ester, Crystal, and Lily were among the first of the flash mob to arrive at the harbor. They strolled the pier, brimming with anticipation while attempting to appear casual. The evening sun maintained its watch, seeming determined to not slip from the sky until it had reigned over the happy occasion.

Ester spotted Allie sitting alone on a bench, going at ice cream in a paper cup. She approached her, but Allie moved off. Ester swerved to the closest section of pier, steadying herself on its railing and pretending to be enthralled by the distant expanse of steel-blue ocean. Seagulls bellyached, loud and piercing. Her chest stirred, as though sections were being rearranged. If the moving parts had a sound, a call, it would be plaintive.

In quick succession, the entire flash mob showed up, forming a deceptively nonchalant tableau of sitting, standing, and walking about.

Crystal, drenched in enthusiasm, said, "They're here," as if Ester and Lily couldn't also see Alejandro and Jacinta materialize at the foot of the pier. Choir members traded stealth, giddy glances. As Alejandro and Jacinta neared the head of the pier, the group filed behind them, and assembled in place. Onlookers, realizing something out of the ordinary was under way, stopped and stared, flushed with pleasure.

Alejandro and Jacinta reached the pier's end and looked out at the broad, peach-streaked horizon, their shoulders and arms touching, as if seamless. The flash mob readied themselves in their respective rows—loosening muscles, clearing throats, licking lips, and smoothing hair and clothing. Monica moved to the front of the group and lifted her arms. Her hands danced midair, as controlled and graceful as a ballerina's, and the choir raised their voices as one. Alejandro and Jacinta whirled around, Alejandro beaming, Jacinta stunned. Jacinta, realizing the choir was singing to her, and at Alejandro's request, pressed her hands to the sides of her face, her eyes and mouth wide with disbelief.

The choir's collective voice climbed, wavering with emotion. Ester felt like the song was coming out of her reorganized chest. Alejandro dropped to one knee and removed a jewelry box from his breast pocket. He opened the small red cube, diminishing sunlight catching the diamond inside and managing to refract tiny, brilliant beams. Jacinta's hands covered her face, and just as quickly she reemerged, pumping her arms overhead and waggling her hips, her whole body serpentine. To widespread laughter and applause, Jacinta completed her joyous dance and Alejandro eased the engagement ring onto her finger. Onlookers videotaped and snapped photos and clapped and cheered. The couple kissed.

Simon had proposed to Ester seated in his chair in a local restaurant, the place long since closed. The unremarkableness of the occasion didn't matter. And it did. The choir sang on toward their rousing finish, several teary voices cracking on the endnotes. Marjorie performed the closing solo, serenading the engaged couple with searing promises of heroic love. Ester wondered if the quaver in Marjorie's voice was about more than the lyrics and the momentous occasion. She sneaked a glance at Allie, who seemed unfazed.

The choir disbanded amid fresh applause and shrill whistles from onlookers. The group surrounded Alejandro and Jacinta, gushing compliments and congratulations and best wishes. Ester waited her turn in the human circle, and hugged the ecstatic couple.

"Thank you," Alejandro said, overcome.

The group escorted him and Jacinta back along the pier, issuing a final round of kudos and farewells in the parking lot. "Enjoy dinner," they chorused.

Alejandro and Jacinta took off, and the choir dispersed, members drifting to their vehicles or out onto the streets. Crystal, about to be chauffeured to an AA meeting, climbed into Lily's beige, battered car—a recent purchase that looked only somewhat less decrepit than Lily's inherited house. Ester issued hasty goodbyes and, her pulse feral, followed Allie through the rows of parked vehicles.

She caught up with Allie and closed her fingers around Allie's wrist. "Can we talk?"

Allie turned around, frowning, and reclaimed her arm. "What's up?"

"I made a terrible mistake."

"Which is?" Allie said flatly.

"I chose what I thought was best for my family and not what was best for me. For us, hopefully."

"I'm really not up for revisiting this right now—"

"Please, hear me out. I keep thinking that if the gunman had gotten into Jason's school and—"

"Why are you putting yourself through that—"

"Let me finish, please." From early on, Monica had taught the choir to let go and hold nothing back. "I need to be brave for real and not like how they're saying in the media. If Jason had died, what would have destroyed me, aside from the obvious, is that he'd have left this world without really knowing me. For years I've been playing at someone, at a life, I've long outgrown, or that was maybe never mine to begin with."

"I have mentioned that you're terribly confusing, right?"

"I'm going home and I'm telling Simon."

"Telling him what exactly?"

"That I kissed you and I liked it."

"Hmm. Smacks of plagiarism."

"Can you be brave and terrified at the same time?"

"You and Simon might work things out."

"No, we're beyond that." *I'm rising up to meet myself.*

"Didn't you swear otherwise, like to God?"

"Under extreme duress."

"Remind me never to stand next to you in a storm," Allie said. Ester's puzzlement must have shown. "Lightning, I'm told it's God's weapon of choice."

Ester's watery smile collapsed. "Maybe I'm being self-serving, but I no longer believe I'm supposed to keep that bargain with God. I'm convinced I should keep the greater contract struck from our beginnings, which is that each of us should live our best, most honest life."

"I can get behind that," Allie said softly.

"Can I come over later?"

"I'll be home."

"I'll be there."

"Only if you're sure."

"I've never felt more sure of anything." Ester touched her hand to the side of Allie's face and traced her cheekbone back and forth with her thumb. Allie's hand covered Ester's, melding them skin-to-skin. Without the other's stabilizing grip, Ester thought they might fall into each other. Even when they steadied themselves and dropped their arms, letting the other go, they were no longer separate.

Ester returned to her minivan as the horizon welcomed back the haloed sun, the last of its fiery light flaring orange-red. She steered for the road, fishing for Allie in the rearview. On finding her, Ester felt like the sun was setting inside her. She drove on, replaying in her head Sing, I's heartfelt performance.

Her memory of "Hero" ratcheted toward its rousing chorus and she joined in aloud, belting the lyrics like an anthem. The surge she felt, the crackling aliveness, was what she imagined Jason and Hildy Hampton experienced whenever they released the macaw and watched the uncaged bird free fly.

ACKNOWLEDGMENTS

My deep thanks to Marisa Siegel for her faith in this book and for her editorial excellence. I'm equally grateful to the entire savvy, dedicated team at TriQuarterly Books/Northwestern University Press, in particular Maddie Schultz, Charlotte Keathley, Kristen Twardowski, and Maia Rigas. Because of you, my second novel is making its way in the world.

My eternal gratitude to the Writers Grotto, San Francisco, with its bounty of marvelous minds and enormous hearts, without whom I would not be the person and storyteller I am.

To Marcy Dermansky, Gina Frangello, Lindsay Hunter, Dominic Lim, Sara Lippmann, Matthew Salesses, and Shanthi Sekaran. Thank you for reaching back for me and providing advance praise for this book; I'm amped with gratitude and admiration.

I'm indebted to Dawn Raffel for her editorial feedback on an early draft of this work, and for her belief even back then that Ester Prynn's story was one worth bringing to readers.

My great thanks to Lily, whose first appearance in these pages surprised and delighted me. A conjured character, Lily embodies Nicole McRory's fierce and fabulous spirit. In fiction and in life respectively, I'm enriched by the time I spent with you both. Nicole, in my thoughts, inside this book, you're forever singing.

This book is also in memory of Noelle Donnelly, a long-ago friend and bright light who died at age twenty-one from "something as stupid as asthma," and who very much wanted to live. Noelle, Bagatelle's "Summer in Dublin" always brings me back to you.

I completed edits on the final draft of this manuscript during a residency at the Tyrone Guthrie Centre, Annaghmakerrig, Ireland. The staff, fellow artists, and enchanted surroundings there nourished and restored me during ill health, and allowed me to make this book better. Similarly, Kew Botanic Gardens, Surrey, England, where I completed the copyedits, was the most wonderful sanctuary.

To readers, librarians, booksellers, and literary champions everywhere, I applaud you, and give thanks for you daily.

My family and friends, I cherish you.

P. M. & T., you are my holy trinity.